Champion! Something comes!
It is not mine.
I fear.
Hurry, Champion!

And so begins the Entean Saga.

Eloch, the Champion of Entean, is asked by the planet who loves him to travel light-years from his home to Spur, a technologically advanced planet whose citizens are determined to colonize Entean.

And because Eloch loves his planet Entean, he goes…only to discover that the vast power flowing through him, power only a Champion can wield, vanishes the moment the spacecraft bound for Spur enters its first wormhole.

Now powerless and alone, how can Eloch stop the colonization, as he has sworn to do?

Meanwhile, on Spur, SubCity Kinlord Wren has her own problems. Sensing the imminent threat of a Culling, in which the strongest of her Folk are taken to serve the UpperUppers who live Above while the weak and old are killed, she must find a way to protect those under her care. How can she give the Martials what they want while keeping those they don't alive?

Eloch and Wren—strangers from different corners of the universe brought together by happenstance. When their paths cross, it will change each's mission to serve and protect, as well as the course of their very lives.

THE ENTEAN SAGA
EPISODE 1: CHAMPION OF ENTEAN

C.B. WILLIAMS

COPYRIGHT

Published by AlChemy Ranch Books
655 Orville Road E., Eatonville, WA 98328
publisher@AlChemyRanchStudios.com
www.AlChemyRanchStudios.com

Champion of Entean
Copyright © by C. B. Williams
All rights reserved
ISBN 978-0-9881814-7-2

Cover design by Al Williams

Edited by Demon for Details
www.DemonForDetails.com

Formatted by My Author Concierge
www.MyAuthorConcierge.com

First AlChemy Ranch Books Edition: May 2015

DEDICATION

For My Team--
Mr. Al, Faith, Maria and Michal
With Love and Gratitude

TABLE OF CONTENTS

Chapter 1: The Star Born

Champion! Something comes!

Eloch shot bolt upright from a deep sleep, Entean's fear burning cold through his veins.

"Where?" he asked, peering into the dark night.

Entean sent him a series of visions.

He cocked his head, not sure what he was seeing. From above? What was coming from above?

It is not Mine. I fear. Hurry, Champion.

He leapt up and threw his pack together while the bedroll disappeared and the circle of fire vanished. Relieved the rain had stopped, Eloch ran to his skiff and flung his pack into the front, then carefully leaned his staff against it. He splashed water on his face before he untied the little boat, grabbed his staff, climbed in, and pushed the boat into the current.

Hurry! It has arrived. It burns. A metal dragon. Hurry, Champion!

Entean's fear was intense, and the clouds roiled and churned, covering much of the night sky while the river flowed faster and faster. Eloch did not even need to steer his skiff. He just had to hold on tight.

~~~

There were only three in the landing party. They fanned out, keeping their backs to their shuttle so they could escape quickly if necessary. But Aiko, the leader, didn't think it would be necessary. From what she had observed while she circled to land, this was a very pleasant little planet with few inhabitants.

She pushed back her helmet, shook out her straight black hair, and filled her lungs with the moist, sweet air. It had been a long flight to get to this small, watery planet the Ring had targeted for colonization. It was the farthest planet on their itinerary, some twenty light years away from Spur. It had taken them just over a year to travel this far. Aiko had volunteered so she'd have the time to think through her domestic problems. If the rest of planet A349 was as serene and peaceful as the landscape before them, she may not ever want to return to the conflict and turmoil of her home life. The meadow was quiet and serene, with wisps of morning fog. And the air! Aiko sucked in another deep breath, savoring the sensation of such beautiful air filling her lungs.

"This is a lovely place," she heard herself say. It surprised her. She had been trained to keep her personal thoughts to herself.

Etsuo grinned in agreement. "The Ring will want to colonize ASAP."

Aiko studied the lush green foliage and the blue of the river rippling past. "Pity," she said. "I wish they could keep it as it is." As soon as she thought of how crowded and dirty Spur was, with its masses of people, she shuddered, remembering the stink.

Not the Above, the City, where the elite lived. But SubCity, where she'd grown up. She didn't think she'd ever get the SubCity stink out of her nose. She swore she would have seduced the fat, greasy recruiter during her last Cull just so she could join the Service and get out of Sub.

She was glad she hadn't needed to resort to that, though. Glad she was smart and things came easy. Glad she had the knack and could fly ships. Lots of Subs became pilots. Lots of Subs who were born with the knack, combined with the will they had to develop to survive in that cesspool. Without the will, there was no managing the knack.

Was that why the government kept SubCity around? No, Aiko decided, the UpperUppers who lived in the highest echelon of the City wanted the Subs to stay where they were—out of sight.

Aiko sucked in some more air. "What's the readout, Genji?" she asked the third in the landing party.

"Not much activity," he replied. "There are sentients to the north and the south, but there's no movement."

"It's early still," Aiko said, curious to find out what the inhabitants were like. If they were peaceful, the Service would capture them, train them, and send them back to Spur, where they'd eventually find their way into SubCity, no doubt. But it was better than the alternative. If they were warlike, they would be destroyed. The Ring did not take kindly to hostiles. It was better to find an uninhabited planet. Less costly. Less trouble. But Aiko knew once the Ring got her report they'd colonize this beauty, inhabitants and all.

Fortunately, Aiko's mission was to gather facts and report back to the Ring's Board of Colonizers on Spur. She didn't like having to make the life-and-death decisions.

"Movement, ma'am," Genji said, just as the scanner in his hand chirped.

"On guard, you two," Aiko said, checking behind to confirm the way back to the shuttle was clear. She unhooked the safety on her holster, just in case.

A being, male humanoid in appearance, stepped out from dense foliage, the branches parting to make way for him, barely brushing his leather garments as he strode past.

Aiko heard Etsuo's gasp mirror her own gulp at the man's size. Etsuo was one of the Service's biggest warriors, yet this man in front of them

3

had nearly six inches on Etsuo, which meant, Aiko guessed, he was at least six foot four. And broad! Such strength in those shoulders. If the other inhabitants were like this one and not hostile, Aiko mused, Spur was on its way to mustering quite an impressive new military. She could practically hear the Service drooling now. No SubCity destination for a man like this.

His face, when he threw back his hood, captivated her with its intensity, the intelligence she saw in the eyes, and its perfect features. . His hair was dark, already damp and clinging around his face from the morning mist. Tendrils of it hung over his eyes, which were deep and green like the forest behind him. They glared at her from under slanting, dark brows. His full mouth was set in a hard line. His jaw tensed, emphasizing high cheekbones and a pointed chin. Power emanated from him. If he didn't have a whole load of knack, she thought, she was a blind-bitched whelp.

The man continued to move purposefully toward them, carrying his heavy staff as if it was a twig.

He spoke in a deep, rich voice, the words rumbling from his chest.

Aiko switched on her translator, noting that Etsuo and Genji did the same. She decided to approach him as one in authority, since it was quite apparent it was what he believed.

"I am Aiko," she said with a quick nod, "pilot and leader of this mission. With me are Etsuo and Genji. I did not have the translator turned on when you spoke. Will you please repeat what you said?"

The man frowned, studying her and her two companions. "Your words are strange, yet I can understand you. How can it be?" he asked in that rich baritone of his. It glided over Aiko like smoke.

She held up her device. "This is a translator. It allows us to speak with one another."

4

He was quick when he moved, somehow covering the distance between them in a soundless instant. When he stepped back, the translator was in his hand.

Aiko closed her mouth and swallowed. "It isn't a weapon," she said, nodding at the translator in his hand. "It merely helps us understand each other."

He nodded, studying the device. Then he smiled slightly and stepped closer to hand it back to her.

"Easy," she whispered to Etsuo when she saw him move. "I don't think he means to harm us." She nodded her thanks when the translator was placed gently into her outstretched hand.

Their fingers brushed.

Oh yeah, he's got the knack in spades. Her hand felt like she'd been burned, his power was so intense, and from the merest of touches! This man was not one to be trifled with. This man was extremely dangerous. Aiko swallowed again, suddenly longing for the safety of the shuttle.

She stole a glance behind her and started. The shuttle was covered with vines, which were now sinuously curling into all its openings.

"Captain—" Genji blurted. She heard real fear in his voice. "What's happening?"

"Stay calm," she ordered, banishing her own fear with the will of a star pilot. She slowly turned her head to look back at the man, and her eyes widened when she saw a translator in his hand. "Where did you get that?"

He held up his own device. "It is helpful to speak with you," he explained.

"What are you doing to my shuttle?"

"Shuttle? The metal dragon is called a shuttle?"

Aiko nodded slowly. "What is happening here?" she asked, willing herself to calm down.

"Fear not," he said. "We will not hurt any of you."

He was commanding them! Shouldn't it be the other way around? She reached for her weapon, only to feel the metal dissolve in her hand like grains of sand. *What was this place?*

"We have no desire to hurt any of you," the man said again. "We just want to understand why you are here, where you have come from, and when you will go away."

Aiko swallowed again.

"Ma'am?" Etsuo said. His voice shook. "My weapon is gone."

Aiko nodded to him. She had to remain calm for her men. "So is mine," she said, keeping her eyes fastened on the strange man.

He was watching her calmly, translator in one hand, staff in the other, waiting for his answers.

She cleared her throat. "Stay still," she ordered her two men, holding up a staying hand. "Who *are* you?" she asked the stranger.

"I am called Eloch. I am the Champion of Entean."

"Who is Entean?" she asked.

He made a sweeping gesture with his staff. "This is Entean. You stand upon Her."

Aiko heard Genji gasp. "The planet is called Entean?"

Eloch nodded. "She is our home, our mother. I am Her Champion. I go where She needs troubles soothed." He nodded to the shuttle, now engulfed with vines. "That was a trouble. It is not a part of Her, and She wants it gone. She wants you gone."

"But," Aiko said, "it cannot fly the way it is. We can't leave."

Eloch's grin transformed his face. "When you are ready to go, it will be ready to fly. Where are you from, and why did you come?"

Aiko shook herself. His power was a heady thing, especially when he smiled. "We come from Spur. It is the capital of the Ring of Colonization, the government seat of the colonized planets. Spur is quite far from your world, the furthest we've ever been."

He nodded, apparently aware there were other planets populated with intelligence. "And why are you here? I have never heard of inhabitants visiting one another."

"I am on a scouting mission. To see if this planet supports life."

"It does. Now you may go," Entean's Champion told her.

"We will go," Aiko said. "But others will come."

"Whatever for? This is not your home. There is no place for you here."

"Our home is crowded, and we seek new worlds for our people. Yours is not the first planet we have colonized. It won't be the last."

Eloch frowned again. "Others are not welcome. You must stay here so others will not come," he decided.

Aiko shook her head, suddenly afraid. "It will not matter. They will come even sooner to discover our fate."

Eloch sighed and leaned on his staff, studying each of them in turn.

"What right do you have to take over another world? What authority has decided this is how it should be without any sort of negotiation? To whom must I speak to make sure no more will come?" he asked, watching the shuttle expectantly, as if someone else might appear.

Aiko shook her head. "You would have to go to Spur to find anyone who has sufficient power to halt the colonization of your planet."

The man paled. It was the first time Aiko had seen any uncertainty.

"I must think about this," Eloch said. "You will remain here."

As he spoke, thick branches thrust themselves up from the earth and surrounded the three off-worlders. Within minutes they were completely caged.

"You can't do this!" Aiko cried.

The Champion gave her a dismissive look. "It is already done." He turned and headed back into the forest. "Eat," he called over his shoulder before pocketing the translator.

"Hoi!" Genji said, looking down at his feet.

Aiko followed his gaze, dumbfounded to see a feast spread before them.

"Can we eat it?" Etsuo asked, eyeing it warily.

Aiko shrugged. "If he never lets us out, we'll die anyway," she said, squatting down and reaching for a piece of fruit.

"Okay, then," Etsuo said, lifting a flagon of ale. "Here's to yer knack," he said and took a healthy draught.

~ ~ ~

Eloch had not gone far, just far enough away from the distraction of the off-worlders. As Champion, he knew what he had to do, and it terrified him.

I will be with you, Entean reminded him, Her energy swirling around him, offering comfort.

8

Eloch smiled and relaxed. He knew She was curious. The translator and the—what had the woman called it?—shuttle? Yes, the shuttle. Entean was fascinated with them both, and after quickly absorbing their essence, nature and functions, She had shared the information with Eloch.

He crouched down, drawing circles in the dirt to help him think. Such a dilemma. As Champion, it was his duty to speak with this Spur authority the woman had referenced and demand that Entean remain untouched. And as Champion, it was also his duty to stay on Entean to do Her bidding. She required his presence in both places. If only he could be! Eloch paused, as he looked at the two figures he had drawn. His face lit up and he laughed. "All I need do is ask," he said, rising to his feet.

Producing a knife, he sliced his palm and allowed his blood to drip on the ground. It stung, but he knew Entean would heal the cut quickly. Already the pain was lessening as he felt the wound close. He asked Entean to create his twin using his blood as a blueprint.

A man rose from the earth, large and broad-shouldered, with dark hair and green eyes. They stared at each other. Then Eloch smiled, and saw his twin smile back. It was like watching himself in a mirror. They both laughed with delight. Eloch reached out, as did his twin, and clasped the man's head between his palms, drawing him forward until they stood forehead to forehead.

"I give you all I know," he told his twin.

"And I willingly receive it," his twin replied.

With the power bequeathed to him by Entean, Eloch shared his knowledge with his twin until they were one and the same, perfectly identical.

"You will be safe now, Entean," he told his planet. "One of us will go speak to the people in power, and one of us will remain."

The energy flowing through him confirmed Her pleasure.

Eloch and his twin walked to the skiff, where Eloch lifted his backpack, pulled out a change of clothes, and offered them to his twin. He'd never been able to watch himself in action, and he was pleased to note his twin's smooth, efficient, and athletic economy of motion. He nodded in satisfaction when his twin pushed the skiff into the water, settled into the seat, and used the paddle to hold the little boat in place. Slinging the backpack over his shoulder, Eloch gently placed the staff in the bow. After a moment's hesitation, he handed the translator to his twin. The shuttle had others, and if not, Entean could make him a new one.

"Say hello to Thaif and his milkmaid for me," he said.

His twin grinned.

"Return soon," the twin replied before setting off to the east, where a herd of wild beasts was causing trouble near where Eloch's old mentor, Thaif, lived.

Pleased with his cleverness, Eloch shouldered into his backpack, which held his personal belongings and went to rejoin the landing party. He frowned, already missing the familiar weight of his staff. Before he could request a replacement, Entean produced a perfect replica.

"Ready to go to Spur?" he asked Her.

~~~

His connection with Entean was fading!

It happened so suddenly Eloch was caught off guard.

Once the probing vines had withdrawn, the shuttle took off without mishap. He and Entean, through Her connection with him, had been fascinated with the docking process as the shuttle was absorbed within a larger orbiting vessel.

10

While Aiko and the others busied themselves with preparations, Entean was transfixed by the sight of Herself floating in space. Just as Eloch had been delighted with watching his twin, Entean was getting a breathtaking, all-encompassing view of Herself. He felt Her pleasure like happy little flutters, flitting and dancing down to a cellular level.

And when they changed course, heading out into deep space, Entean's delight was palpable.

The stars blurred and the ship jumped.

Eloch felt the severing.

"No!" he shouted out his agony. "No! Please!"

But after a final burst of images and instructions, all traces of Entean's consciousness vanished.

Eloch groaned so loudly that Aiko shot a worried glance in his direction.

"The shuttle!" he shouted, catching her eye. "Take me to it."

At first she refused, thinking he would attempt to escape, but then she realized it was impossible while they were in hyperdrive, sluicing through a wormhole. Her craft was sealed shut. Locked down.

"Take him," she nodded to one of the crew who stood idly by. "Find his translator. Make sure it's turned on and working," she added. The man was babbling like a lunatic.

When they got to the shuttle, Eloch shoved past the crew member.

She shouted.

Eloch paid no attention.

The crew member shrugged and trailed timidly after her charge.

Eloch went directly to where Entean had left the gift She showed him in that final burst of communication. There it was, tucked deep within the wiring for the landing gear. It was a seed, which Eloch promptly swallowed. He choked when it stuck in his dry throat. He swallowed again, and kept swallowing and choking until he felt the seed reach his stomach. He sank into an available seat and glanced at the bemused crewmember.

"Leave me now," he told her, his voice hoarse. "I crave solitude."

She nervously shook her head. "I can't keep the shuttle open. You must come with me. But first…." She reached into the shuttle's small galley and handed him a container of water.

He nodded his thanks and drank it all, sighing his relief.

"Keep it," she said when he tried to return the container. "Now, come with me. I know a place."

In spite of his need for immediate solitude, Eloch followed the girl out and watched, fascinated, while she locked down the shuttle.

She glanced over her shoulder, making sure he followed, before she left the shuttle bay and headed to the crew's galley. Until the next shift, he would have his solitude. She pointed to a table. "Sit there. I will tell the captain where you are, and someone will retrieve you when we've got a berth ready." She didn't know what the plans were for their guest, but she felt she had to tell him something. She stood watching him a moment longer, a little disappointed to realize this very handsome man had already forgotten her.

~~~

The seed was sprouting. It left Eloch deaf and blind to the outside world while it took root, grew, and flourished within him, pushed and thrust up and out to fill him. The pain was so intense it was a blessing when he lost consciousness, leaving the growing plant to surge unimpeded up his central nervous system, into his brain, winding within the soft, spongy folds, where it fastened onto the neurons and spread through the connecting dendrites.

As he slumped to the floor unconscious, information flooded him—terms, functions, labels, languages, names of places and titles of people, mathematical equations, measurements of distance—all spiraling out of the seed, into the plant, and into Eloch's mind, all the information Entean had absorbed from the shuttle while She explored it with Her vines.

But the seed didn't merely transfer the collected information. Throughout his whole body, the plant pushed and coiled, redesigning Eloch's senses, attuning him to the natural world in a way he had never known before, but in the way Entean knew, allowing Eloch to interpret the subtleties and nuances of his natural surroundings as Entean would.

When the shift changed and members of the crew entered the galley, they found the strange man sprawled on the floor, his legs tangled in chair legs. Thinking he had died, Aiko ordered the fallen Champion to be taken to Sick Bay, where he was laid on a pallet. Someone draped a sheet over him.

Aiko reported the incident in her log, disappointed she would not witness his confrontation with the Ring Colonizers. She also instructed Genji to report in his science journal the possibility that, if removed from their planet, the inhabitants would die. The Ring Colonizers would like that.

While they flew onward to Spur, Eloch dreamed an endless stream of dreams, memories orchestrated by Entean as final instructions to Her Champion.

Eloch's skiff bumped gently against the mossy bank. Murmuring a word of thanks to Entean, the planet Who loved him, he slid his paddle under the wooden seat and climbed out.

With the towrope in his hand, he stretched the kinks out before fastening it to a low-hanging branch, and swore when it sprayed icy water down his exposed neck.

Droplets slid down his back, adding to the chill and discomfort. It had rained unceasingly for days, and he was sure moss would begin sprouting from his sodden clothes any moment now.

Eloch adjusted the waxed-soaked canvas sacking he used to cover his meager supplies. He didn't need much when he served the planet Who loved him, he thought. The essence of a planet, he corrected himself.

When he was satisfied the canvas would keep the dampness at bay, Eloch straightened. He stomped and shook the water off and, rubbing his hands together, looked around, squinting into the gloom.

He knew his mentor was somewhere nearby. He felt his presence.

After five years of traveling the face of Entean, wending his way through Her waterways—for the voice of Entean, when She whispered Her wisdoms to him, was female—he was eager to talk to Thaif. He had many questions for his mentor, and even more adventures to share.

The scent of wood smoke and something else that quickened his hunger caught Eloch's attention. Taking careful note of where he left his skiff, Eloch wended his way through the thick foliage and finally spied a small campfire with a blackened kettle hanging over the flames. A familiar figure rested beside it, smoking a long-stemmed pipe with his legs stretched out toward the warmth.

"Thaif!" he called.

His mentor straightened, peering into the gloom. "That you, Eloch?" he asked before taking another puff from his pipe. "Took your sweet time getting here. The porridge is near burned. I've been keeping it warm."

Eloch chuckled. "Burned or no, it's a welcome sight," he replied as he stepped into the circle of light created by the fire.

"Well, come in. Sit down," his mentor said, making room. "Hang that sopping wet skin you call a coat on that branch there," he added, gesturing with his pipe. "Don't want it to drip on my sweet fire."

14

Eloch did as he was told. Shivering from the wet and cold, he hastily moved closer to the fire, immediately feeling his muscles begin to relax when its warmth greeted him. He sighed with pleasure and sat down across from his mentor to pull off his boots.

"You don't know how I've yearned to be dry," he told Thaif while he arranged his boots by the fire. "She's not taught me this trick yet." He looked up and saw the rain was still falling…everywhere except within the fire's circle of light.

"Not a trick, boy," his mentor said, watching Eloch tug off his socks and wring them out. "'Tis a gift from Herself. All you needed to do was ask."

Eloch snorted, shaking his head as he draped his socks over his boots and watched the steam rise when they began to dry.

Thaif barked out a laugh. "You didn't think to ask, did you, boy? Thought all things were done with a command, didn't you?"

Eloch looked up at his mentor from under the shock of thick black hair clinging and dripping onto his forehead and neck. "I did, I suppose," he answered sheepishly.

"Oh, boy!" Thaif chortled as he tossed a bowl to Eloch. "Fill your belly and tell me some of your other crazy mistakes. I know I trained you well, but Entean has Her ways to keep you humble, and it looks like She's found an easy target in you, all right." He laughed merrily as he watched his student tuck into his meal. "You've not thought to ask for food, neither, I suppose."

"I've asked for game and grain," he replied, his mouth full. "I've asked for a safe and easy journey and a dry place to rest," he continued after he swallowed. "Thanks," he said, accepting ale from his mentor, the ale that had magically appeared in the old man's hand. "But I never thought to ask for a meal. Nor for a warm, sweet fire. And to be sure," he said, after taking a swallow of the smooth, bitter draught, "I'll be asking for some ale now I know."

"As Her Champion, lad, all you need to do is ask," the old man replied. "You already do much for Her, and will do far more in time, and She loves you for it."

"I'd do it for Her anyway," Eloch replied.

Thaif smiled softly. *"Aye, we all would, and She knows it, too."* He lifted his pipe to his mouth, *"That's why all you need do is ask,"* he said before he drew in the aromatic tobacco.

Eloch set down his bowl and leaned back against a log. He smiled with contentment while he watched his old mentor blow smoke rings as the rain continued to pour down outside their circle of warmth. *"I've missed you, Thaif."*

"Have you, now? Well, I'm here. Why don't you tell me what you've learned since last we met?" Thaif blew another set of rings, watching them expand and dissipate.

The two talked long into the night while Eloch told of his adventures. He'd visited every village and city along the lakes and waterways of Entean. He described the wonders of all Her peoples, the diversity of lifestyles. He spoke of the marvelous animals, plants, and trees, and how they arranged themselves along the latitudes and longitudes according to their preference. He spoke of the bounty everywhere, and then he was silent for a while, deep within his memories.

"I almost caught up with you a couple of times," he told Thaif.

Thaif lifted an eyebrow. *"Indeed?"*

"Yes. At Thule, and then again at Falk. Both times they said the Champion had just passed through. At Thule you created a dam. And at Falk you discouraged a dragon from feeding on their livestock. At Falk you had turned east, they told me. I tried to catch up, but I couldn't find you."

"It was not yet time for me to be found, boy. But now's the time."

"I'm glad, too. I've grown weary of traveling alone."

"But you're never alone, Eloch."

Eloch ran his fingers through his hair, which had finally dried. *"Aye, I know. But, you know what I mean."*

"I do, boy, I do." Thaif replied, relighting his pipe and puffing till the dottle glowed. *"But ye best get used to it, although 'tis better when you truly step into my place. Your time is nearly here."*

Eloch sat up. "Me? Champion?"

Thaif grinned. "I've only a few things left to teach you. And then I will be leavin' to set down my roots. I'm thinking about Vernoch. I like how lazy the river is there, and the milkmaids are all rosy-cheeked and willing. One once promised to wait for me," he mused, taking another puff. "She would be nearing her twilight years by now. Perhaps she'd enjoy ending her days with the likes of me. And if not?" Thaif shrugged.

"But Master, I'm not ready. Not nearly," Eloch exclaimed. "You've only just told me. These past five years, especially when I heard about your deeds—the things you have yet to teach me," he shook his head. "Not nearly ready."

"Eloch," Thaif said quietly. "It's not up to me to determine your readiness. It's up to Her. And She says it's now."

Thaif produced two bedrolls and tossed one over to Eloch. "Get some sleep, lad. We will discuss it some more in the morning." Thaif put another log on the fire and then squinted up at the rain. "I suspect it'll dry out now you've learned to ask." He chuckled as he settled himself on the ground, laying his pipe near the Champion's rune-clad staff.

Between the constant stream of other dreams and memories, Entean continued to remind him, "When you awaken, my Champion," She said, "remember the many lessons you have learned. They will serve you again."

CHAPTER 2: SUBCITY

Flick snickered and Wren kicked him out of their bed.

He landed on his backside with a curse. "Aww, Wren, there's no call for that," he complained, his grin twitching to life at the corners of his mouth.

She glared at him until his grin faded again.

"All right, I apologize," he said, hoping her good nature would bubble up again.

Wren continued to glare, her grey eyes flinty. "I'm serious, Flick. If we are to become like them," she jerked her chin upward, to Above, where the ruling classes lived, "we are going to have to behave like them all the time. And," she pointed a finger at him, "no wind should ever come out of your ass in the presence of a lady. Ever."

"Ass?" he asked, rubbing the offending bit of his anatomy. "You mean where I just landed? You can still call it an 'ass' up there?"

"Bottom," she amended. "You just landed on your bottom. Or backside. We don't say 'ass' either. Argh!" she sighed, scrubbing both hands over her long mop of coilmats. "It's so hard to remember all these futing *niceties*."

"I don't think ladies are supposed to swear, Wren," Flick commented, accepting when she held out a helping hand.

She grunted as she hauled him up. "If the lady is a leader, she is permitted to speak in a manner her subjects will understand," she told him. "And you understand, me, right? No. More. Bottom. Wind. Or I will be forced to find someone else to share my bed."

"No more, I promise," Flick replied.

Such a little, thing he thought, their leader. Wren claimed to have no knack, but he was pretty sure she was wrong. She had the knack of leadership, and a powerful good leader she was, too.

Her sparkle came back. "Good. I'd hate to lose such a cuddlesome bed warmer," she replied. "Let's begin the day, shall we?"

Not waiting for his reply, Wren left Flick's room and walked down the short hall to her own. They weren't lovers. She didn't have a lover. Didn't like to be touched that way. But she hated to sleep alone. After the childhood she suffered, nobody blamed her, especially Flick, who had watched it all.

Wren shook off the chill of childhood memories and pulled off her nightshirt, stepping naked into her bathing pool. With a sigh, she eased down the two steps and curled into the warm, fresh water.

When the water felt this good, she thought while shampooing her coilmats, gratitude trumped guilt. She knew how hard it was to come by fresh water every other day for her bath. She also knew it was a tribute from her Kin, a way for them to show their respect and affection for her. If she asked them to stop, it would do more harm than good. And did she really want to go without her bath? Decidedly not.

She finished washing and ducked under the water to rinse. Resurfacing, she leaned back against the pool's ledge to think.

Her Folk were in trouble. There would be a Culling soon. She felt it coming. It had been too long since the last one. Maybe she should send Mouse and Flick out to gather information. Maybe she would go on a solo, too. It would be a good excuse to take a little trip Above and get out of SubCity for a span.

Gods, she hated SubCity. Hated the stink, the brutality. Hated the fact that no matter how hard she tried, her Folk were never truly safe. So easy to get hurt in Sub. It was why she had decided to try something new—teaching them how to blend in Above and act more like an UpperUpper. If they were successful, maybe they'd finally get off Spur, live on one of the colonies. Wouldn't that be something?

Wren reached for the towel someone had left folded by the pool's steps, climbed out, and dried off before wrapping it around her. With quick strides, she went to where her meager wardrobe was slung haphazardly over clothes pegs, grabbed an undershirt, tunic, vest, and leggings, and pulled them on. Then she crossed over to a tarnished mirror and finger combed her damp locks. Making a face at herself, she turned and headed downstairs.

A few of her Kin still lingered at the table, although most had gone about their business. Some thieved, some begged, while others had honest jobs that unfortunately paid very little, jobs that no one Above wanted to do, such as cleaning the cesspools, dressing the dead for burning, or whoring. People living in SubCity had to do whatever it took—no matter how unpleasant—to survive.

Flick and Mouse looked up when she entered.

"Morning," Mouse said while she picked at the few remaining crumbs on her plate. Like Wren, she was slight and delicately made, with pale skin and huge eyes. Unlike Wren, her eyes were dark, and her straight dark hair was gathered into a short braid at the base of her graceful neck. She was dressed in grey, a color that helped her move invisibly through the murky streets of SubCity. Looking at her, it was hard to believe Mouse was one of Wren's most competent assassins, but she was. Wren had two, and she used them both when necessary. She didn't like giving a kill order. But she would. She had.

Wren sat across from them, placed a napkin in her lap, and accepted the plate of bread and cheese Flick handed her with a nod. Mouse poured her a flagon of diluted ale.

"Feel like taking a little stroll?" she asked while she piled a thick slice of cheese on a piece of bread and took a bite. At least the pungent cheese masked the bread's stale taste.

"Where to?" Flick asked. He touched his napkin to his mouth while he watched her with calm grey eyes.

She smiled at her cuddlesome bed warmer, appreciating both his loyalty and his attempt at good manners.

Flick had been with her since the beginning. His round, open face concealed a fluid intelligence and a steady heart. He was large for someone born and raised in SubCity, with thick, meaty hands that could punch and strike. They were hairy hands, light brown to match the hair on his head. She sometimes teased him that his father had been some huge, hairy beast his whore-of-a-mother had lain with. She wasn't swearing. Most of the KinFolk's mothers were whores.

"I'm going Above," she answered. "It's been some time since the last Culling. I have a feeling we're due."

"Might be," he replied. He laid down his napkin and stood, holding out a hand for Mouse to hand him her plate so he could take them both to the sink.

"Where do you want us? Above or Sub?" asked Mouse.

"Sub," Wren replied. "But have a care if you go beyond the borders of my KinSpace. Fergus and MacMichaels are talking about banding together again to take me out."

Flick snorted. "I'd like to see them try."

"Yeah, well," Wren replied. "It's hard enough to survive without adding a border war. I'd hate to have to go on a killing spree on account of them hurting either one of you."

Wren herself was the other competent assassin.

"Not to worry, Wren," Flick said. "Mouse and I will take good care of each other—er, one another."

Mouse looked at him and smiled.

"We'll accompany you until the tunnel, then," Flick said.

Wren nodded, washing down her meal with the rest of her ale. "Your company would be most pleasant," she said, dabbing her mouth daintily with her napkin. She rose and carried her plate to the sink to soak with the others. "I'll just fetch my knives."

~ ~ ~

There were two ways to get Above. One used the many moving stairways and checkpoints, which were monitored by the Martials, and were intended for those who had legitimate business Above. The other was through the tunnels. Within the borders of Wren's KinSpace there were five such tunnels, all guarded by her KinFolk. These tunnels were long-forgotten passageways housing now-defunct electrical cables or dried-up sewage systems which had been boarded up and blasted closed.

Wren and her Folk had painstakingly dug through the debris and reopened every one of them. Not only did they now serve as secret entrances to Above, but they also provided storage chambers for food, water, weapons, and clothing, as well as places to hide the very old, the very young, and the infirm during a Culling.

Flick and Mouse walked with Wren to one of the tunnels before heading off to loiter at various checkpoints and eavesdrop on the Martials.

Since she was there, Wren went over the stored supplies to see if it was time to organize a food raid. Stale bread was common, but the bread she'd eaten this morning bordered on moldy. She eyed the surplus.

"What do you think, Skip?" she asked her Grainier while they studied his list of stored items and circled those needing replenishment. "Think we should find something a little better packaged?"

Skip tugged his ear. "P'raps in a day or two I'll send the runners to forage."

"Make it a day," Wren replied. "I don't want us to get so low our bellies fuss."

"Will do, m'lady," Skip said with a brisk nod, jotting it down on the list. "I'll send my runners tomorrow at first light."

His two young sons were the runners. They were good at their job, little thieves that they were, but Skip worried. This worry sometimes hampered his judgment. Wren knew this but didn't hold it against the man. She would have killed to have a father like Skip.

She patted him on his shoulder. "You're a good man, Skip. I'm going Above next. Not sure what route I'll use on the way back, so I'll say good-bye for now."

The reopened tunnels were in reality a warren, and it was easy to get lost. But Wren had made it a point to know every passageway and where it led from each of the tunnels within her borders. She could lose herself within them, but she was never lost. Lighting a torch, Wren entered the black and began the climb to Above. Since some tunnels were pitch-black and others shadowed and grey with Above light eking through, it was always prudent to use a torch.

She could have found where she was going this time blindfolded, even though it was a long trail through a labyrinth of twists and turns. Some tunnels were dank and slippery and forced Wren to tiptoe to avoid splashing her clothes, her fingers lightly skimming a slimy wall for balance. Others tunnels were dry and dusty, her feet making little puffs of dust with every step. If she walked too briskly, the puffs could make her sneeze. Occasionally she came across still-active tunnels, with the energy humming through cables looped and bracketed along the walls. Those were the tunnels where she was most cautious. Active tunnels meant there were other, known, openings from Above.

For more than an hour she walked, the flickering shadow cast by her torch her only companion. And her thoughts. She could always think better when her body was in motion.

There *would* be a Culling soon. She could feel it; she just needed the confirmation she'd get when Flick and Mouse returned later tonight. She should also know then how much time she had. But she would still have enough time make plans. How much time would determine how to plan.

With each wary step closer to her destination, Wren wove different scenarios, and by the time she reached her destination, she had a number from which to choose. By the time she came to the entrance of the last tunnel, felt the dry wind on her cheeks and smelled the fresh air, one decision was finalized. She had decided where to hide her Kin during the next Cull.

This tunnel's opening was hidden behind metal latticework. Out of habit, Wren hesitated, keeping to the shadows until she was certain she was alone. She had never found anyone in this particular part of the Above, but she wasn't about to take chances. *Caution First* was her number one rule. She demanded it of all in her Kin, especially herself.

Seeing and hearing no one, Wren slipped from the shadows and came around from behind the lattice to stand in the middle of a lovely little square which the moveable City of the Above had long since abandoned for newer, more modern residences. A circle of ramshackle stone buildings that had once been proud homes enclosed the little square. Now only empty windows stared blankly down at her. But to Wren's eyes they were still beautiful. The rosettes and carved vines trimming the sides and outlining each of the windows, and the rusty, curlicue iron railings on balconies charmed her. The stones were cream and grey. Although cracked and old, their grandeur was undiminished.

In the middle of the square was a fountain, in its center the figure of a woman, a pitcher in her hand. Water bubbled out of the pitcher and pooled around the woman's feet, a little oasis in an abandoned square. When the City had moved on, no one had even taken the time to disconnect the fountain from the water supply.

Wren crossed over and dangled her fingers in the water. Precious water some fool had forgotten to redirect. Their loss, she thought, her gain.

Wren had found this square in an hour of need when she was very young. When her life was bleak. When she lived in constant pain from daily beatings—gifts from her whore mother and her drugged-out father. One day she had been beaten unconscious. It had been one of those occasions when her parents simultaneously had a go at her. Thinking she was dead, they had tossed her outside to be carted away with the rest of the garbage. When she came to, she was buried underneath refuse and debris and other things she would rather not remember.

She did remember crawling into the nearest tunnel. And crawling, and crawling, willing her damaged body to obey her. Throughout the dark of the tunnels she crept, determined to keep moving until she could go no farther, crawling as far away from the ugliness as possible. When she heard the liquid sound of a gurgling fountain, she followed it until she finally came upon this abandoned square.

Wren reached over and touched the center figure. The lady with her pitcher, and the fool who left the water on, had saved her life. It had taken her weeks to recover, most of which had been spent huddled in the shadows, close to the fountain, trapping small birds and rodents who came for a drink. She ate them raw.

As she grew stronger, she began to explore her surroundings, both the abandoned square and the tunnels. She found a room overlooking the square she claimed as her own. She learned to merge with the crowds, and to steal food from street vendors and clothes from merchants. Always a quick learner, she imitated the mannerisms and speech patterns of those in the Above.

After watching and listening, she slowly and carefully selected new companions while she redesigned her life. She met Mouse in a pub where she often worked for food. It was one of those instant friendships, and Wren readily agreed to let the girl recruit her as an assassin. Since she'd vowed never to be helpless again, she became quite skilled in the trade, quickly surpassing Mouse.

She joined the guild, was invited to social gatherings among the UpperUppers. Did favors. Called in favors. She created her own network of those loyal to her in the Above. And then, fifteen years later, with Mouse as a companion, she abruptly vanished back into the tunnels.

She soon reconnected with Flick and a few others who remembered her from her childhood, but to her disappointment, she learned her parents had been Culled and died shortly after her disappearance. She would have liked to have killed them herself.

For several months she observed the KinLeaders, explored the tunnels, and accepted assignments from the UpperUppers in both the Above and SubCity, efficiently building a reputation as someone it was best not to trifle with. When the time felt right, she challenged Jig, the KinLeader of the tribe she had been born into.

It had taken mere seconds to dispatch Jig. He had grown old and soft, too dependent upon cruelty to get his way. She took his seat without challenge and with Mouse and Flick by her side, began to implement what she had learned in her years Above, creating as safe a haven as possible in SubCity for those KinFolk under her protection. The numbers in her tribe doubled and then tripled, and as they did, so did the responsibility of keeping them safe during a Cull or a KinLand dispute. Thanks to her tunnel system and the rigorous training she insisted on for all her Kin, they all knew the closest escape routes.

Wren was known to be fair-minded, but firm. If her rules were broken, she did not hesitate to punish the offender to the degree she felt necessary to keep the peace and her leadership intact.

She did not trust many of her Kin. It wasn't that she doubted her Kin's loyalty, but the simple truth was, loyalties shifted like sand. Her profession had taught her how cheaply life could be bought or sold.

Caution First.

~~~

"And you say you have no knack," Flick, who was sitting across from Wren at the dining table, scoffed. "Culling will happen in a month."

She laughed as she popped a bit of dried fruit into her mouth. "No knack, just keen observation skills," she said between chews. "There hasn't been one for a span, and it's getting crowded in SubCity. The Martials don't like it when there are too many of us to handle. We're not so easily controlled."

When she was finished with her snack, Wren put her hands on the table and rose, nodding to the Kin who gathered her plate and utensils. "Okay, then, Flick, let's call for a KinTalk in thirty."

"Wait," he said. "Mouse found out more. She's waiting for us in the Narrows."

The Narrows wasn't a place. It was their code word for privacy. Wren would find Mouse in her bedroom, the safest place in their compound for a private talk.

Wren nodded and waited for Flick to join her. Together, they made their way up the stairs to her sanctuary.

They found Mouse, arms folded, gazing at Wren's bathing pool.

"I'd love to have one of those in my room," she said without turning.

"You can always use mine."

Mouse shook her head, her dark braid swinging slightly. "Couldn't. Wouldn't be fair." She flashed the smile that made her beautiful. "But your offer means a lot. My thanks."

Wren smiled back and nodded in acknowledgment. "Flick said you had some news?"

Mouse nodded. "Flick was doing so well pumping the Martials I decided to take a little solo through some other KinLands."

Wren's couldn't hold back a frown but said nothing. Mouse had her invisible ways.

"Some deal has been cut, Wren. I don't know all of it, but the Cull will go after only your KinFolk."

Only her Kin? Culled?

For several moments Wren couldn't think of a word to say. "It's either Fergus or MacMichaels' doing," she spat, then felt a chill course through her. "Or both," she added.

"I'll find out more," Mouse promised.

"It's one way to increase your KinLand," observed Flick. "It is pretty crowded down here."

"It's crowded everywhere on this planet," Wren said, "except for Rubble."

"Which doesn't help us much with our current situation," Flick replied.

"Maybe not this time, but it will," Wren said.

Mouse raised her eyebrows.

"My plan is getting more and more real," she told them both with a smile. "But we need to solve this problem first, or there won't be any KinFolk to help make it happen."

"And what are we to do?"

"We have a KinTalk in thirty in storage room Five. Spread the news. I need to think," Wren answered.

After the two left, Wren sank into a chair and ran her hands over her coils. Assuming Fergus and MacMichaels had indeed banded together with the Martials, there was a good chance they would succeed in eradicating her Kin. Wren would admit her fears only to herself. And only allow the luxury of fear to fill her just this one time.

If it was only her or even a handful of others, they could easily slip through the cracks. But her tribe numbered nearly five hundred now. And it was growing.

"Should have stopped accepting Kin at three hundred," she mumbled to herself. It would have been wiser, but she couldn't. When they came begging, she saw the beaten, starved child she had once been in every alone and desperate face. Felt their hopelessness.

And knowing she was the last resort for many, she agreed and admitted them, even though it meant she was adding burdens for those Folk still healthy and strong enough to work.

With a sigh, Wren went over to her basin, poured in a little water from the pitcher, and, scooping it up with both hands, splashed her face and patted more cool, refreshing water on back of her neck. After blotting with a towel, she looked deeply into the wide grey eyes reflected back at her from the cracked mirror hanging above the basin.

"They're your Kin," she told herself. "You take care of them."

~~~

30

In the storage cellar, it was noisy, hot, and smelled like five hundred unwashed bodies. Because she was so small, it took a few moments for her Kin to realize Wren had arrived. Bracing herself on Flick's broad shoulder, she hopped lightly up onto a crate filled with dried fruits one of her runners had nabbed that very day. Wishing she'd worn something brighter and more eye-catching than her usual assassin greys, she raised her arms and waited for the crowd to notice her and calm down. When it was quiet, she spoke.

"There's to be a Culling in a month. We must make preparations," she announced, "and give the Martials a nice selection."

Her proclamation was greeted with more groans than cheers, which spoke volumes about the demographics of her Kin.

"But I thought Cullings were good things," a young boy said. "I know I've got some knack in me."

"If you've got knack, or a good strong back, or something else of value to the Martials and the UpperUppers, yeah, Cullings are good things," Wren answered. "It's the others I'm worried about. If we don't protect our own, we'll lose them."

"It's not fair!" someone groused. "Just because we're old or sick."

"Or crippled, or slow, or a baby, for futing sake!" someone else added.

The crowd murmured in agreement.

"We all know that," Wren said, feeling her face flush with anger. "But SubCity is crowded, and the UpperUppers have only one way of dealing with those who can't be of service to them. And complaining won't save a single soul. It's time to be proactive and make our plans. We've all experienced the Culls. Since I've been your KinLord, we've survived five of them with very little loss of life. And after each one, there were more of us remaining. Why? Because we're smart, and we've got closed mouths, and we've got our tunnels, and we know how to hide."

31

She paused, suddenly feeling drained as she strove to boost the hopes of her KinFolk. "And we also give the Martials the best knackers, so the first thing we do is test you all. And the next thing we do is prepare the others to disappear for a good, long hide. A hide for as long as it takes."

She scanned the crowd, searching for her Grainer. She spied him standing toward the back, an arm casually draped over each of his boys.

"Skip!" she called over the crowd's hum. "Send your runners out tonight. It's time to stock up for a three-week hide."

Skip raised his burly arm, acknowledging he'd heard.

Toward the front of the crowd stood lean and rangy Spider, with his hip cocked and arms folded. Wren locked eyes with him. With a nod, he disappeared into the crowd. She'd find him in her rooms when she returned.

After Flick and Mouse, Wren trusted Spider the most. A few years after she'd taken over the Kin, he'd appeared, requesting an audience. In his blunt manner, he told her he was from Above, a born and raised UpperUpper, and a student at the university with an inconvenient conscience. In exchange for asylum, he offered her his knowledge of how the UpperUppers' governing bodies functioned. He explained he had led a group of protestors during the last Culling. The situation had turned violent, Spider killed a man, and now, despite his family's high rank, there was a price on his head.

Their relationship had begun on rather shaky ground. Neither could fully trust the other. The reward for Spider's capture would have earned Wren several favors. And how could Wren be sure Spider hadn't come solely to learn her methods and worm his way in behind her defenses?

Wren took it upon herself to go Above to see what she could discover about the young, unassuming, blunt man. It took her longer than she would have expected to learn Spider's real name. And when she did, she'd been shocked to learn how much he had sacrificed for his ideals As soon as she was convinced of his authenticity, she relaxed and began using his knowledge to learn everything she could about how an UpperUpper operated on Spur, the governing hub of the Ring.

Before Spider, all Wren's focus had been on survival and the dynamics between the Above and SubCity. After Spider, Wren's focus expanded to encompass the Ring.

During her walk to Above earlier that day, Wren had decided to use Tunnel One as the place to hide during the Culling. However, Mouse's information changed her mind.

"We will fix the hide in Tunnel Two," she announced.

"Tunnel Two's a swamp! What's the matter with One, or even Three?" a swarthy man with a pocked face asked.

A chorus of agreement followed.

Wren glared until the noise died down. It didn't take but a moment.

"Since we know Two is a swamp, we can prepare for it," she stated.

"But why Two?" the swarthy man asked again.

"Because I say, Weasel," Wren snapped, "and if you don't wish to chance the Cull, you will keep your thoughts to yourself."

She glared again at Weasel until he dropped his gaze with a nod.

"Flick," she said, "you stay with Cricket and assign tasks. Mouse and I will plan the knack tests."

"Why Two?" Mouse quietly asked as they wended their way back to the compound.

"It's the last place they'd think to look," Wren answered. "Plus the tunnels are so twisty, it's easy to escape and hide in them if we're forced to flee."

"I'd best find my waxed canvas sacking, then," Mouse said.

Wren grinned at her friend. "You're lucky you have some. It's going to be a rather cold hide this time. I'm not looking forward to it."

"But it's better than death."

"It's better than death," Wren agreed.

They were silent while they threaded through the alleys and warren of shanties comprising her KinLand. Their shadows occasionally flickered while the bare bulbs strung to light their way did the same. Overhead, the cavernous SubCity's ceiling climbed high into the dark. It was always dark. And it always stank. The huge fans that filtered the air did little to relieve the stench.

When she was small, Wren had once climbed all the way up to one of the fans, which was at three times her height. She thought if she was the first person to breathe the incoming air, it would smell as sweet as she imagined the Above would smell. She was so very wrong. The air blowing into SubCity was filled with dust and grit and oil. It gave a very different impression of what Above was like. On both counts, she had been wrong. The air of Above was somewhere in between.

"I'm making the move sooner, Mouse," she told her friend abruptly.

"Are we in the Narrows?" Mouse asked, cautiously scanning their surroundings.

"I didn't tally, but I'll wager all the Kin are still back at Five. We'll be fine if we talk softly."

"The Culling's got you jumpy?" Mouse asked, her voice barely above a whisper.

"More like the banding together of the other KinLords," Wren replied just as quietly.

"We don't know for sure."

"True, but it's pointing that way."

"It is, isn't it?" Mouse mused. "So we're moving to Above, then?"

Wren nodded. "Might as well think on it. Tomorrow I'll take you and Flick to the abandoned square with the fountain. You two memorize the route. It's a twisty one, but you can get to it from either Two or Five. If anything goes wrong, that's where I want you to take the others."

Mouse halted and peered at Wren. "What's going on in that head of yours?"

Wren shrugged. "Caution First, is all. Whatever happens during this Culling, Mouse, to my way of thinking, the leaders will be a nice, juicy target. There are three of us. If we all know a way out to Above, it's more likely some of us can make it there."

"What if all of this is in your head, Wren? What if it's not as bad as you think?"

"My friend Mouse," Wren said. "You're the one who found out a bargain had been struck. How can you not believe it won't be as bad as I think?"

Mouse shrugged. "I'll believe whatever I find out to be truth. Until then, I will keep an open mind."

Wren threw her arm around her friend as they began walking again. "And that is why I'm the KinLord and you are the best eyes-slash-assassin I've got. We'll know more tomorrow. For now, let's organize the testing.

~~~

"Have you ever heard of two KinLords making an agreement with the Martials?" Wren asked Spider while she shrugged out of her jacket. She draped it over her chair and took a seat facing him.

Spider had made himself at home in her room, where he lounged on the small couch she had in a corner of her sitting room. His arm was slung over the back and he slouched against a cushion, one leg crossed over his knee. His thin, angular face gave nothing away as he shook his head in response. "I used to have a friend whose father was on the Board of Culls. He told me they were open to whatever would keep the Scofflaws thinned out. So I wouldn't be surprised," he paused, looking at Wren as she shifted to sit beside him. "I told you we call KinFolk 'Scofflaws' so you needn't look so baffled."

"I'm not baffled, Spider," Wren answered, feeling her face flush. "I was trying to imagine someone other than a Martial coming to SubCity for negotiations if they didn't need to. I suspect Fergus or MacMichaels approached them. They hate my tribe that much?"

Spider patted her on the shoulder, ignoring her warning glance. "I don't think they hate your Kin, Wren. I think they hate you. Your clan is always increasing. What do you think is happening to theirs?"

Wren shifted very slightly so Spider couldn't touch her again and said, "Good point."

"So what are you going to do?"

"What you heard at the KinTalk. Pick the knackers and others the Martials will want to recruit. The rest will go into a hide. We're starting tomorrow. There are some we know wouldn't live through this Cull, so they'll be the first to prepare." She glanced at him. "And since you are technically not here, you will go with them."

Spider bowed his head. "Thank you. It's hard not to be afraid at times."

"Too true," Wren answered, her thoughts flickering back to earlier that day, when she had been alone. "But fear is a luxury in SubCity."

Wren fell silent, long enough for Spider to ask if he should leave.

"Oh, sorry, Spider," Wren smiled, tugging on a coil. "There's more thinking and planning to be done. Please close the door on your way out, and tell Flick when he's back I want to see him."

She didn't hear him leave.

CHAPTER 3: RETURNING, REAWAKENING

"Ma'am?" Genji asked.

Aiko held up her hand, too focused to speak. Her knack had found their next jump, and she needed all her concentration to guide their vessel to the wormhole's opening. Once there, she locked the coordinates and the ship hovered, poised.

"You were saying, Genji?" Aiko asked, swiveling her pilot's chair to face him.

"There is something I'd like to show you, Captain."

"Can it wait until we're through the jump?"

Genji shrugged. "I suppose."

"Good," she replied, swiveling back to face the view port. "Why don't you sit and buckle in? She's a straight shot, short, and should be no trouble. And," she couldn't keep the excitement from her voice, "when we get through, we should only be a couple of months from home. It's been a long time."

As Genji sat and strapped himself into a chair, Aiko flicked the com switch and announced the jump to the rest of the crew. She glanced sideways at Genji. "Ready?" At his nod, she asked, "Care to do the honors?"

Genji grinned and gave the countdown over the ship's com system.

At one, Aiko slowly guided her ship into the chaos of the wormhole. When the current caught them, she smiled, cut the engine power, and leaned back to enjoy the show. Once the coordinates were locked in, she trusted the ship's navigation system more than her own skills to keep them on track. During training she had actually flown through a wormhole unaided, and it had taken all her concentration and skill to get out alive on the other side. But she had done it. And sworn she'd never do it without Nav again.

The ship funneled through and out into a universe where the star systems were much more familiar. With a sigh, Aiko silently greeted them as old friends. She turned to Genji with a grin. "Okay. That was the last jump for this trip. In…" she studied her data screen, "…exactly two and a half months' time, you'll find me at the port bar getting drunk off my ass."

Genji snorted and unstrapped from his seat.

Aiko unbuckled her harness, stood, and stretched before she sat down again to set the coordinates for Spur. "Let me radio ahead to the Colonizers and announce our arrival date, and then I'm all yours," she told him.

"Fine," he said.

Genji stood by the door to the bridge and watched while Aiko sent her message. *I'm all yours*, she'd told him. He wished. They'd been on many missions together over the years. She had never once noticed him as a man. He was simply Genji. Or Genj. Still wasn't how he wanted to be known by her.

He watched her stand and turn with catlike grace, her uniform hugging her curves. Before she could catch him, he switched his gaze to the view.

"I think I see our sun," he said pointing to a star in the distance.

"Close, Genj. Just a little more to the south, and you should see her. Use those three stars round 'bout two o'clock, there," she pointed, lightly touching his shoulder with her other hand. "The ones in an inverted triangle? See them?"

Genji nodded.

"Good, now just use the point and track due south. That bright star about two fingers' width down is Unukalhai."

"I see it!" Genji smiled. "Thanks, ma'am. I've never been much of a star gazer."

"You don't need to be, Genji. You're the best research scientist and med tech I know. You keep reading the data, and I'll keep reading the stars."

He saw Aiko realize she was touching him right before she dropped her arm and ducked her head, hiding her expression. "So what did you want me to see?"

Genji cleared his throat. "If you'll follow me to Sick Bay, ma'am. I do believe I will be forced to alter my report in the science journal."

"What are you talking about?"

"It's best if I just show you, ma'am."

Curious, Aiko silently walked beside Genji down to the second deck, where Sick Bay was housed toward the center of their craft.

The door hissed open and Genji led the way into the bay and down a corridor, where he stopped in front of the familiar draped figure of the Champion of Entean. For nearly ten months, the Champion's body had been canistered in a pod, kept off to the side and out of the way. It had become such a permanent fixture, Aiko had scarcely noticed it on the few occasions she'd made a trip to the bay.

She glanced at Genji. "So?"

His eyes were fastened on the body. "Don't you see anything?"

She followed his gaze, and after a few moments noticed the barest of movements, an extremely slow inbreath followed by an equally slow outbreath.

"Well, I'll be damned," she breathed. "I may get to witness a showdown with the Ring Colonizers after all."

Genji laughed. "Couldn't believe my eyes. Since I was bored, I thought to dissect the body and preserve the organs for study." He glanced at her. "You can tell a great deal about a culture from what they eat. Anyway," he continued, "I came down here to prepare him and," he swept his hand in front of them, "found this."

Aiko peered closer. "Will he awaken?"

"Don't know, but I've got a couple of months to see what I can do to prod him awake, now, don't I?"

"Yes, Genji, you do." She glanced at him in amusement. "Shall I leave you to it?"

He was already reaching for his instruments.

~~~

He lived and marveled that he did.

He sat weakly in a chair, wrapped in a white robe with a bowl of broth on his knees, and savored the astringent smells of medicine, the rich flavor of the broth he'd been given, the drone of the engines, and the star fields out the porthole. Savored it all because yet he lived.

The one who woke him, Genji his name, told him he had been in a coma for nearly a year. To him, his body felt like it had been in hibernation rather than a coma. He had not been ill. Although weakened and thin, he did not feel unhealthy. The bowl warmed his hands, reminding him to eat. He lifted a shaky spoonful to his lips and

42

sipped, feeling the warmth and salty goodness trickle down his throat and explode into hunger in his stomach. He smiled, enjoying the feeling of hunger, and took another sip. And another, until he had drained the bowl.

"More?" Genji asked. He had been sitting quietly off to the side of the Champion, taking notes.

Eloch nodded and handed him the empty bowl. "Please," he said. His voice sounded rusty.

Genji set his tablet aside and reached for the bowl. "Keep the spoon," he said as he handed it back to Eloch. "When I return, I will bring visitors." He paused at the doorway and then his head whipped around to look at Eloch again. "You don't need a translator." He sounded surprised.

Eloch shook his head. "No, I do not." He was equally surprised.

What had happened to him?

He searched his memories, cobbling together what he could remember from before his hibernation. He ate a seed, he recalled. Entean's gift. A seed filled with knowledge. It had sprouted and grown. He remembered the pain and was grateful for the pain's absence. It had been extreme, he recalled. It was what had sent him into the hibernation.

And now? What of now? What had he become? And what was to become of him? Genji had told him they were near the invading planet. Entean had sent him there to champion Her, to tell them to stay away from Her. But without Entean, he was helpless and weak. Weak in limb. Weak in power.

As if in response, deep within his lower abdomen, something fluttered, a tightening, like a fist preparing to strike a terrible blow.

The seed making itself known.

Eloch relaxed. Perhaps he could not wield Entean's power, but She was still a part of him. "I can speak and understand without translation," he reminded himself out loud. Inwardly, he reminded himself how, before becoming Entean's Champion, he had been a proud warrior, an expert with the staff. She had purposely selected Eloch for his stature and strength.

He knew with time he would regain that strength. He had been wounded before, this weak before. He would become strong again, with time. With time, too, he would understand everything Entean's seed had planted within him. He'd learned and adapted before. He would learn and adapt again.

Eloch stood shakily and crossed over to the window, touching the bulkhead to keep his balance. Transfixed, he watched the stars outside, losing himself in the wonder of traveling in a small craft through stars, planets, galaxies, and solar systems that glimmered against the black. He ached with the beauty of it.

Perhaps this invading planet, this Spur, would not be as dreadful as he had anticipated. Perhaps the Ring Colonizers were reasonable individuals.

CHAPTER 4: SPUR

They were laughing at him. All five of the men and women on the Board of Colonizers were laughing at him. One woman in particular actually sobbed with glee.

It was extremely irritating, but Eloch stood quietly, shoulders squared, staff in hand. With effort, he loosened his grip.

When the laughter died down, Eloch repeated what he said. "You do not belong on Entean. You are not a part of Her. She does not want you."

The sobbing woman, blew her nose in a kerchief. "Is he mad?" she asked her neighbor, a grin tugging at her lips. She started to giggle again.

Her neighbor barked out a laugh. "Not mad. Delusional perhaps?"

"Let's not forget who we are," the Chairman said, with a light tap of his gavel. "We've had our fun. Let the man speak."

"I am the Champion of Entean," Eloch began again. "Entean has sent me to tell you that you may not live upon Her, and to keep you from attempting to do so."

"And how do you propose to stop us?" the Chairman snickered, his eyes wandering up and down Eloch's gaunt form. Although much stronger, Eloch still had not regained his natural weight.

Before he could answer, Aiko, who had brought him to meet the Board, stepped forward and stood beside him.

"I have seen this man do some amazing things," she began. "Our weapons disintegrated in our hands. Just fell apart. He needed a translator and it appeared. He imprisoned us in a high fence that grew instantly from the earth. So we could not fly, our shuttle was encased in vines."

As she spoke, the Board members stopped their chuckling and leaned forward with interest.

"You say your weapons disintegrated?" the laughing woman asked, suddenly quite serious.

Aiko nodded. "We were helpless," she said. "We are only here because he allowed us to return so he could come as well. Please, I think we should take this man very seriously. He's filled with knack."

"Can you show us something?" the Chairman asked. "Perhaps make my gavel disintegrate?" He held it up.

Eloch shook his head. "I cannot. I am not on Entean. I need Her power. I am Her Champion," he explained.

Someone started to snicker again.

The Chairman smiled the smile of a predator. "Well, then," he said slowly. "I think we should keep you here on Spur. Problem solved."

"Unacceptable! I do not belong here. Return me," Eloch commanded, thumping his staff.

Ignoring Eloch's outburst, the Chairman turned to Aiko. "And how did you find planet A349?"

Eloch groaned, and Aiko peeked worriedly at him before addressing the Chairman. "It is a remarkable place," she answered, a small smile

46

playing about the corners of her mouth. "Beautiful. One large landmass, laced with lakes and rivers. Life is abundant."

"And inhabitants?"

Aiko glanced again at Eloch, who looked as if he was made of marble, pale and expressionless. "It's lightly populated. We were not on planet long enough to read them," she answered quietly. "You see, we had barely touched down when," she tilted her head at Eloch, "he arrived."

"I see," the Chairman murmured, idly toying with his gavel. "Apparently our greatest kerfuffle with regard to colonization stands before us," he said with a snort. "I will put a vote to the Board. Do we or do we not wish to send a second scouting mission?"

"You shall not colonize Entean!" Eloch roared. He took his staff in both hands, preparing himself.

Aiko's hand darted out and grasped his arm. "Psst," she hissed and gave his arm a little shake. "Now's not the time. Think."

Eloch glanced down at her, surprised she would offer any advice. He listened though, and lowered his staff.

"We will conduct our meeting in private," the Chairman declared. "Leave us."

"But what of him?" Aiko asked. "What of the Champion?"

The Chairman barely hesitated. "I care not. He looks too used up to be of any use to the Service. Since you brought him here, he is your responsibility. Use him as you wish, send him to SubCity, dispatch him, whatever you wish." He gave Aiko a dismissive wave with his gavel. "Take this bone puppet away."

Aiko looked up at Eloch. "Come," she said under cover of the renewed laughter.

Head high and back ramrod straight, Entean's Champion exited the Boardroom of Ring Colonization, determined to return.

~~~

Back aboard her ship, Aiko held her own meeting. With the exception of Etsuo and Genji, her crew was on leave. The corridors were eerily quiet as she and Eloch made their way to the bridge. Aiko liked it that way. The empty vessel was her asylum from Spur's endless crowds.

Etsuo and Genji had been playing cards while they waited. When the door whooshed open, Etsuo quickly bunched the cards and his winnings together and tucked them into his tunic pocket. Both stood at attention.

"And because we are docked and between assignments, this means you can bend my rules to please yourselves?" Aiko asked, scooping up a card that had fluttered to the bridge deck. By their expressions she knew she had made her point, so she returned the card to Etsuo.

It disappeared into his pocket to join the others.

"Take a seat," Aiko said. "You, too," she added, glancing up at Eloch.

"What'd the Chairman say?" Etsuo asked. It was the reason he and Genji had remained behind. They had also witnessed Eloch's powers.

"Told us to get out while they voted on whether to send another scouting mission to A349."

Genji glanced at Eloch and back at Aiko. "That's all?"

She nodded. "That's all. Oh, and they laughed at the Champion."

"You let them laugh at you?" Genji asked, eyes wide.

Eloch shrugged. "I am not at my peak," he said hesitantly.

"Of course you aren't," Genji soothed. "You've only been out of your coma for six weeks. It takes time to regain your strength."

Etsuo glanced at Genji. "When did you decide to champion the Champion?"

"Since Aiko made me responsible for his health and his indoctrination into Spur's regulations," he huffed, glancing at his commanding officer.

"It's fine," she told Etsuo. "The Chairman made him my responsibility anyway."

"This is not what I expected to hear," Etsuo said. He squinted at Eloch. "No vines? No food suddenly appearing? Weapons disappearing?"

"Nothing like that," Aiko replied. "They just laughed at him."

Eloch rested his staff across his lap. "It does not work that way," he explained. "Only on Entean can I do those things."

"Then why did you come?" asked Etsuo.

Eloch grinned ruefully. "I wish to Entean I had not. But She asked me to, and so I came. I did not know Her power would withdraw from me," he added.

Aiko studied him while they talked. "But you still have the knack. I can feel it. Powerful knack." She shook her head. "Just as much as before. I don't understand."

Eloch was silent.

"Maybe his knack works differently here. Maybe he just hasn't harnessed it yet," Genji offered.

Eloch glanced at him. "That is possible, but I don't know where I would begin."

"What are you going to do with him?" Etsuo asked suddenly.

Aiko shrugged. "Turn him loose, I suppose."

"You can't do that!" Genji said. "Where would he go?"

"Is there someplace quiet?" Eloch asked. "Someplace with trees?"

Aiko snorted. "Why do you think the Ring wants to colonize? There's nothing but rubble. City and Rubble Above, death and violence in SubCity. Hasn't Genji told you anything?"

"I hadn't gotten that far," Genji mumbled in self-defense.

"Then drop me off in the Rubble," Eloch said.

"And what will you do?" asked Aiko, suddenly afraid for the tall, gaunt man who was light-years away from everything he knew.

"I will endure," he replied.

"I can't in good conscience just leave you in Rubble," Aiko said, flinging up her hands.

"It's my wish," Eloch said.

"At least let me supply you with food and water. At least allow me to look in on you from time to time, bring you more supplies," she said.

"And me," said Genji, "to make sure you stay well and all."

"You will keep me informed of the Colonization plans?"

"Better than that," she replied. "If there's another scouting mission, I'll make sure you come with us."

"You can't promise him that," Etsuo said. "There's no guarantee you'll be assigned. We've been gone two years. We're entitled to some R&R."

"Doesn't matter. Even if there is another scouting mission, I cannot go back until I have at least tried to stop them," Eloch said.

"But your planet is without you, her Champion," Aiko argued. "What of that?"

"Entean is safe enough. I would not leave Her vulnerable," Eloch replied.

His look told her the discussion was over.

Aiko sighed and smoothed her dark green uniform. "Okay, then. Tomorrow morning Genji and I will take you to Rubble. We will leave you with enough supplies to last for a couple of months." She surveyed him. "We can provide something for you to wear as well."

"I will wear what I brought," Eloch said, "but I gratefully accept the supplies."

"Are you sure I can't fit you with a uniform?" Aiko asked. "You look…" Her voice trailed off.

"Like a bone puppet?" Eloch supplied.

Etsuo laughed.

"Not funny, Etsuo," Aiko said with a glare.

"It is a little funny," Eloch said. "It's what I look like. But not for long. I will rest and regain my strength. I just need the time."

"Which we can easily supply," Aiko said.

~~~

In the morning the ship's shuttle flew over the planet's surface, carrying Aiko, Genji, and Eloch. No one said much, each preferring his or her own thoughts to conversation. Occasionally Aiko and Genji glanced over at their taciturn passenger, who gazed fixedly out the shuttle, his face a mask.

"There!" Eloch said suddenly, causing the shuttle to tilt when Aiko jumped.

She righted the craft and aimed it where Eloch was pointing.

"Why here?" Genji asked when they had landed. "It looks like all the other places in Rubble."

Eloch glanced around. "It feels right," he answered. "It feels like what I need."

"Okay, then," Aiko said, tossing three duffle bags down to the men as soon as they reached the ground.

She watched while Genji showed Eloch how to operate the radio, whose signal was tuned to her ship. She wondered why she felt so protective of the Champion. She noted how quickly he grasped new concepts. He seemed to adapt to their technology much faster than she would have expected. All in all, Eloch seemed quite capable of taking care of himself.

"Let's go, Genj," she called when he continued to dawdle over details, and she fired up the shuttle to encourage him to hurry. It shook a little when the engines activated, and she made a note to have it overhauled. "Time for our R&R."

As Genji scrambled in and sealed the door, she watched Eloch. He stood with his hands on his hips, surveying the supplies. He glanced up. Their gazes locked. A tremor of power pulsed through her. Had she not been born with a considerable gift of knack, she might not have known what it was. She shivered, then slowly returned his wave.

"You told him we'd check in on him in a month?" she asked as the craft took off and banked sharply.

52

"I did," Genji replied. He watched the lone figure fade into the Rubble as the shuttle climbed higher. "I feel sorry for him. He looked lost."

Aiko shook her head. "Don't feel sorry for him. That man's so full of knack he's like a volcano ready to explode. He said he would endure. Hell, he'll be doing way more than that. I need a drink, Genji. I'm heading for the nearest bar as soon as I dock the shuttle."

~~~

For the first time since he had stepped on the shuttle for his voyage to Spur, Eloch relaxed. He was alone, and would be left alone, which provided him with the time he needed to understand what Entean had done to him. For him? Perhaps. Entean had Her agendas, some hidden, some not. Her Champion was not privy to them unless he was a necessary part of Her plans.

And apparently, Eloch thought as he unpacked his supplies, he was a necessary factor in this case. He might have failed with his first task, but he had not begun the second.

For his second task, Entean wanted him to learn why a planet would allow its creatures to colonize other planets. She wanted him to ask Spur and then return to Her with the answer. Hence the seed, packed with both knowledge of Spur's inhabitants, all She could glean from Her minute examination of the shuttle, and the ability to communicate with Spur in the same way Entean spoke to Her creatures.

"Assuming all planets talk with their creatures as you do," Eloch said out loud. His voice echoed slightly around the broken-down walls and resounded in his ears.

Eloch marshaled his thoughts. It was time to make his encampment. He had already emptied and organized all his supplies according to their various functions, now spread in a semicircle in front of him. He squatted down and filled two of the duffle bags with his food, making a mental note to find somewhere close to stash one of them. He always felt better having a cache of food hidden nearby. The other food duffle he tossed in the corner, leaving the rest of the supplies spread out.

He had a tarp and a bedroll, as well as some basic survival equipment. He had made a list, worrying that some of the things would not be available, but Aiko assured him with a snicker that scouting ships were well stocked with a variety of supplies, even the antiquated ones on his list.

As he walked around surveying his surroundings, the gravel crunched under his feet. As far as he could see were dilapidated and abandoned buildings, some just shells. He glanced up and shielded his face. Not a cloud in the sky. Nor a bird. *What kind of planet was this?*

What had felt right to him from the vantage point of the space shuttle was a half-demolished one-story building. The roof and half the walls were gone, but two sturdy walls still stood. It was on a slight rise and a little apart from the other dilapidated buildings, thus providing Eloch with a view of his surroundings. If anything intruded on his domain, he would be able to see it and prepare.

He spent the rest of the day creating his home, although in his weakened condition it took him longer than he had anticipated. By nightfall he was hunkered down in front of the fire he had made from debris. It crackled and popped, sending sparks high into the sky. He leaned back with a sigh against a portion of the wall and reached for one of the meal bars in his food duffle. It was nearly tasteless but nutritious. He hoped he would learn to appreciate what flavor there was.

Darkness had fallen fast, and with the night came a chill as the day's heat rapidly dissipated. He glanced back at his bedroll, which was nestled underneath the tarp he had fastened to the two walls. He was tired and sore. The bedroll beckoned. Meal bar eaten, Eloch rinsed his mouth with a swig of water and put another board on the fire before he climbed into the welcome warmth of his bed. He watched the fire until his eyes grew heavy and he drifted off to sleep.

In the morning, he looked for tracks around his encampment and found none. The Rubble appeared to be empty of all creatures, animal and human alike. But a light mist was falling, and it gave him hope.

In the most recent evolution of their City, the people of Spur had insulated themselves so completely from the environs of the planet Eloch had been unable to determine before he arrived here if weather still happened outside. Since there was rain, even if only a fine mist, things could grow. Eloch decided to search for signs of life. He slipped an oilskin poncho over his clothes, retrieved his staff from where it leaned against the wall within easy reach of his bedroll, and set out into the mist.

Rubble spread to the horizon in all directions, nothing but old, abandoned buildings in different stages of collapse. Genji had explained to Eloch that the City of Spur was a continuous collection of buildings. When the ruling classes were tired of where they lived, they built new buildings and moved themselves and their possessions into the new, leaving the old to become a part of Rubble, a place for those less fortunate to scavenge. This was how it had been done for thousands and thousands of years, until the City had finally covered the entire face of the planet.

"The entire planet, covered by one City?" Eloch had asked. "It cannot be." He had been thinking of Entean, and Her many waterways winding through the green. "But how can you grow your food? Graze your beasts for meat?"

"We have glass houses, rows and rows of them, where our plants grow. Our technologies have cloned meat portions we keep alive until harvest. Meat cloned from animals became extinct long ago."

"It cannot be true," Eloch repeated.

"It *is* true," Genji replied. "You will see soon enough. And now, for nearly a thousand years, we have been building on top of the old City. That is how SubCity was formed, where those who are not ruling class are forced to live."

"In the dark?"

"It is lit," Genji laughed. "And many work in the Upper, so they see the light of day on their way to and from work."

"And so you have used up your planet and are now finding other planets to use up," Eloch said with disgust.

"It was why the Ring was formed," Genji explained. "We had too many people. There was a panic that our greenhouses couldn't feed everyone. People began hoarding their food supplies. Skirmishes broke out. We were on the brink of total chaos. Since the Ring Colonization, that fear has been put to rest and we've settled down. Now only SubCity gets overcrowded. But the wars between the KinLords keep them thinned out fairly well. And those with enough knack in them, like Aiko, are trained to be pilots."

"But what of your planet?" Eloch asked, ignoring the rest of Genji's lesson. "Is your planet still alive, Genji?"

Genji had merely laughed and said Eloch had a lot of strange notions. The lesson ended shortly thereafter.

Now Eloch set off toward the east. After a few miles, he noticed the buildings were not as dilapidated as in his section. He paused by a pool of water, gently lifting debris from around its edges, seeking signs of life. He soon discovered the pool was man-made, and so trudged on, leaning more heavily on his staff.

The mist had cleared when Eloch stopped for lunch at noon. He dug into the pocket of his poncho and pulled out another near-tasteless meal bar. Then he stripped off his poncho, since he no longer needed it for warmth, and used it for a cushion. From where he sat, munching on the bar, he could see the spires of the new City in the distance.

The people of Spur reminded him of the coral growing in some of Entean's lakes, vast colonies living on top of the skeletons of their ancestors. Whole islands had been created by the coral. "But not here," he whispered. "Nothing good has grown from these skeletons."

He suddenly felt very far away from home and very alone.

Something stirred and fluttered deep within his center. Eloch put his hand over his middle. Not alone, he mused, just very far from home.

Finished with his so-called meal, Eloch carefully folded the wrapper and stored it in a pocket of his jerkin. He tied the poncho around his waist, picked up his staff, and retraced his steps.

The days flowed into weeks, so much the same he wouldn't have known a month had passed if a shuttle hadn't appeared out of the blue sky, touching down lightly next to his encampment.

When Aiko and Genji emerged, his shout of greeting was spontaneous.

"Brought you more supplies," Aiko said.

"My thanks," Eloch replied. "Every day, I have walked in different directions to find food. I have found nothing, again and again."

"I told you," Genji said. "The only food is in the glass houses." He handed Eloch two duffle bags. They felt heavy. "There's some fresh food in there. Best eat it first."

"We've received an assignment," Aiko told him, "so we'll be off planet for several months. Hope that's enough food."

"I'll make it enough," Eloch replied. He'd been frugal and still had most of his original food cache.

"If it's not," Aiko continued, "head northeast until you come to the new City limits." She dug into the breast pocket of her flight jacket, removed a small plastic rectangle, and handed it to Eloch. "Give the guard this, and he will tell you where to go."

Eloch took the rectangle. "What is it?"

"A voucher. Says you work for me. Also, an address of a man named Manabu. Old pilot friend of mine. Retired. He'll let you stay with him until I get back. I'll look for you here first. If you're not here, I'll go to Manabu's."

Eloch nodded and placed the rectangle in the inner pocket of his jerkin. "Thank you, Aiko, for your kindness."

"Don't lose it."

"I won't."

She scanned him and then glanced at Genji. "He looks good, doesn't he? Filled out some."

Genji nodded. "You do look much better."

"I feel better. Stronger," Eloch said. "Come see what I've done."

He led them through his encampment to another abandoned building. "I constructed a bathing pool," he said, unable to conceal his pride. "I capture rainwater in this black sacking I found. During the day, it heats up, and at night I spill it into this tub so I can clean myself."

Aiko raised her eyebrows. "That's quite clever, Champion. I'm not sure it would have occurred to me."

"You don't need it, Aiko," Genji laughed. "We've got the shuttle."

"True, Genj," Aiko agreed. "Speaking of which, time to get back and prep."

"What do you plan to do next?" Genji asked while Eloch walked with them back to the shuttle. "Surely a month of solitude has given you time to pull together some ideas."

"To keep on what I'm doing," Eloch replied. "I'm learning your ways by exploring what you've abandoned. Tomorrow I head south, where it appears to be older."

"All you'll find is more rubble," Aiko told him. "I've flown all around Spur in all directions, and that's all there is. Rubble and City."

"Nonetheless, it is my plan," Eloch said.

He watched them climb aboard and strap themselves down.

"Be well," Genji said before the door was sealed.

"And you," Eloch replied.

As before, Aiko and Genji both watched Eloch's retreating form until the shuttle banked.

"He seems less scattered," Aiko commented.

Genji shrugged. "He still looks a little lost to me."

"I disagree," Aiko replied. "He seems to have purpose now. The way he looked at us, I caught glimpses of the man we met on A349."

"Entean."

"Hmm?"

"Entean. His planet. Not A349."

Aiko glanced at Genji and grinned. "Who's the Champion's champion now?"

Genji met her smile with one of his own. "There's just something about him. You want him to succeed."

Aiko surprised herself by reaching out to lightly touch Genji's knee. "I know," she said. To cover her awkwardness, she changed the subject. "When we get back, I'll start going through the prep list. I want this trip to be flawless. Perhaps it'll convince the Colonizers to give us some business other than the scouting missions."

"I thought you liked to scout."

"I do, but…" her voice trailed off.

"But what, Aiko?"

She hesitated. "I'm not getting any younger, Genj," was all she said. It didn't feel right to tell one of her crew she wanted a home and a family.

~~~

In the evening, before he settled into his bedroll, Eloch made a backpack out of one of the duffles, since he planned to travel for more than one day. He filled the pack with a couple of water bladders, food, a change of clothes, and a cape to wrap up in at night. Then he set the pack by his staff.

Since the temperature had dropped by then, he put a board on his fire and settled down to sleep, planning to get an early start in the morning.

It never happened.

Chapter 5: The Culling

Wren whistled in appreciation when she saw what her Kin had done with Tunnel Two. Everything was suspended off the ground, all their supplies bundled on little platforms constructed high on the tunnel's walls. And not just their supplies, but sleeping platforms as well, all connected with rope ladders leading from platform to platform.

"Good defense, too," she said to Cricket and Flick. "Looking up seems to be the last thing people think to do when attacking." She cuffed Cricket playfully in the arm. "Don't forget that. Something Auntie Wren has used most effectively on more than one occasion. Good job, boys," she added. "I think we'll have ourselves a quite cozy hide in dank and drippy Tunnel Two. Now, what about escape routes, should we happen to need them?"

"We've made everyone memorize at least three routes. They'll be able to scatter like cockroaches when the light's turned on."

Wren made a face. "Cockroaches? Really? Couldn't you have picked a different critter?"

Flick laughed. "Well, there aren't many to choose from. Anyway, most of the routes will lead to other tunnels, but a few lead to Above. They had to memorize at least one route to Above."

Wren nodded. "Good thinking. Let's hope our Kin won't need any of them, and we have a nice, quiet hide." She hesitated. "And I don't want them to think if they make it Above, they're automatically safe. Not on the night of a Cull. None of us will be safe anywhere."

"Especially you," Flick muttered.

Wren silenced him with a look. "Narrows, Flick," she warned.

Cricket gave them a glance but said nothing.

"Again, well done, boys. When will it be Kin-ready?"

"Nearly there," Cricket answered with a glance at Flick. "This afternoon?"

"Sounds 'bout right."

"Great!" Wren replied. "I'll tell Spider to gather the old and weakened and start the move." She winked. "If they begin now, those slow folk should be here by this afternoon."

With a wave, Wren set out for Tunnel One to find Spider, since she'd seen him heading in that direction when she went to Two. She hoped she could catch him before he darted somewhere else.

She found him in a heated, whispered discussion with Mouse, their heads together. They jumped apart when she made herself known.

"What's up?" They didn't say anything, but they looked so guilty, Wren's suspicion went on high alert. "Keeping something from me, I suspect. Neither of you look too happy I'm here." She folded her arms. "But since I am, let's hear it."

Mouse kicked Spider's boot. He cleared his throat and glared at Mouse before he spoke. "We were talking about how to protect you, if you must know."

Wren shook her head. "I'm not the priority, here. It's the Kin. Always the Kin."

"And Caution," Mouse countered. "Caution First. Your words. Your rules."

62

"And you don't think I'm cautious enough to look after my own person?" Wren challenged.

Mouse gave a little smile. "You've got this weakness, Wren," she said gently.

"Yeah," said Spider, not gently at all. "Your Kin. With you it's Kin first. And that's when Caution gets slaughtered."

"I can take care of myself," Wren said quietly. "I don't step out of our compound without my knives. There are eight knives hidden on my body this very moment. Eight knives. And a few others tossed into my pockets." She patted her jacket's two pockets. "I'm feeling pretty secure, here, folks."

"But it might not be enough," Spider told her. "This isn't just a KinLord battle we're talking about. We've got Martials. And Martials use weapons that make your knives about as effective as blunt sticks."

Wren straightened. "I do just fine with these knives, Spider. I wouldn't want to meet me in a dark part of SubCity. Or anywhere else, for that matter."

Mouse touched her shoulder. "Look, Wren, we know you're skilled. We know you know how to take care of yourself. But this is going to be different." She lifted her arms and then let them flop down. "I can't seem to get through to you. We're not going to be on a Kill. We're going to be *attacked*. They're planning to raid our tunnels, Wren. Lots of Kin from two other KinLords, and lots of Martials. All armed."

"You forget something, Mouse," Wren said. "These are our tunnels. And I know these tunnels through and through. We all do, but especially me. We're going to survive this. All of us are. Now, if you'll excuse me, I need to talk to Skip. Oh, and Spider, we're starting the move this afternoon, so rouse the Kin." She turned away, heading for Tunnel Five.

"I want to put more booby traps in the tunnels!" Mouse called after her.

"If you feel you must, you have my permission," Wren called back over her shoulder as she continued on.

~~~

Tunnel Five buzzed with activity.

The minute she stepped in, Wren was forced to duck around a man carrying a flour sack and then dodge a runner with a box of meal bars.

"Good swipe!" she called after the runner. Meal bars were hard to come by.

The young runner glanced at Wren as she passed by and lifted his chin in acknowledgment.

By the time she reached Skip, she was grinning. "Saw your boy, Rabbit. Nearly ran me down, he was in such a hurry."

Skip glanced at her. "Not hurt, are you?"

Wren waved a hand. "Not at all. There's quite a commotion in here," she commented, as she looked around.

Skip grinned. "A huge haul today. Found an overturned delivery shuttle early this morning. We were all over it like that!" He snapped his fingers.

"Lucky us. How's Guy?" Guy was Skip's other son. He'd taken a fall and had broken his collarbone.

"Guy's good," Skip said, his smile strained.

"Listen, why don't you get Guy's gear together and take him over to Spider? We're beginning the hide this afternoon."

"This afternoon? So soon?"

"Yep. And it looks pretty good, if you haven't checked it out. Quite cozy."

"I haven't left this Tunnel since this all began," Skip answered. "Too much to do."

She patted his shoulder. "Then you take the time now. Go get Guy and check out Tunnel Two, get him settled. That's an order."

He nodded. "Thank you, Wren. Just have a few more things to do, and then I'll take Guy to Two.

She watched him walk away, a concerned father, shoulders stooped with worry.

"Don't worry, Skip!" she called. "I had a broken collarbone once. Hurts like crazy but it heals. Guy's going to be fine."

She wasn't sure he heard her over the din.

~~~

It happened fast.

Wren shot out of bed and vaulted into her clothes, slipping her knives into their sheaths as she ran, Flick close on her heels.

"Mouse!" she cried.

"Here!" Mouse shouted.

"Need eyes. Go high. Relocate at Tunnel Five."

Mouse gave a quick nod before scrambling up to the compound rooftops, where she could get a clear view of what was happening and report to Wren when they met in Tunnel Five.

Soundlessly, Wren and Flick crept down the steps, where a group of her frightened Kin waited, eyes wide.

"What's going on?" Ilsa, a young girl, asked. Her lips trembled. "It sounds like it's coming from Tunnel Two. My grandparents are in there."

"I'm about to find out," Wren said, placing a hand on the girl's shoulder. "Flick, take these and any others you gather along the way to Five."

She turned to her Kin. "Listen to Flick. If he says, stop, stop. If he says duck, duck. We know our KinLand. That's the only defense we have when we don't know what's happening. If you trust Flick, he will get you to Five. I'll see you there."

With a nod to Flick, Wren silently slipped out the back and into mayhem. Shouts, gunfire, torchlight, flickering figures. And screams. The screams of her Kin in Tunnel Two.

Wren ducked behind a fence to get her bearings. A group of Martials ran by in that jerky trot-march they seemed to believe looked threatening.

Their guns were what made them threatening.

And their destination was Tunnel Two.

She had to get there first to have any hope of saving even a few of her Kin. From the sounds, hope was fleeting.

Like a lizard, Wren shimmied up a rusted drainpipe barely attached to her compound, a reminder that SubCity had once been the City. Like Mouse, she had been trained to use rooftops as highways for her work. Ever aware that someone might look up, she darted from rooftop to rooftop, and arrived at Two before the Martials. She speculated she had five minutes at best to get in and get out with whatever survivors she could find. She was most worried about Spider. She needed his knowledge, especially when they moved to Above.

The opening was unguarded and she slipped in...and her heart plummeted as her stomach heaved at what she saw.

Her Kin were putting up a good fight. There were several Martials sprawled on the floor, some still alive, most dead. But her KinFolk were still vastly outnumbered, weak to begin with, and losing quickly. From what Wren could patch together in the few seconds she had, the tide had turned against the Kin when the Martials managed to burn the rope bridges and ladders, trapping them up near the ceiling. Through the smoke and flickering firelight, she frantically searched for any who were escaping, hoping Spider was one of them.

When she heard tramping feet, she melted against the tunnel and held still, just as the group of Martials she had outdistanced made their entrance.

And then the carnage began in earnest. A nightmare unfolded before her eyes.

All the defensive plans she, Flick, and Cricket had devised. All the escape routes they had made the Kin memorize.

Useless.

Why didn't we think to use chains instead of rope?

And there was nothing she could do to help her Kin except keep herself alive to lead the survivors out of SubCity.

The bile rose in her throat so quickly, she fell to her knees and emptied the contents of her last meal.

As soon she could move, she slipped out and made her way to Tunnel Five.

Flick was waiting for her just inside the entrance. He stepped out of the shadows, a gun resting comfortably in his hands. She was beyond words and merely shook her head at the question on his face.

"Oh, Wren," he said and slid an arm around her.

She momentarily allowed herself the luxury of leaning against his familiar strength. Then she stepped away and ran her hand over her coils.

"There wasn't a thing I could do, Flick," she told him. Her voice sounded hollow in her ears. "But we're going to have to mourn them later. How bad is it?"

"It's bad, Wren," he told her while they hurried deeper into the tunnels. As her eyes adjusted, she noticed Flick had positioned sharpshooters in key positions. "We've been ambushed. It looks like they've got two groups going. From what the eyes have told me, the Martials are focused on Tunnel Two."

"Yeah, I saw that," Wren said. "And the second group?"

"Well-armed Kin. Both Fergus and MacMichaels. They're sweeping the KinLand, capturing, not killing, hunting for our compound." He smirked. "Went to the biggest, fanciest house first. You were so smart to pick a more modest headquarters."

Wren nodded. "It saved our lives," she told him. "That big mansion made a perfect decoy. At least they're not killing Kin." She stopped walking, forcing Flick to follow suit. "We've got a chance against Kin, Flick, but not against the Martials. Once they're done with Two, they'll start a sweep of our KinLand. Are all your eyes out?"

Flick nodded. "I'm expecting Flea back soon."

"When Flea comes back, send her out for a final sweep. Have her spread the word we're going to blow the main entrance of Five, so go to the side entrance. Move your snipers into position to the side. It's narrower and easier to defend," She shook her head. "I doubt very much there are many survivors left. Did many Kin make it to here?"

"A few, Wren."

She shook her head. "This morning there were nearly five hundred of us." Her voice cracked.

"Don't go there, Wren. We need your wits."

"I'm not going there, Flick. Where's Mouse?"

"Mouse went through the tunnels back down to Two to see if she can find any survivors."

"Cricket?"

"In the main cavern, where we're arming ourselves."

"That's where I'll be." She pulled out her timekeeper, wiped the lint off its cracked face. Flick did the same. "Let's get out of here. Meet me there in twenty. We'll blow the tunnel in fifteen, starting the count now." They synchronized their timekeepers. "Get your snipers stationed." She gripped his meaty arm before he could move away. "What I want to know is who told the Martials where we were holding our hide, and that we were beginning tonight. This is no coincidence."

She watched the blood drain from his face.

"Go follow your orders, Flick. I'll handle this part." She gave his arm a little push. "No traitor's going to come with us when we move out, I can promise you that."

~~~

The main storeroom was lit with both electricity and torches, usually a cheerful sight after walking through the gloom. Now it stood as a beacon for any survivors, although there were only a pathetic few. Wren found Skip handing out blankets. Rabbit, his son, headed to a bench where five wide-eyed people sat huddled together.

"Don't get comfortable," Wren shouted before Rabbit could hand out his first blanket. "We're not staying here."

Heads turned when they heard her. Her Kin began to bombard her with questions.

"Not now," Wren said, raising her hands. "We've things to do, and not much time in which to do them." She looked at the small crowd around her. The last time her Kin had gathered, it was hot and crowded. Now Tunnel Five looked cavernous, ready to swallow them up.

"Has anyone taken a head count?" she asked.

"Thirty-five," Cricket said, appearing at her side.

Her chest ached.

"Listen up, everybody. We'll leave as soon as we can. The main entrance to Tunnel Five will be blown. When it goes, it will give us a little bit of time to get out of here."

"Where will we go?" someone asked. "There's no one in SubCity who'll take us."

"We're not staying in SubCity," Wren said. "We're going Above."

"Above?" Rabbit asked, glancing at his father. "But we don't know anything about Above."

Wren snorted. "Would you rather stay here?" She didn't wait for an answer. "Mouse has gone over to Two to bring back survivors, if there are any." She glanced over at Skip. "I'm sorry. I know Guy was there. I wouldn't hold out much hope."

"Guy's not there," Rabbit said. "Guy's here." He pointed to a boy, his arm in a sling, who stood just behind Skip. From where Wren stood, the boy had more than just a broken collarbone. She'd seen that look in her own eyes.

Wren turned slowly to face Skip. His face was a white mask. "It was you, wasn't it?" Wren said through gritted teeth. Her hand moved to one of her knives.

"It was him, what?" asked Cricket. His Adam's apple bobbed as he spoke.

"Not now," Wren said. She took a steadying breath. "Too much to do. Cricket, do not let Skip out of your sight. I want you glued to his side."

"Skip." She forced herself to look at him. "This is not finished, but for now I want you to fill as many runners' packs as you can with foodstuffs and hand them out." She looked at Skip's two boys. Their round eyes looked darker against their pale faces. "Boys," she said, "hand out blankets. Each person gets one until they're gone."

"Listen up, Kin," she called, addressing the survivors. "We're all in shock, and we're all scared. We will not survive unless we override that fear. Get in line. Get your pack of food and your blanket. When Mouse and Flick get here, they'll take you to safety. In the meantime, I want you quiet and ready. I repeat, we will not survive unless we override our fear. Now, line up."

She turned back to Cricket. "Stay glued to that man," she said, jabbing her finger. "I'm going to find Mouse."

She darted into the warren of tunnels that led to Two, praying Mouse had found at least Spider alive. Halfway there, she intercepted Mouse *and* Spider, who was carrying a small boy on his back.

Relief washed over her, followed closely by sorrow. "I hoped there'd be more," she said, feeling hollowed out.

"It happened so fast," Spider rasped. "I did what I could. It just happened so fast," he repeated.

"It was a massacre," Mouse said.

Wren nodded. "I know. I saw."

"What now?"

"We move to the Above, like we planned," Wren said, leading them back to Five. She fed Mouse and Spider details as they went.

"You realize we've been compromised," Spider said.

"I know. It was Skip, and I should have seen it coming. Should have read the signs," Wren replied.

Mouse touched her shoulder. "Don't beat yourself up. Save it for later."

Wren barked out a laugh. "Right."

The explosion rumbled through the tunnels and they staggered. Wren looked at her watch. "Tunnel Five's main entrance. Right on schedule. Which means Flick will be on his way. Let's hurry. I need to deal with Skip before we move out." Her teeth clenched with the thought.

~ ~ ~

"But what could I do?" Skip's voice was a little more than a whisper. "They had my son. I had no choice."

"Of course you had a choice," Wren spat. "You could have told me immediately. Both your boys are my Kin. I would have protected them. We could have used your boys against Fergus and MacMichaels. We could have made a plan, fed them information. Manipulated them. But now? Now? Now one of my best runners has been injured. Tortured for information. And you, my Grainier, have forced me to kill you."

She grabbed his face on either side, compelling him to look at her. He struggled, but two KinFolk held him fast.

"And the Martials know where we are hiding. Every last one of us is on the Cull list. Because you didn't trust me to take care of my own."

72

Abruptly, she dropped her hands and turned, blinking to clear her vision. Her Kin watched her silently, fearfully.

"Gather your things," she told them. "It's time to move out. We're not going to make this easy for them."

"What about Skip?" someone asked hesitantly.

Wren sighed, the weight of her decision so heavy she wished she could sit. "Betrayal means death," she answered, "but frankly, I am so tired of death…" One of the Kin gasped when a blade appeared in her hand.

Knife in her hand she turned back to Skip. "I can always kill you later, Skip. But I am done with it this day."

With a swift movement, she wedged Skip's mouth open and cut out half his tongue.

His cry was thin and reedy.

"Father!" Rabbit cried. He looked at Wren. "You cut out his tongue," he said, incredulous.

"And he's still alive," Wren told him. "Count your blessings, boy."

"Someone cauterize the wound," she commanded, wiping her knife on Skip's shirt before throwing the tongue to the far end of the cave. "We will leave in ten. Flick, Mouse," she said, re-sheathing her weapon.

They stood off to the side, trying to make their plans in spite of Skip's anguished cries…which eventually turned into whimpers when someone told him to shut it, and that he could have been dead like the ones in Tunnel Two.

Wren glanced at Flick. "Not a good night," she said.

He nodded, his expression gloomy. "I've experienced happier times."

"Ditto," Mouse agreed. "Why'd you do it, Wren? Cut out his tongue?"

"Just couldn't kill him, Mouse. He loves his son. He was scared."

"I could have done it for you, Wren," Mouse said softly.

"I know, and I thank you for it. But we need him. Only have one Grainier. Besides, I think he understands my intentions."

"And he won't be able to rat us out no more this way," Flick added.

"Truth," Mouse said.

"So, we take to the tunnels," Wren told them. "You both know the way to the fountain square. Get them there. Get them settled like we planned."

"What about you?" asked Flick.

"I'll create a diversion so you won't be followed."

"It should be me," Flick protested. "You're needed to lead."

"No, Flick. Me. I know these tunnels, and I'll lead the Martials on the merriest chase of their blighted little lives. Then I'll meet you back at the square. And you, you know explosives. Mouse, you take the front, and Flick, when it's all clear, blow the tunnel to Above so you can't be followed."

"But you'll be stuck," Mouse said.

"I know the tunnels, and I know the Above," Wren told her. "I can't be stuck," She paused. "But if it takes me more than a week, contact Max. He owes me quite a few favors."

"Max? Who's Max?" Flick asked.

"Someone I knew from my time Above. Mouse knows him. He can't be trusted any more than anyone can be trusted, but he's been a good bloke to me. And he owes me."

"I don't like it," said Mouse, shaking her head.

"Got a better plan? We haven't got much time to argue. Are the snipers in place, Flick?"

"They are."

"Any hope for stragglers?"

"Flea confirmed the other Kins are recruiting our survivors."

"That's good, means they're safe from the Cull. Get your snipers back."

Flick called over to Flea to give her the instructions. With barely a nod, Flea was off.

Wren scanned her Kin while they gathered their meager supplies, and shook her head. "Out of all my Kin, these are the only ones left. How many, Flick?"

"If you count the snipers, forty-five."

"That's all?"

Flick sighed. "'Fraid so. We got slammed."

Wren felt her throat thickening. She covered her face with her hands and silently counted to five.

Flick touched her arm. "They're not all dead, Wren. Most are just being recruited. Think on that."

Wren smiled at him and nodded. "You take the rest, then, and keep them safe." She flung an arm around each of them. "They're my Kin, but you both are my family. Keep yourselves safe, too. And Spider. Trust Spider. He's our best asset for understanding the Above. No risks, none of you. Just survive." She released them, and stepped back. "Let's pack up. The Martials won't wait for us to escape."

Wren crossed over to where Skip and his sons were loading a distribution cart with the last of their portable supplies.

She studied his bruised and swollen face. There was fresh blood at the corners of his mouth. Inwardly she cringed. Outwardly, she waited, hoping her judgment had been sound.

When he noticed her, Skip nodded, looking at her warily. His boys did the same.

"I need a pack of the basics," she said quietly. "Then you and your boys get in line. You've filled that cart enough. It's time to go."

Skip motioned to Rabbit to bring him a pack, and he filled it with meal bars and a bladder of water. When he handed it to her, Skip grasped both her hands and squeezed them tight before releasing them.

She felt her tension dissipate. She nodded to him, showing that she understood, and slung the pack onto her back.

He saluted her in return and then motioned to his boys to hurry.

She crossed over to Flick. "Skip's going to be okay," she told him. "I'm fetching more knives for my merry chase. You leave. Now."

Before he could answer, they both heard deep, roaring growls reverberating through the tunnels.

They froze, their expressions identical.

Someone screamed.

Wren pushed him. "Go, Flick. There's barely enough time."

"But Wren, they're sniffers."

"All the more reason to stop wasting time."

She looked for Mouse, relieved to see she and Spider were already leading the surviving Kin into the tunnel.

"Blow the tunnel, Flick, as soon as it's clear."

"Wren—"

She grinned. "I know, Flick, sniffers. We do what we need to do. Now go." She saw their fear "Go. I do *not* want any more Kin to die."

She didn't wait, but hurried toward the growling barks, determined to make the sniffers catch her scent first. On her way, she risked a brief stop at the arsenal to shove a handful of throwing knives into her pockets.

She didn't want to die, either.

~~~

Two knives left. Wren leaned against the tunnel wall and sucked huge gulps of air into her exhausted lungs. She squinted through the endless grey, grateful she'd finally found a tunnel that wasn't pitch black. It meant there was some hope she might escape. She wondered what time it was. Near dawn, she suspected.

The sniffers were closing in again. She had managed to keep ahead of them as she raced through the tunnels. Barely. They were faster. But she was smaller. When she came to an intersection, she had chosen the tunnels with the smallest openings, forcing the sniffers to dig to before they could fit through. It bought her some time.

In the beginning, there had been eight of them following her trail. Now there were three. The odds were still not in her favor. If she was lucky, and her aim was true, she would have only one sniffer to deal with in the end.

They were larger.

Much larger.

And faster.

And she was so tired.

Her only hope was to get out of the tunnels and somehow trap the sniffers inside.

The problem was she was hopelessly lost, and in completely unknown territory. So her scent would be the only scent for the sniffers to follow, she had chosen tunnels she had been in the process of exploring for future use, far from her Kin's escape routes. It hadn't taken her long to come to the limits of her knowledge, and she had been running since then on instinct more than wits. But maybe, just maybe, her instincts had been leading her true. Wasn't that a breeze on her cheek?

Wren held her breath, held still, and waited.

Yes!

Softly, she crept further, using her feet to feel her way along the dusty floor while tapping the fingers of her left hand on the wall. Her right hand gripped her second to last throwing knife.

From behind, she heard the sniffers whining and digging, enlarging the opening she barely managed to squeeze through. She'd heard those sounds before, and knew eventually they would find a way. Then their whines would become bays. She hated the sound, knew if she survived the memories of this night and the relentless baying of the sniffers would follow her into her dreams for years to come.

If her hand had not been tracing along the wall, she would have walked smack into the tunnel's end. Her heart plummeted when she realized what the sudden stop meant. Fear squeezed her throat and she shook her head to clear its grip.

There was still a breeze. It meant this was an opening and not an end. It meant she still had hope.

With her hand, she traced the end of the tunnel. When she crouched down, her fingers located a grill bolted to the far side. Moving swiftly, she pivoted on her butt and braced herself on her arms, right fist still gripping her knife, and began kicking at the grill, willing the bolts to release their grip. They did, and the sudden lack of resistance sent her sprawling onto her back with an "Oomph."

The baying began.

"Hurry!" she scolded herself. She scrambled to her knees and crawled toward the opening.

The baying was louder already, and she heard their claws digging into the dirt just a few yards behind and closing fast.

The sniffers were nearly upon her, and their excited yowls and snarls filled and echoed around the tunnel, coming at her from all directions.

Her survival pack made it impossible for her to wriggle through the grate. With a frustrated cry, she ripped it off her shoulders and threw it through the opening, then dove headfirst after it, only to be stopped in mid-air.

She screamed.

A sniffer sank its teeth deep into her left calf, and then chewing down to the bone while shredding her flesh with its claws. Without thinking, she rammed the heel of her other boot into its muzzle.

With a yelp it loosened its grip enough for her to rip her leg free. She screamed again, this time in defiance. If they wanted to rip her apart, she was not going to make it easy.

The scent of her blood drove the three sniffers into a frenzy. They snarled and barked and bit each other bloody while they fought to reach her through the opening, their lethal claws ripping out giant clods of dirt, making it wider.

She scrambled to her feet and backed against a pile of rubble, leaving a trail of blood.

So much blood. No wonder she was about to pass out.

The blood catapulted the sniffers into an even greater frenzy. Their growls rose into crescendo of howls as they redoubled their efforts to reach her.

Wren took a calming breath and ignored both their howls and her pain as she'd been taught. She took out the first sniffer through the hole with a dagger in the heart. It dropped at her feet.

The other two paused and began to circle, sniffing warily.

Keeping her eyes on them, she stooped and tugged her knife from the dead sniffer.

"One for each of you," she told them.

One of the sniffers growled a challenge.

She growled back.

Her throbbing leg finally broke through her concentration. Wren glanced down to see blood pooling at her feet. Another wave of dizziness struck. She took a deep breath and refocused. Pocketing one of her knives, she picked up a rock and sent it flying at the nearest sniffer.

She hit it squarely on the head.

It yelped, shook its head and stood still, studying her, nostrils distended.

The other sniffer paused just out of range.

Smart beasts. If only they could have been less so.

She felt for her belt, loosened it and stooped to tie it tight around her left thigh, making a tourniquet in order to staunch the flow of blood.

She only dropped her gaze for a moment.

Reflex made her duck and roll.

With a yelp, the leaping sniffer smacked into the rubble pile Wren had been leaning against. Before it could recover she was on it, slicing through its sleek hide, going right for its jugular.

Its blood mingled with her own as the creature bled out.

With a grunt she rose, pushing herself off the creature, and faced the final sniffer.

She blinked, but her vision kept going in and out of focus while spots danced around her in little explosions of color. She sucked in another breath and reached for the second knife.

Do Not Faint.

The sniffer paced a few steps, scenting again, sniffing its downed companions, its growls interspersed with whines and whimpers.

Watching it move its sleek body back and forth was almost hypnotic.

"Come on!" she taunted. "Get on with it." She was surprised to hear her shout emerge as a thready whisper.

The creature's ears pricked in her direction. Through her wavering vision, she saw its muscles bunch.

I should be throwing my knives, she thought, feeling her knees give way.

The beast snarled and launched itself.

Chapter 6: The Sausage

At least he had his strength back.

Eloch wrestled with the creature while it writhed and snapped its great jaws. Even though he was strong, Eloch knew he needed to come up with a plan fast to quell its battle madness. Otherwise he would be forced to dispatch it, which was not an option. Spur needed Her creatures.

He could feel its claws digging into him, returning his lethal embrace. Fortunately, his tough leather clothes held fast. Elbow on the beast's neck, he first clamped one hand over its muzzle, and then the next, holding its jaws shut. The creature thrashed harder. Eloch began to sing the crooning song he used to soothe Entean's beasts.

The creature stilled, but Eloch suspected it was more from surprise than pleasure. And perhaps fatigue. He kept singing, and was rewarded when the muscles under him relaxed into sleep.

Keeping one hand clamped around the sleeping beast's jaws, he pulled a cord from his tunic and wrapped it tight around the beast's muzzle, knotting it securely. As soon as he moved, it woke up, and its growl turned into a whine when it couldn't open its mouth. It started to struggle again, trying to use its claws to tear at the binding, but Eloch was ready, using another cord to bind all four paws together. When he was convinced the beast could not escape its bindings, he rolled off it and stood to retrieve his staff.

He watched it for a while, ready with another cord should either of the two snap.

But the beast lay silent, its sides heaving, while it watched Eloch warily.

Although Eloch suspected it would try again after it had recovered, for the moment, the beast was quelled.

It was time to tend to the girl who lay in a crumpled heap, a throwing knife loose in her outstretched hand.

From what Eloch could patch together, the beasts had been hunting the girl, and if he had arrived a moment later, the remaining beast would have successfully completed their hunt.

The howls and snarls had attracted his attention. Eager to meet the wildlife of Spur, he had changed course immediately. The ferocity of the baying alerted him that a hunt was on. He broke into a run when he came around the towering heap of rubble and saw their prey was human. And when he saw her waver, he knew she wouldn't survive the remaining beast's attack.

Flinging his staff and pack aside, he flung himself at the springing beast to save her. Now he knelt down to examine her quickly, impressed that she'd known to tourniquet her wound in spite of being under direct attack. It was probably why she still had a chance to live, despite the terrible wound. Quickly he scooped her up, retraced his steps, and collected his belongings before he jogged with her back to his encampment.

~~~

He'd done all he could for the girl.

The medical kit Aiko gave him was equipped to handle only the most minor of injuries. He had been forced to use up all the cleaning and clotting spray to get the wounds to finally stop bleeding. He'd used all the wound sealant as well. Her poor calf muscle had been shredded to ribbons.

Eloch had no idea if she would ever be able to walk on it again.

If she lived.

If she lived was now up to her.

For the moment, she had a slight fever but was sleeping quietly. He hoped the fever would not worsen.

Eloch rummaged around in the medical kit and found two syringes loaded with antibiotics. As a precaution, he injected her with one. Then he wrapped her in his blanket and left her sleeping on his bedroll.

After one last look, he went to the broken-down building housing his makeshift shower. The building next to it had a roof, and seemed sturdy. If he planned to befriend the beast, he would need a very sturdy enclosure. He would also need a floor. Its claws told him it was a proficient digger.

Good. The building still had a floor, and would be perfect for his needs.

It took him nearly two hours of diligent work, but when Eloch finished he was satisfied he could keep the beast contained. After checking on the girl, he returned to the skirmish site to fetch the beast and make things right.

It was none too happy to see him, rumbling deep in its throat when he approached. From the churned-up earth, he could tell it had struggled against its bindings, even managed to flip itself around before it gave up. It continued to growl while he stood over it. But when he reached down to assure himself the knots were secure, the beast flinched, as if it expected a beating.

Instead Eloch stroked it gently and told it how magnificent it was. Its hide quivered under his touch, and the beast growled another warning. Eloch kept stroking it, feeling for any signs of bruises or other wounds. He kept his touch gentle and his voice melodious until it began to relax again. Satisfied the animal needed no care other than food, he stood to survey the scene. The beast still watched him with a malicious glint, but it had stopped growling.

It was time to honor the fallen. As it appeared somewhat intelligent, he wanted the remaining beast to see what he was doing, so he dragged the bodies of its two fallen comrades where it could see them.

The beast whimpered.

"You do have intelligence," Eloch mused. "You recognize them."

The creature eyed him warily.

Eloch ignored it and began his ritual. If he were back on Entean, the bodies would have already been returned to Her care. With a sigh, he picked up the small shovel he'd brought and dug a large grave. He gently arranged the two creatures within it and then covered them. When he had finished, he outlined the two graves with bits of rubble.

"I thank Spur for the gift of your life and I re-gift you back to Her," Eloch said, making the sign of gratitude for life. He glanced over at the bound beast.

It was watching him.

"You were excellent brethren. I suspect you will be missed," he added to the buried creatures.

Eloch ended the ritual by smoothing away evidence of the mêlée and burying the spilled blood while he thanked Spur for the gift of life.

Next he picked up the pack the girl had dropped, collected her throwing knives, wiped them clean, and put them in her pack, glad to find additional meal bars, water and a blanket inside.

"I will not be cold tonight after all!" he exclaimed as he reclosed the pack and tossed it near his shovel.

The tunnel opening had been torn apart by the frenzied beasts. So none could follow, Eloch filled the gap, building a wall of rubble and permanently sealing off the tunnel. When he finished, he mopped the sweat from his eyes, grateful the girl's water bladder was close at hand.

As he took a long, refreshing drink, he noticed the beast's eyes following his movements.

He went over and squatted down by its head.

"You're won't bite me if I free your jaws to drink?" he asked it as he loosened the leather cord.

The beast was quick, but Eloch was quicker. He held the jaws closed until he felt its surrender.

"We will do this one more time, Beastie," he told it. "If you act up again, you'll be thirsty for a little while longer."

It was docile enough for him to get one good squirt down its throat before it erupted in a frenzy of snarling and snapping, ripping the bladder out of Eloch's hands and showering them both with its contents. With considerable effort, Eloch was able to re-bind the beast's jaws and leave it to thrash out its frustration while he surveyed his handiwork. Except for the graves, there was no evidence that anything out of the ordinary had taken place here.

Deciding to let the beast tire itself out, he scooped up the empty bladder, slung the pack and shovel over his back, and returned to his encampment.

The girl's fever was worse. When he forced water down her throat, she cried out at his touch and struggled weakly. Eloch moistened a rag and wiped her face, speaking as gently to her as he had to the beast.

She slowly quieted and sank back into a fevered sleep.

While she slept, Eloch went back for the beast. It had turned itself around again, its sleek hide now covered with dust. Its flanks were heaving, its nostrils expanding as it tried to catch its breath.

To a chorus of snarls, Eloch scooped it up and slung it over his back as he had with the girl's backpack, surprised to find it was lighter than he'd expected. Its ribs dug into his shoulder. "Poor Beastie," he murmured.

Feeling the need to hurry back to the girl, he jogged back to his encampment.

"I'll see to you later," he told the beast as he laid it gently within its new enclosure.

It answered him with a snarl.

She was sleeping, even hotter to the touch. Eloch gave her the second injection of antibiotics. After soaking them in water, he used shreds from her bloodied leggings to wrap her ankles, head and neck. Before he went back to the beast, he forced her to drink more water.

The beast he fitted with a metal collar and harness he created from the bits of metal he found strewn about the encampment. He was rather proud of his handiwork as he hammered it shut and saw the pieces were snug and secure around the creature's chest and shoulders. He next manacled all four legs and chained it to the wall by its hind legs. Since the beast was still bound, he took the opportunity to trim its claws with one of the girl's knives.

"Quit your fussing," he told it while he worked. "They'll grow back before you know it."

Then he slowly unbound it, jumping back from its lunging reach, holding his staff between them. The chains held firm, yanking the beast's paws out from under it and throwing it to the ground when it reached the chains' limits. With a smooth, liquid motion, it was up again, only to be thrown to the ground again. And again.

"I'll let you struggle with it for a while," Eloch called over the angry din. Satisfied the chains would hold, he returned to the girl.

Eloch's first night with his new companions was spent nursing the girl and minding the beast. In time the beast, weakened and defeated, had quieted enough for Eloch to remove the leather binding from its jaws. Of course it snapped at him, but was more interested in the food and water he'd brought. He discovered the beast would eat the meal bars, and was again grateful for the additional ones the girl had with her.

On one of his returns from visiting the beast he found the girl was up, braced for an attack, her injured leg held up as she wavered on the other. The cooling strips of cloth were scattered everywhere, and her eyes were glazed with pain and fever. She was obviously out of her wits.

"Don't come any closer," she told him. "I will kill you."

"I don't doubt it," he replied conversationally.

She reached into an imaginary tunic pocket. When she brought it out, her hand balanced for a throw. "Not one step closer. I won't warn you again."

He took a step.

She threw and then gasped when he kept coming. "You survived!" she said, eyes wide. "But that can't be."

He caught her before she hit the ground, assuming she had finally passed out from the pain. He carried her back to the bedroll and gently laid her down. Before he covered her, he checked the wound. It looked angry but did not smell of disease. Her forehead was still blazing with fever, though. He rinsed and then reapplied the strips of cloth, then removed them when she started shaking with chills. He forced her to drink. He took it as a good sign when she swore at him and called him Flick.

The fever broke a few hours before dawn, and she began sweating profusely. He bathed her unconscious body and dressed her in his spare leggings and tunic, rolling up the shirt and legs. He hoped the looseness of the leggings would make her wounded leg more comfortable.

Now she was out of danger, he took the time to study her. She was small and strongly made, all muscle and lean lines, reminding him a bit of the beast. Her small nose was straight, her mouth a little bow. As she slept, the little bow parted and she sucked in air like a small fish. The thought made him grin.

Still grinning, he reached out and stroked her damp, coiled hair. "Stay out of trouble, little one," he said.

After collecting the blanket from her pack, he wrapped it around his torso, brought his staff within easy reach, and drifted off using his arm as a pillow.

~~~

It was either the throbbing pain shooting up and down her left leg or the gnawing hunger that woke her. Wren couldn't decide which. Both were equally distracting, enough to yank her from the warm floaty place where she had been drifting.

She didn't open her eyes right away. Rather, she lay still and attempted to patch together what had happened and where she was. She remembered racing through the tunnels. Running to near exhaustion. She remembered a sniffer had latched onto her leg, had almost succeeded in hauling her back into the tunnel when she finally kicked herself free. She remembered battling the sniffers.

She remembered she should be dead.

Yet she wasn't dead.

So what happened?

Wren opened her eyes…

… and stared up at a tarp that shielded her from the sky. She wasn't in SubCity. Upper? Had one of her Kin found her, then? She turned her head to look out. Her neck was so stiff it felt like she hadn't moved her head in weeks. The light slanted in, like late afternoon. Her view showed her nothing but broken-down buildings.

Rubble. She was in Rubble.

How?

"Hello?" Was that her voice? It sounded like an old woman. She cleared her throat and tried again. Better.

There was a whisper of leather and a figure blocked the light. A large figure. An enormous figure. Maybe three times her size. She had never seen anyone that large before. Maybe she was dead after all, and she was in the holding place the priests always talked about. "Am I dead?" she croaked.

The figure squatted down beside her and reached out to feel her forehead. She tried not to flinch.

He quickly pulled his hand back. "I'm sorry, did I hurt you?"

His voice was the rich rumble she remembered from her dreams. Perhaps she hadn't been all that asleep.

"You didn't hurt me. I just don't like to be touched is all."

"I see," he replied, and she thought he really did see…which was rather disturbing.

"I'm not dead, am I?" she repeated.

He chuckled. It was low and gentle. "No, you are not dead. But you were very close to it at one point."

She thought for a moment and swallowed. "What happened?"

"Would you like a sip of water first? Some food? I can tell you while you eat."

Her stomach cramped and she nodded. "Please."

"I'm sorry, but I'm going to have to touch you to help you sit up. You have been asleep for nearly four days. I expect you are very weak."

She nodded, and he wrapped his arm around her shoulders and smoothly moved her to a sitting position while she tried not to groan.

"Your face is white. Do you feel faint?" His arm tightened, supporting her.

Wren took a breath, letting it out slowly. "No. It's the pain."

He nodded gravely. "I see. Shall I fetch the food, then? It will take a moment."

She nodded and closed her eyes briefly, listening to the rustle as he moved away. So weak. She'd never been this weak before, even after her parents had beaten her nearly to death and she had crawled to Upper and found the fountain.

"Here," he said, startling her. "Sip this until your food is ready." He helped her curl her fingers around a cup.

She nodded her thanks.

The water helped. She sighed at the sensation of cool liquid gliding down her throat. Her stomach lurched and then settled. She sipped more and watched the giant man make a fire. For one so large, he moved with an effortless ease she could appreciate. No wasted movement. No wasted energy.

He was very beautiful, she decided, even with the growth of beard covering his cheeks and nearly hiding the slight cleft in his pointed

92

chin. His deep-set eyes were the most brilliant green, and glittered like precious stones. And the strength of him when he lifted her. So warm and strong. Quick, deft fingers. Gentle touch. No, she wasn't dead when she could still respond to such glorious maleness.

The man glanced up, cocked his head at her. "You're smiling! This is good," he exclaimed, smiling in return.

Who had teeth that white? she wondered, feeling the flood of warmth rising up her face. The man was waiting for a response. She had none. "It's nothing," she said. "Just realizing I'm not dead is all," she took a sip of water and closed her eyes, listening to the spoon scrape against the sides of the pan as he stirred while heating its contents.

"Nearly ready, and afterward you can rest again," he told her.

She opened her eyes to let him know she wasn't asleep already. Her leg was so painful she wasn't sure she could go back to sleep. Nearly four days, he'd said. "My leg. How bad is it?"

He looked grave. "It is not infected," he told her.

"But?" she prompted.

"But it is bad. I am not sure if you will be able to walk properly. I am sorry."

She nodded. "But I will walk?"

His face gave nothing away. "I am hopeful you will, yes."

"I want to look at it," she said abruptly.

He crossed over to her, carrying a bowl with a spoon stuck in it. "Eat this first," he said as he took the cup from her and replaced it with the bowl. "And then you can look at it."

She sniffed at the bowl. Her stomach rumbled. "What is it?"

"A porridge I made out of a meal bar."

"You can do that?"

"Eat," he told her. "It's rather good." He spooned a small portion and aimed it for her mouth.

She opened her mouth to protest and was greeted with a mouthful of warm, soupy meal bar. She swallowed. "Not bad," she commented.

"You sound surprised," he said spooning up another portion.

"I am," she said before she took a second bite.

He spooned up a third bite and offered it to her.

She reached for the spoon. "I can do it myself," she said.

"You sure?"

She nodded and he handed her the laden spoon. Her hand shook as she leaned forward so she wouldn't spill anything. Pain shot through her leg and she gasped, nearly dropping her food. He reached out to steady it and she flinched, spilling porridge on her blanket.

"Let me help you."

She sighed and nodded, waiting for the pain to settle. "I'm sorry for the mess," she told him.

"Nonsense," he said and produced a rag from his tunic, deftly, cleaning up the spill. He paused to study her. "You realize the weakness is a result of your wound and is not something to be ashamed of."

"I make it a point to never show weakness if at all possible."

Without answering, he picked up the spoon and resumed feeding her.

She ate in silence until she was full, only a few bites. She shook her head at the spoon. "I'm sorry. I can't eat any more."

"I'll save it for later," he told her.

She nodded, her eyelids feeling heavy. She willed them open. "What happened? How did I get here?"

"Why don't you rest so your body can recover? When you awaken, I will answer all your questions."

She stifled a yawn. "I want to see my leg now."

"That can wait as well. Let me help you lie down."

It was an effort not to cry out.

"Now sleep," he said as he drew the blanket to her chin.

She didn't know if she actually slept or passed out from the pain, but when she next opened her eyes, it was dark. She glanced toward the shelter's opening and saw his profile reflected in the firelight. "Has it been dark long?" she asked, pleased her voice sounded stronger.

"Not too long," he said. "Would you like to sit up?"

"Yes, please."

He crossed to where she lay and helped her up. Her leg hurt just as much as before. It was hard, but she managed to ignore it. "May I have water?"

"What about some hot tea instead?"

"That sounds nice. Yes. And some meal bar mush?"

While he was gone, she found if she held her leg very still with it turned inward, the pain lessened.

He returned, using a board as a tray. Squatting next to her, he placed the tray on the floor and handed her the tea.

She nodded her thanks and shakily lifted it up to drink. It smelled of happier times with her Kin. The warmth spread down her throat and throughout her body. She sighed and looked at him. "This is nice."

He nodded.

"So what's your story?"

"My story?"

"Yeah, who are you? What's your name? How long have you lived here?"

"I am called Eloch, and I have not lived here long. A little over a month maybe."

"Where are you from, then? I'm assuming from Upper, because I have never seen anyone as tall as you in SubCity."

He shook his head. "I am not of Spur. I come from Entean."

The way he looked when he told her made her feel like crying. She swallowed.

"Entean?"

He nodded. "I am her Champion."

"I don't understand. Is Entean a planet or a woman?"

"A planet. I serve Her. Protect Her. Make things right upon Her surface."

Was he touched in the head? "But how did you get here? In Rubble? I assume we are in Rubble."

96

"Yes, this is Rubble. I thought you wanted to know how *you* came to be here, not me."

"I want to know both."

His eyes narrowed as he studied her. "I will make you a deal," he said and picked up the bowl of porridge. "You allow me to feed you, and I will tell you what you want to know."

"Both your story and how I got here?"

"If you finish the meal, yes."

"I'm not sure I can finish all that," she told him, frowning at the bowl. "You added to it. It's much fuller than before."

"You need to eat to heal. You're much stronger now than before, yes?"

"Yes." Careful not to disturb her leg, she straightened and held out the tea mug. "Okay. Talk."

He took the mug, set it down, and spooned up the first bite of her meal.

As he fed her, he told her his story. It was remarkable, even if she didn't believe half of it. People didn't talk to planets. They just didn't. She suspected he was one of the off-planet Martials who had fallen on hard times.

Perhaps he had been wounded in the head, which made more sense than him actually being able to do the things he described. She knew he believed what he was telling her, so decided to play along. After all, he had saved her, patched her up, and, despite his strength and size, she was not afraid of him. He was too gentle. And too beautiful, she added to herself.

"And so you were on your way south when you heard me fighting the sniffers?"

"Sniffers? Is that what they are called? The beasts?"

"Yes. They're bred to track and attack. But never in SubCity. They've never been used in SubCity before."

She grew silent.

"This is the last bite," he told her as he offered the spoon.

"It is? Really?" She ate.

"My story captured your attention, and now your meal is over. More tea? I can reheat it."

"No, I like it that way. Name's Wren" she told him as he handed her refilled mug. "You never asked me what my name was."

"I assumed you would tell me when you were ready."

She shook her head. "I don't understand you, Eloch of Entean."

"I know." He rose. "I will wash these and come back to get you resettled for sleep."

"I want to look at my leg first," she told him and took a sip of the tea. It still reminded her of her Kin.

"After you've slept. It will be daylight then, easier to see. Enjoy your tea. I will return."

As soon as he left, she set the tea down and flung back the blanket. A smile tugged at her lips when she saw how many times he had needed to roll up the leather leggings she wore. Her grin faded when she realized he had dressed her. Gingerly, she pushed up the left legging, glad to find it was loose. Her leg throbbed. She closed her eyes then opened them again. "Coward," she muttered and looked. Encased in its clear bandage, it looked like an uncooked sausage.

Her stomach heaved.

With shaking hands, Wren rolled down the legging and tugged the blanket back up.

"All done with your tea?" Eloch asked as he walked back into the encampment.

She nodded mutely, staring straight ahead.

He re-shelved his items and came over to her. "Ready to sleep?"

She pointed at her leg. "How am I ever going to walk on that?" she asked, her voice sounding hopeless to her.

"You couldn't wait until morning when it was light?"

He sounded disapproving.

"Oh, it was bright enough."

"Firelight can be deceiving."

"I'm not easily deceived." She looked at him. "I'm useless if I can't walk."

"Your leg is healing. You don't know what will happen until it heals and strengthens."

She nodded, her heart thudding dully in her chest. She felt very tired.

"I suppose I should try to sleep."

"I think it's what you need most right now." His voice was calm and gentle. "Let me help you lie down."

Now she'd seen her leg, Wren was afraid to move. She allowed Eloch to give her more help than she normally would have allowed. "This is not one of my best days," she told him.

"I expect not," he said as he smoothed the blanket around her. He reached out and wiped the tear that leaked from her eye.

"Don't."

"Good night, little Wren. Sleep well."

She didn't answer him, willing him to leave so the tears could just come. It was a relief when she heard him walk away. She stole a glance and saw he was getting ready for sleep himself. He'd taken off his tunic. She closed her eyes again, wishing his broad chest and hardened muscles could have distracted her.

"It looks like a sausage," she said suddenly.

"What did you say, Wren?"

"My leg. It looks like a sausage. Like something you'd cook and eat."

"Go to sleep, Wren. Your leg is healing."

"My sausage, you mean," she muttered to herself.

No, it hadn't been one of her better days.

CHAPTER 7: LITTLE SISTER

"The Sausage needs help!"

Eloch grinned. Wren never asked for help. It was always The Sausage. He gave the sniffer one last stroke behind the ears the way she liked and went to collect Wren and her Sausage.

He found her sitting in the bath, water drained and modestly dressed in her borrowed tunic top, a towel carelessly tossed over the tub's rim. She glowered at the sleeve she was attempting to roll up. Noticing him, she made a face. "I don't mean to be ungrateful, but I wish you were closer to my size."

"If I was closer to your size, I wouldn't be able to do this," he told her as he lifted her from the tub and helped her balance on her good leg. His tunic fell to her knees.

"True."

"How is the Sausage after your bath?"

She held it out to him. "See for yourself. Hey!"

He had wrapped his fingers around her thigh to get a closer look at the wound. It still looked angry but less swollen. "It seems to be healing faster with this bandage."

"The Sausage Case?"

He snorted. "Exactly so. I've never seen it used before, but it appears quite effective. Without it, your leg would have needed a lot of stiches, and it would have been a nightmare to do. Yes. It's healing quickly and cleanly." He released her thigh.

"Not quickly enough. I still can't put any weight on the thing without wanting to scream in pain."

"In a few more weeks you should be able to."

"A few weeks more of you carrying me all over the place? I'm not sure if I can handle a few more weeks."

He shrugged and lifted her. "Perhaps it will be an incentive to heal faster."

"As if I have a choice about how fast I heal. Don't lift your eyebrow at me. I have no healing knack."

"But you have a strong will."

"So I've been told. What's that?"

"What's what?"

"That sound?"

He had carried her past the sniffer's enclosure.

"My other guest."

"Another guest? I didn't know there was anybody else here."

"That's because it didn't feel like the right time to introduce you. But since you're stronger, here we are."

He set her down and chucked to the Beastie. "I've named her Little Sister."

All Wren's muscles locked on high alert when she saw what Little Sister was. "No. No. Eloch, No. You can't keep that thing here. You have to kill it."

"I will do no such thing."

The sniffer growled low in her throat.

"Eloch, you don't know what those things can do."

He chuckled. "Of course I know what they can do."

It growled low again and bared its teeth.

"Little Sister, calm yourself," Eloch told the sniffer. "This is Wren. She will not hurt you."

"Give me a knife and I will."

The sniffer bristled and snarled. Her tail whipped back and forth. Her muscles bunched.

"Little Sister, stop. Now. And sit."

The beast whined at Eloch and sat, glaring at Wren.

"No, Wren, I will not allow you to hurt her. Little Sister's life is as precious as your own."

"But they're killers, Eloch. I told you. They're bred to track and to kill. Do you know what they eat? They eat people. We are their food."

"This one eats meal bars."

"It would eat you if it could."

"I think not. Let me prove it to you."

Before she could protest, Eloch set her down, helping her brace herself against the wall. In his fluid fashion, he walked in.

Wren cried out.

"Hush, Wren, all is well. Just watch."

Eloch knelt down on one knee and held out his arms. "Little Sister, let's show Wren what you're really like, shall we?" he crooned. The great beast stood and walked into Eloch's embrace, rubbing her head over his chest and nuzzling his neck.

Wren sucked in her breath, speechless.

A great rumbling came from the sniffer's throat while Eloch scratched her ears and rubbed her sides. Her tail wrapped sinuously around Eloch.

"When she first arrived, Little Sister was exactly as you described, Wren," Eloch told her over the escalating rumbles.

Wren gasped as the sniffer plopped on her side and rolled onto her back, offering her belly to be rubbed.

Eloch stroked her belly and rubbed her ribs as he continued to talk. "She tried to kill me several times. She was chained to the wall over there and she would lunge at me. But in time, we came to an understanding which has since grown into a friendship."

"How much time?" Wren said, pulling in her breath as she watched the sniffer's paws grasp Eloch's head.

His answer was muffled. "You've been here three weeks, yes?"

"You tamed her in three weeks?"

"Little Sister, that's enough" Eloch laughed as the sniffer bathed his face with her tongue. He moved to rise and she backed away, allowing him the room. Mopping his face, he walked over to Wren where she leaned against the wall.

The sniffer sat back with half-closed eyes, then she stood and followed Eloch, slipping her head under his hand so he would fondle her ears.

"Little Sister is not tame, Wren," Eloch said. "We are companions. Friends. Like you and I," he explained as he fondled the sniffer's ears. "Here, you pat her. She's very soft."

Wren shook her head, her eyes wide. "I can't."

"She won't hurt you, Wren, I promise."

Wren looked at the sniffer who was making her rumbling sound again. "No, I'm sorry, but I just can't. Not right now. I'm feeling too—" She held up her leg.

Eloch nodded and sighed. "I understand. Maybe later."

"Maybe. Now can we please get out of here?"

"Of course." He gave Little Sister a final stroke and then let himself out of her enclosure. "Soon," he told the beast. "It will be soon."

"What will be soon?" Wren asked as Eloch carried her away from the enclosure.

She glanced back and saw the sniffer watching her. Her ears were up, her head cocked to one side. She didn't appear threatening, but Wren knew what they could do. She glanced down at her leg.

"I'm planning to let Little Sister out so she can hunt." He felt Wren stiffen. "She was starving when she arrived, Wren, and the meal bars won't last. We need the meal bars for ourselves. Little Sister needs to hunt."

"Hunt what? Only thing out there are rodents and people, a few birds maybe. You want her killing more people Eloch? She might be your friend, but she's nobody else's, I can promise you that."

"She wouldn't hurt you, Wren."

They'd reached the encampment, and he set her down on a chair he had found and mended. She reached for her leggings she'd draped over it and put them on, pulled the drawstring tight against her belly. Eloch had cut the length to fit her, but they hung loose. Two of her could have fit in one leg with room for a third.

"I'm not so sure."

"If you don't threaten her, she won't hurt you."

Wren shrugged. "I will never turn my back on the creature, that I can promise you." She hesitated. "And I will try not to be a threat. I know our food supply is important, and what you suggest makes sense." *And maybe it will run away and that's the last I will ever see of it.*

Eloch smiled, which always made Wren uneasy. His smile made her belly quiver with warmth. She didn't want to feel that way. Not with anyone. Ever.

He stopped smiling. "What, Wren?"

She shook her head. "Nothing. When are you planning to let the sniffer out?"

"As soon as you're comfortable with the idea."

"I'm never going to be comfortable with the idea, Eloch. But if you promise you will protect me if it attacks, then I'm okay with it now."

"She won't attack. But if she does, I will protect you with my life. I promise."

She sat back and folded her arms. "Okay, then. Why wait?"

With a nod, Eloch reached for his staff and handed it to her. "Why don't you hold onto this? And I'll set Little Sister free."

"I'd rather have a knife," Wren muttered as she accepted his staff. She balanced it on her knees.

"I'll be right back," Eloch promised her.

Eloch quickened his pace as he approached Little Sister's enclosure. His heart leapt. How could Spur not provide for one of its creatures in need? Little Sister had need, and he hoped her need would help Spur wake up and provide for her.

Sensing Eloch's excitement, Little Sister paced back and forth at the enclosure's gate, whimpering.

Eloch laughed when he opened the gate and she shot out and raced in circles. She stopped short and looked back at him over her shoulder, her sinuous tail waving like a flag. With a burst of speed she changed directions and hurled herself at him. Knocking him off his feet she landed on top of him to lick his face and nibble on his ears.

Eloch laughed and pushed her off. "Be gone with you, Little Sister," he said as he scrambled to his feet. "Hunt well, my friend."

She woofed and darted off.

Wren watched the sniffer run by the encampment's opening. "So beautiful," she whispered.

As if sensing her, the sniffer paused and turned her magnificent head toward Wren.

Wren sucked in her breath and gripped the staff.

The sniffer's nostrils flared and then she dipped her head and remained still, as if waiting for a response.

This is crazy. Wren raised her hand in a salute and wondered why she did. *Can you catch crazy from another person?*

The sniffer dipped her head again and with a little *yip* turned and ran south.

~~~

"Why did you do it? Tame the sniffer?"

They sat across from each other at a table Eloch had dug from the Rubble. One leg was bent, and it wobbled if there was too much weight on it.

Wren nibbled on her meal bar while she waited for Eloch to answer.

He chewed carefully, studying her. "I didn't tame her."

"Well, made friends, then." She shook her hair from her eyes.

"Life is precious, Wren," he told her. "A life should never be taken if there is another way."

"It could have killed you."

"No." He flashed his grin. "I'm smarter. I knew what she needed."

Wren's stomach fluttered at the smile. "Needed?"

"She's a pack animal. She needs to belong. And she wanted a leader. I filled that place for her. Which is why she won't hurt you. I won't let her."

"How can you be so sure?"

Eloch pushed his hair from his face and sighed. "I just know, Wren."

"But how?"

She watched him smooth the meal bar's wrapper with his strong, gentle hands. Long fingers. He seemed fascinated with its design.

"You wouldn't understand," he said finally.

His eyes flicked up at her.

She felt the pull of their intensity. *So very green.*

"I know you think me mad, Wren. You are entitled to your opinion, of course. But because it's your belief, I don't feel free to share my deepest thoughts with you."

Wren felt her face warm and she lowered her eyes. "I don't think you're totally crazy," she said.

He laughed. "You would if I told you everything I know, everything I plan to do here, on Spur, before I go home."

"Try me."

"Another time, perhaps," he said gently. "For now, why don't you tell me a little about yourself?"

She narrowed her eyes at him. "Why don't I tell you something about me, and then you tell me something about you? Tit for tat."

"Tit for tat. What does that mean?"

Wren shrugged. "I don't know exactly. I think it means I'll tell you something about me and then you'll tell me something about you, and we'll be on equal footing."

"Okaaay," he said slowly.

"And it has to be the truth."

"Of course, but we both have the option to retain our privacy. Meaning, if I don't want to discuss something, I don't have to."

"Deal." She spat on her hand and held it out to him.

She burst out laughing at Eloch's expression. "Spit on your hand, Eloch and shake mine. It seals the deal."

Reluctantly, he followed her example.

"Good. I go first," she told him.

"You already asked me something."

"Doesn't count. We weren't playing the game then."

Eloch sighed. "Very well. Proceed."

"What is Entean like?"

"Entean is beautiful." He began.

Fascinated, Wren watched his whole demeanor soften. *How can I be jealous of a planet?*

"She is smaller than Spur," he continued. "It can take me two years to circumnavigate her. But if she wants me to arrive somewhere sooner, she will change her currents to get me there."

"Currents?"

"Water. We travel by canoe and small ships. There are no oceans, just lakes and waterways and rivers. The land is green and lush. The temperature varies, colder at her poles and much warmer at her equator. There are many creatures, and many people living in small communities."

"And everyone gets along and they live happily-ever-after."

Eloch chuckled. "If I said yes, I'd be lying. That's why Entean needs a Champion."

"You."

"Me."

"But you're here. What's happening there?"

"It's my turn."

Her brow furrowed. "What?"

"My turn to ask you a question."

"Oh, sorry. Ask away."

"Why were the sniffers tracking you?"

Silence greeted Eloch's question.

"Wren?"

"Yes, I know." Briefly, she put her head in her hands, elbows on the table. "Why don't you put something under that leg?" She glared when it wobbled, sloshing her mug of tea.

"Excellent idea, Wren." Eloch glanced around and picked up a board from the stack near the fire ring. He broke it in two with his foot and slid the half he held under the table. "Better?"

Wren nodded. "Until I trip over it."

Eloch cocked his head at her, reminding her of the sniffer. "Perhaps you need a rest," he suggested.

"It had been such a good day," she began, ignoring his suggestion. "We had moved all the old and weak Kin into Tunnel Two. They were well prepared for a nice, long hide. More than prepared. Had three weeks' food supply. When Mouse, Flick, and I left them, they were laughing and joking while they settled in for the night, the old ones taking care of the very young and the sick. We had made these platforms with rope bridges so they'd be off the ground. Tunnel Two is so damp, you see. The Martials burnt the bridges. Trapped my Kin on the platforms, those who didn't fall."

Eloch watched her hands fidget with her meal bar wrapper. Her head was bowed. He couldn't see her face.

"I must have been asleep for about two hours when the screams woke me. And from then on, it just got worse," she looked up at him.

"They Culled my Kin. I was supposed to keep them safe. When we went to sleep that night, there were more than five hundred of us. Not all in Tunnel Two, of course, but home in bed. Safe. The ones in Tunnel Two were the ones the Martials wouldn't want, you see. The rest would be okay. We knew they'd make it through the Cull.

"At Flick's last count, just before we parted ways, there were around forty-five of us left. Over four hundred either slaughtered or recruited into other Kin that night. I don't know how many survived.

"Don't touch me!" Her arm shot up, blocking his hand. "I don't like it."

She swiped at the tears, rested her face in her hands. "And then they sent in the sniffers to get the rest." Her voice sounded muffled. "I wasn't going to let that happen. We had an escape plan in place, only it didn't take into account a sniffer pack. I distracted the sniffers. Took to the tunnels, keeping them fairly close behind me so my remaining Kin could escape." She took a deep breath and finished on the exhale. "I just hope it worked."

"Wren, I—"

"No, there's nothing you can say to make it better. That's just life in SubCity. I never want to see SubCity again. For as long as I live. I tried to make it better down there, and you just can't. You just can't. I'm such an idiot." She slammed her hands down. "I'm tired of this game. I want to lie down. Can you help me with this blasted Sausage?"

"Wren—"

"Just help me, Eloch."

Without another word, he scooped her up in his arms and carried her to the bedroll. He knelt down so she could slide into it. He steadied her when she flinched.

Even though it was still warm outside, she yanked the blanket over her head and turned toward the wall, her back to him.

He watched her curl into an even tinier ball, knowing she was hurting her leg. With a quiet sigh, he returned to the table and gathered the shredded wrapper to use as kindling for that night's fire.

It's going to be like befriending Little Sister all over again, he thought as he went out into Rubble to find a new table leg.

She wasn't asleep. She heard him go out. She heard him come back in, move around a while, and then go out again.

The Sausage was throbbing. Was it ever going to heal? Which was a silly question. In time it would heal. Too much time.

And meanwhile, what of her Kin? By now they thought she was dead. Hopefully, it wouldn't stop them from proceeding with her plan, settling in the square with the fountain. Never to live in SubCity again. Never to be under the Cull.

With Flick's leadership, Mouse's surveillance skills, and Spider's knowledge, she thought they'd be okay. They could stay hidden for years, learning to mingle with the UpperUppers. Then finally going off-planet to a colony, far away from Spur, which meant far away from SubCity.

Gods and goddesses, she missed them. Missed Flick's heartbeat and warm, sleeping presence. Missed Mouse's sudden smiles. Missed sparring with her. Missed joking with them all, eating with them.

"Stop it," she said out loud, her voice sounding ragged and raw.

She rolled over and sat up, pushing the blankets off. "You and I are going to get back to them," she told The Sausage. "And we're starting now."

With a grunt, she flung her legs over the side of the pallet and stood.

Oh the pain!

A million stabbing needles.

Her vision wobbled, but she refused to sit. Refused to faint. She waited until she could withstand the needles stabbing up and down her leg. She took a deep breath and, arms stretched out, took a step.

The Sausage collapsed beneath her.

She passed out.

When she opened her eyes she was being held by strong arms, listening to a steady heartbeat.

"Easy, there," Eloch murmured softly. "Let me get you to a chair."

She shook her head. "No. Help me get up."

"Wren—"

"Help me get up. I'm done with lying around in bed. Having to wait for you to take me to the bathroom. Take me anywhere."

"It's too soon."

"No, it's not soon enough. Help me, Eloch. It's not easy for me to ask for help. So just do this, okay?"

After a moment he nodded and helped her to her feet. She stood, balancing on her good leg, gripping his arm with one hand. She took a couple of deep breaths.

"Okay, don't move your arm. Let me set the pace."

He held strong, feeling her fingers dig into him.

"Okay," she said again. Using his arm as a crutch, she took a step.

They both hissed out a breath.

She glanced at him and flashed a smile, her face white. "Just be glad you don't have the empath knack. This does not feel good," she told him through gritted teeth.

But he did. One of Entean's parting gifts. The longer he and the plant were merged, the more he came to understand Entean's way of knowing. Wren's pain was a white, hot heat that he would have given anything to soothe away from her.

All he could do was will it away from himself and remain strong for her.

She amazed him, how she managed to walk to the table and sit in the chair, step after halting step. With a groan, she released him, to cradle her head in her arms on the tabletop.

The only sound was her panting.

"Wow," she finally told him. "That was extremely unpleasant." She looked up at him. "But now I know what to expect. I promise you, by the end of the week, I will take myself to the bathroom when I need to go."

He studied her, took in her ashen, sweaty face, her set jaw, her scowl.

"I'll go find you a walking stick," he told her and left without a backward glance.

She snorted and laid her head back on her arms. "Stop whining," she told The Sausage. "I don't feel sorry for you."

~~~

It was dark and the world smelled of dust and age. She paused and lifted her muzzle to the slight breeze, yearning for some other scent. Still, only dust and age. Yet, something called her, something urgent within her breast.

She ran, feeling her muscles flex and release. She'd never been able to run like this before. Alone, without the scent of her prey filling her nostrils. Alone, without her brothers and sisters. She whimpered a little as she ran.

Come it called her.

She ran.

Toward dawn, she found a new smell. Something unknown.

She stopped, her sides heaving as she brought the new smell into her lungs. It smelled alive and warm. It smelled close.

She put her muzzle to the ground and sniffed, picking up the scent traces.

Had she been with her pack, she would have begun baying. But she was alone, so she hunted quietly, moving forward softly on padded paws following the scent's trail.

A little creature bolted from its hiding place.

Her head jerked up, startled. Recovering quickly, she followed.

The thing darted and wove about the rubble, disappearing and then reappearing.

116

Even when she couldn't see it, she trusted her nose and ran, closing the gap. Muscles bunching, she pounced on it, gripping it with her claws.

It was hard to grip. The man had filed down her claws until they were dull. They would grow, he had reassured her.

She needed them now.

Fearful of losing her meal, she bit hard, sinking her teeth deep into the creature's flesh.

Warm blood gushed down her throat.

She settled onto her haunches and fed, purring her pleasure as her strong jaws crunched through bones.

It didn't take long to finish, but she had eaten enough, and she somehow knew there would be more creatures to hunt. She decided to remain where she was and hunt them.

For now, she curled up where she lay and slept, committing the new smell to memory.

Miles away, warm in his bedroll, Eloch opened his eyes and smiled. Little Sister had fed.

CHAPTER 8: IT MATTERS

By the end of the week Wren could walk to the outbuilding with the bath and pit toilet. It took her nearly fifteen minutes to reach it, but she did.

She stood braced against the doorway, leaning heavily on the staff Eloch had made for her while she peered into the space.

From behind, she heard Eloch clapping and she laughed.

"By the end of next week, I will be able to walk here and back," she tossed over her shoulder. "But for now The Sausage and I need a lift home."

"Well done, Wren," Eloch told her as he bundled her up, walking stick and all.

Without thinking, she curled her hand around his upper arm and leaned into him. "Careful you don't trip over my staff."

"Keep holding it the way you are and I won't."

She glanced at the sniffer's enclosure as they passed by. "Do you think we'll ever see her again?"

"In time, I'm sure. She is learning to be free and enjoying it."

"How do you know? How can you possibly know that, Eloch?"

"I just do."

Wren sighed. "I'm getting tired of that answer. You say it a lot."

His chuckle vibrated against her back.

"How is The Sausage?" he asked as they neared the encampment.

"Hurts."

"Does it feel stronger?"

She sighed. "Yes, but I worry if it will ever be as strong as it once was."

"It will be."

She laughed. "Because you know?"

"Because I know *you*. You won't accept less. The Sausage has met its match."

She laughed again.

"Ready for dinner?" he asked as he set her down at the table.

"I suppose," she said, handing him her staff.

He leaned it in the corner beside his own and went to fetch two meal bars.

"Thanks," she said as she took hers. "Are there many left?"

"A few. Enough for a couple more months."

"That many? I had no idea."

"I still have my cache. Plus, Aiko left me with enough to last several months. She didn't know when she would be back."

He had told her about Aiko and about Genji and Etsuo. He had told her about his journey from Entean to Spur. He had even told her about his meeting with the Board of Colonizers.

She had been outraged on his behalf.

It seemed he couldn't stop telling her things.

"I appreciate them, but I am also very, very tired of them. Once I get back to my Kin, I'm not sure I'll ever want to eat another one ever again." She took a bite and chewed it thoughtfully. "Are you coming back with The Sausage and me when I can finally walk far enough to get to the City?" Suddenly she was afraid of his answer.

He was silent long enough for her to feel an unusual crushing feeling in the pit of her stomach. She set down the meal bar.

"I don't know, Wren. Perhaps."

"Yeah, well, I can understand you being as tired of me as I am of these meal bars," she drew her legs underneath hers and braced to stand. "In fact, I think I'll just save the rest of this one for later."

Eloch put a hand out and covered her own. "Wait, Wren. I would very much like to go with you. Meet the people you have told me about." He hesitated. "But I have an obligation, and I fear it will carry me south."

She sat again. "South? There's nothing in the south but more rubble. Why would you want to go deeper into Rubble? What obligation?"

He withdrew his hand, but its warmth lingered on her skin.

"If I told you, you wouldn't believe me. You would think me more mentally unbalanced than you already do."

"Try me. I couldn't possibly think you're crazier than I already do." Her heart felt lighter when he smiled.

"Oh Wren," he said shaking his head. "Why do I find myself telling you things I would rather keep to myself?"

"Because I'm a good listener? Or because I keep nagging you until you do?"

"Perhaps a little of both," he said softly.

"Look," she said after a moment. "For what it's worth, I tell you things I don't normally tell people, too. Not even Flick knows everything I've told you."

"Like what things?"

"Like the only reason I want to mingle with the Upper Uppers and learn their ways is so I can get the Kin off this planet, get as far away as possible. Only the Upper Uppers are allowed to colonize."

His eyes widened. "You never told me that."

"I just did."

"But why? Why do you want to leave your home planet?"

"Why do you want to go south, Eloch? I will answer you if you answer me." She folded her arms and sat back.

He smiled wryly. "It's like that, is it?"

"It most definitely is, my friend, it most definitely is."

"No more secrets between us, is that what you want?"

He knew her so well, she thought. Yet it didn't seem to matter that he did, which surprised her. He deserved an answer. "There are things, Eloch, that I don't like to talk about. Things that happened to me when I was young. Things I want to forget. I don't want to tell you those things. Ever."

"Whatever happened," he said after a pause, "must have been terrible, and I am sorry you suffered."

"I survived, and that's what counts. Made me pretty good at it, too. So, why do you want to go south?"

"Entean asked me to find out why Spur allows Her creatures to leave Her."

"Excuse me?"

"You see? I said you would think me madder—sorry, crazier—than you already do."

"No, I don't," She caught herself and grinned. "Well, maybe a little. But why does Entean want to know?"

"Because planets are supposed to care for and nurture their inhabitants. They maintain the balance so everything can thrive. If things were thriving on Spur, there would be no need to colonize. So why is Spur allowing it to happen? Entean wants to know. And I cannot return home without an answer."

"And you will find Spur in the south?"

"I don't need to find Spur. Spur is all around us. But I believe if I go farther away from the City I will have a better chance of being heard by Her. And Little Sister is thriving in the south. Spur is caring for her. So Spur is not completely unaware of what is happening. She's waking up."

"Wait, how do you know the sniffer is thriving? I really want an answer this time."

"You won't believe me. You don't believe me now."

"But I believe that you believe it, Eloch. And I don't *not* believe you. Not anymore. I just don't have any proof. I've never been to Entean. I've never been off planet. What if Entean is the only planet that maintains the balance? There are other planets out there that we've colonized. The Ring is made up of several planets. This is the first time I've ever heard of a planet that talks."

"I don't know about all the other planets. I don't. I only know Entean wants me to get an answer for Her from this planet."

"And how are you going to talk to Spur?"

"I'm not sure, exactly. I'm learning."

"Learning?"

He took a deep breath. "Entean changed me so I would be able to, but She didn't tell me how."

"Changed you? How?"

He looked at her with a crooked smile. "You may be sorry you asked, Wren." And he told her about the seed he swallowed that grew into a plant and merged with him.

"Well," she said after he was finished. "I'm going to have to think about that one for a while. I guess you warned me, didn't you?"

"Have I frightened you?"

"Frightened me? No. But I'm not sure what to believe right now. Are you sure you didn't get hit in the head somewhere between Entean and Spur? At takeoff, maybe? You said you were in hibernation for several months. Are you sure you weren't in a coma and, I don't know, this is your mind's way to cope with being taken from your home planet?"

"I wish you could talk to Aiko. She could verify everything I've told you."

"Believe me, so do I. I know you believe all this, but I'm not sure I do. At all."

He was silent for a moment. "What if I bring Little Sister home? Would you believe then that I'm different?"

"I believe certain people are born with knacks. It's one of the things the Martials look for during a Cull. They say the best pilots come from SubCity. So," she continued, "you could have a knack that tames and talks to beasts, I'll grant you that, but talking to a planet?" She shook her head.

"I will ask Little Sister to be home tomorrow evening," he told her, his jaw set. "When she comes as I ask, perhaps it will help you begin to believe."

"Perhaps," she said. "But honestly, why should it matter whether I believe you or I don't?"

He looked at her with those deep green eyes of his, nearly taking her breath away. His answer did, heating her soul and waking something buried there.

"It matters," He told her.

~~~

The next evening, as promised, Little Sister bounded into the encampment, carrying two bloodied carcasses in her mouth. She dropped them at Eloch's feet and sat with head cocked.

"She looks like she's smiling," Wren commented as she watched Eloch squat down to appraise the sniffer's catch.

"You hunt well," he praised her. "Thank you for your gifts." He reached out and scratched Little Sister behind the ears.

The creature leaned into his hand. With eyes half closed she crooned her pleasure. Then with an excited *yip* she put her paws on his shoulders and tumbled Eloch backwards and began licking his face.

Watching the two wrestle on the floor, Wren warred between fear and laughter. And she didn't relax her grip on her walking stick until Eloch told the sniffer he'd had enough and the beast allowed him to get back on his feet.

He stood, grinning, as he swiped the dust from his clothes.

"I'm surprised you managed to not squash whatever it was she brought you," Wren said dryly

"Me too," he replied and picked up Little Sister's kill. "Well done," he told the sniffer.

Little Sister sinewy tail skimmed back and forth as she settled on the ground, near the opening of the encampment.

"What did she bring you?" Wren asked.

"Us, Wren. She brought us dinner."

Wren wrinkled her nose. "And you expect me to eat that?"

"It will be much better than a meal bar after I've cooked it, I assure you." He reached for a knife. "I'm going to go skin these. Will you light the fire? We will need to cook them right away. Fresher the better." Eloch turned to leave, but Wren's voice stopped him.

"I don't know how to light a fire."

"Just feed it. The coals are still warm. Come, Little Sister, I will share this kill with you. The liver and the heart. "

Wren scowled at his receding figure. "Just feed it," she muttered, grunting as she eased herself onto a stool next to the woodpile. "Easy for you to say, Mr. He-Who-Talks-To-Planets."

~~~

126

"Better than a meal bar?" Eloch asked. He tossed a bone to Little Sister. Her jaws snapped it in two and she began sucking out the marrow.

Wren stared at the sniffer and grimaced at the sounds. "Much better than a meal bar," she answered, pausing to lick her fingers. "Although the sniffer still makes me nervous."

"You're part of her pack, Wren. She proved it by bringing us her kill. One animal for each of us."

"I think I'd need a bit more proof," Wren said, glancing over at where Little Sister lay licking her paws.

The sniffer extended her claws so she could clean between her toes.

The Sausage twitched when Wren tensed at the sight.

"Why don't you throw her some of your bones?" Eloch suggested. "As a sign of your appreciation."

Wren did so, gingerly, and winced at the snap of the jaws.

The animal neatly sucked out the marrow before crunching and eating all the bones.

"You're sure thorough," she told her. "I'll give you that. Oh—"

At the sound of her voice, the sniffer had risen to her feet and padded over to where Wren sat.

They were eye to eye. Wren could smell its meaty breath. She held her own, feeling very naked and vulnerable without her knives. Her walking stick was close at hand, but it wasn't a knife.

Little Sister whined and took another step closer, nuzzling Wren's hair, the coils brushing her face.

Very slowly, Wren lifted her hand and stroked the sleek head, scratching behind the ears, imitating what Eloch had done earlier. The great beast started to rumble deep in her chest and she flopped down at Wren's feet, exposing her underbelly. Wren glanced up at Eloch and found him smiling.

"She wants you to rub her belly, Wren."

Wren stretched out and began to stroke the sniffer. She felt her lips curl up at the corners. "She's so soft!"

The sniffer continued to rumble.

"She is. And sleek. Her ribs no longer show. Wherever she was in the south, she found good hunting. This is a sign to me."

Still engrossed with the sniffer, Wren didn't hear him. "She really won't attack me?" she asked as she stroked the length of a foreleg and studied the enormous paw.

Eloch laughed and she quickly glanced up at him.

"You destroyed her old pack. She knows your merits. No, to her mind, she's found herself two strong pack mates and is pleased to let us lead. All she wants is to hunt and receive our affection."

"I guess I'll just have to trust you on this," she replied, watching as Little Sister captured her arm between her two immense paws to lick her hand. Wren wiggled her fingers and the sniffer positioned her ear underneath them.

"You can."

"Hmm?" Wren asked as she leaned forward to scratch the other ear with her other hand and evoked the telltale rumble from Little Sister.

Eloch shook his head and with a smile took the opportunity to go out of the encampment to relieve himself.

Neither noticed him leave, nor did they notice his return.

He sat and leaned against one of the two wooden benches by the fire and watched the woman and the sniffer and reflected on his own thoughts.

In the south, Spur had provided for Little Sister.

Perhaps Spur was ready for his visit.

Chapter 9: North

Mouse shook her hair out of her eyes and sat down beside Flick, who gave her a tight smile and returned to the watch list he was working on.

"It's not the same, is it?" she asked.

He set his pencil down. "Not nearly," he answered with a sigh. "The worst part is I keep expecting her to just pop in one of these days, like she used to."

"Yeah, I know. It's been two months, Flick, and I've heard nothing on my walkabouts. Just got back from SubCity."

"Mouse, no. It's too crazy down there. You can't take those kinds of chances, not when it's just the two of us."

"Three. Don't forget Spider."

"Oh, right. Spider. I don't trust that one. He's hiding something."

"Or from someone. But Wren trusted him. She risked her life that night to get to him. And it's obvious he's an UpperUpper. A way up there UpperUpper. The guy just has to say one word and—"

"I see what you're doing there Mouse. You don't want me to talk to you about SubCity. It's dangerous down there, isn't it? You nearly got caught, didn't you?"

Mouse studied his open face and the dark circles under his eyes. "It's harder to get down there since we blew so many tunnels getting out of there," she agreed. "But I had to see what had happened. What they'd done to our KinSpace."

"And?"

"They're going to have to run the SubCity fans for months to get the smell of smoke and—" she glanced at him "—cooked meat out of there."

Flick covered his face with his hands. "I can't stand to think about that," he told her.

Mouse put her small hand on his shoulder. "They've raided all our stores, the other two Kins. I heard that some of MacMichaels' Kin are going to move into our space as soon as the smell goes away. Which won't be anytime soon, I can promise you that."

She paused and sighed deeply. "They're digging through all the things we left behind. Ignoring the bodies. They are still lying where they fell. It tore at my heart, Flick. Saw some fights break out over some stupid dress I used to see what's-her-name wear. Vicko. That's right. Vicko. Yeah, ol' Vicko loved her fine clothes and baubles. Did plenty of favors for them, too. Made me feel so bad seeing those women fighting over ol' Vicko's clothes."

"Aw, Mouse," Flick covered her hand where it still lay on his shoulder. He gave it a small squeeze.

She kept her hand there for a moment, might even have given him a small squeeze back, before she withdrew it.

"I found these," she said and took out two throwing knives. "They were Wren's. See? Her mark is scratched on them."

"Where'd you get them?"

"I went to our compound. They were hidden in the wall behind the door of her room. She showed me where she'd hidden all her weapons, just in case." She held a knife out to Flick. "Here, take it. One for you, one for me. To remember her by."

Flick took it with a short nod. "Thanks," he said, swallowing and blinking rapidly. "Thanks," he repeated.

"Sure, Flick. Of course." Mouse paused. "They shit in her pool. Filthy bastards. She loved that pool." She fell silent.

"Well," Flick said after a few moments. "The best revenge is to carry out Wren's plan. All she ever wanted was a better life for her Kin. So, we'll make her better life happen." He grinned suddenly. "Remember how she'd force us to be all polite? Eat just so? Say the proper words?"

Mouse giggled. "She got so mad at us when we acted out, didn't she?"

They watched each other's smiles fade, then disappear.

Flick picked up his pencil. "I better get back to this. I need to relieve Cricket in an hour. You?"

"Going to keep searching for Max." She shook her head. "He's relocated so many times, I'm still having trouble picking up his trail. I think he's slipped into the UpperUpper. Don't want to ask too many people. Don't want him knowing I'm looking for him. Don't want to spook him."

"But he was a friend of Wren's, wasn't he? I thought he'd want to help her Kin."

Mouse snorted. "Max's no friend of nobody's. But he did owe Wren lots of favors. So let's hope he'll honor them when he learns she's—" Mouse couldn't find it in her to finish.

Flick nodded slowly. "Well, you know what's best. I'm a stranger to the workings of Above. You and Spider find Max and make your plans. I'll focus on keeping the rest of the Kin safe and fed."

"You're good at it," Mouse said quietly.

With another squeeze of his shoulder she slipped out of the room, down the stairs, and into the square with the fountain to search for Spider.

It felt good to be living in the Above again, she decided. She'd always thought Wren's plan was crazy, but if it meant living in the Above, she was all for it. The open air, whether hot or cold, was such a welcome difference from the stench of SubCity.

A couple of the Kin were gathering water at the fountain when Mouse passed by. They gave her a wave and a cheerful hello. Seemed like the Kin liked it in the Above just as much as she did. Already they were losing their pallor. All of them. Soon they could start blending. For now, though, until they had their new idents, only the runners and the eyes were out.

The runners were having a hard time finding food, so it was fortunate there were so few Kin left to feed. They'd known SubCity. They'd even known the area surrounding Sub's entrance. But here, and without any escape tunnels, the runners were a little lost. And afraid. She was doing the best she could to teach them about their surroundings.

The eyes were having an easier time of it. Probably because they used the rooftops as their highway. Whoever looked up? Hadn't Wren kept telling them that? "Just as long as you kept your tread light, minded where your shadow fell and knew where the lose tiles were, you'd be good."

As Mouse entered the building across the way and began to climb the stairs, a sliver of an idea took shape. Why couldn't the runners use the rooftops as well? Instead of escaping into tunnels, they could escape to the roofs. She'd talk with the eyes, see if they could map out some sturdy roofs with solid drain pipes a runner laden with food could scramble up.

Mouse found Spider where she thought she would, propped up on his bedroll in the semi-isolated room he'd chosen a short distance from the other Kin. Although the door was open, she knocked softly on its frame and waited for Spider's nod before she entered.

Spider watched Mouse cross the short distance from his doorway to his bedroll. Her size and movements reminded him too much of Wren. Made him sad. He composed his features.

"Greetings, Mouse, pull up a floor, or sit by me on my luxurious bedroll if you dare."

Mouse snorted. "You sound exactly like the spoiled UpperUpper that you are, Spider. At least *you* have a bedroll."

His eyebrows shot up. "You don't have a place to sleep? I didn't realize."

She waved a hand as she settled herself beside him on his bedroll. "I've a room, but no bed yet. I'm good at finding little nooks and crannies. The bed at the compound was the first I ever had."

He looked at her with schooled features. Only his silence gave him away.

"I'm not here for your pity, Spider." She nudged him. "Nor your bedroll. I've come to pick your brains. I'm stuck."

He straightened. "How so?" he asked, closing the book where he'd jotted down everything Wren told him about her plans.

"I know a lot about the dark alleyways of Sub and Upper, and I've searched everywhere I know for Wren's contact, Max. He's vanished. Word on the street is he's called in some favors and gotten himself moved up the ladder. Word on the street says he's retired. Then the word on the street won't say any more. All hush-hush. A big ol' wall of hush that I can't seem to climb over or go around. So where does a retired forger go if he's living up the ladder, Spider?"

135

"Wren told me to trust you and Flick," Spider said slowly.

"Yeah? She told us to trust you, too, so I'm trusting. You? You trusting?"

"Wren brought me in when no one else would touch me. It's hard to trust, but I've got nothing left anymore, and no one to turn to. Up here, without the Kin, I'm a dead man. So, yes, you can trust me, Mouse, because of that. And I can trust you, because up here is the City and it's got a whole different set of rules."

"I know those rules. I lived here most of my life. I've worked here all of my life," she shook her head. "But there's the wall of hush that I suspect you know how to scale. I suspect you once lived behind it, Mr. Spoiled UpperUpper." The grin she flashed took out the sting.

"Guilty," he said self-mockingly. "And I knew a couple of forgers. They came in handy when I was a young, punk student wanting to go for a little ramble. Perhaps they'd know where Max is."

"Can you take me to them?"

"Sadly, no." He glanced at her. "Here comes the trusting, Mouse. That young, punk student I was telling you about? He organized a demonstration. Funnily enough, it was against Culling. Anyway, someone was killed. And since I thought I was untouchable because of my family's connections, I took the blame. Only," his mouth tightened, "the dead one had family connections as well, and his connections apparently trumped my own, because I am now a wanted man with a price on my head."

It took Mouse a few moments to process this news, leaving Spider with an edgy feeling growing in his stomach.

"Well," she said at last. "I guess I'll have to rethink all those opinions I had about you, Spider. It was a brave thing to take the blame. Brave to oppose the Culling. They were both brave things. Stupid, but brave."

He shook his head. "Brave when you thought your father could bail you out? No, it took far more courage for me to go to SubCity and hide with Wren."

"Perhaps," Mouse mused. "And now you're stuck with us, and we'll help you while you help us."

She spat on her hand and stuck it out to him.

He responded in kind.

They shook hands and sealed the pact, both ignoring the electrical current that sparked the instant their fingers met.

Suddenly aware she was sitting next to Spider on his bedroll, Mouse rose and wiped her palm on her leggings. "Well," she said into the silence. "I think I'd better go and investigate what lies behind the wall of hush," she said, making her way to the door.

"Wait," Spider called. He set down his book of notes and stood.

Mouse paused, one brow raised.

"Don't you want the names of those two forgers?"

Mouse laughed, feeling the warmth creep up her face. "I would need that, wouldn't I?"

"I could sketch what they look like if you'll wait a second," Spider offered. "It's the least I can do, since I can't go with you."

"Why not?" Mouse said suddenly. "You can go with me if you're disguised."

"Disguised? I dunno," he said slowly. "I don't want to be spotted. You forget about that price on my head."

A smile quirked at the corners of her mouth. "You forget, they're looking for a skinny student, not an ugly woman."

"A woman? You want me to dress like a woman?"

"Why not? What's wrong with women?"

"N-nothing," Spider sputtered. "But to dress like one?"

Mouse put her hands on her hips and grinned as she looked him up and down. "You'd be pretty ugly, but you've got good legs. Men will forgive a lot of things if you've got good legs."

"Mouse, come on! You can't be serious."

"I am. Very. Wouldn't it be fun to be free for a day? To be able to just walk around without worrying that someone will spot you? Just for a day."

"I'm going to have to think about this one."

"Well, don't take too long," Mouse told him as she stepped out of his room. "One of Wren's last orders was to find Max, and I'm going to find him, if it's the last thing I do."

Spider gazed at the doorway and tried to hear Mouse's footfalls, her silent assassin's walk. With the tiny woman gone, the room suddenly felt very large and empty.

~~~

"Leggings," Mouse said, flinging a pair at Spider. "Skirt," she said and flung that as well. "Tunic, long enough to cover your man bump,"

"Hold!" Spider said, bending down to pick up the skirt he'd dropped.

Mouse waited, arm raised, then flung the tunic with a grin as soon as he straightened.

The tunic hit his chest in a wad and slid through his hands while he groped for it. "Ah! Dammit, Mouse, wait." Spider glared at her.

"And a scarf to cover up the neck bump," Mouse said. She dangled it on her finger and waited for him to organize the outfit to his satisfaction.

He took a step toward and snatched the scarf from her finger. "Now go away so I can put them on," he told her.

"You sure you know how? Sure you don't need any help?"

He glared again. "You're really enjoying this, aren't you?"

"Sure am, Mr. UpperUpper. Sure am."

"Just leave."

Mouse giggled. "I'll be right outside if you need me."

"I said leave, Mouse! Now!"

"Okay, but don't take too long making yourself pretty. It won't help."

Mouse left, feeling satisfied. She always thought anger was the best way to overcome fear. She'd seen how white Spider's face was when he let her into his room.

She listened to him muttering and throwing things around. Couldn't have stopped her grin if her life depended on it. He sure had a righteous mad going.

The door opened, slamming against the wall, and she walked back in.

Spider scowled at her from the center of the room, hands on his hips.

She studied his slim form. He would be tall for a woman, but otherwise it wasn't too bad. She nodded. "I knew you'd look good in a skirt. It's the legs. And you've got really pretty eyes, too. All dark and lashy. Gotta do something with that hair, though."

"I'm not going to braid it or anything," he told her taking a step back when she crossed over to him.

"I wasn't thinking of a braid. Hold still. I'm not going to bite." She withdrew a comb from her pocket. "I think if you parted it on the side," she said, doing just that, enjoying its soft, silky texture. She stood back, and surveyed him. "Okay. That works. I like how it keeps falling over one eye. Very sexy."

"Very annoying, you mean. I feel ridiculous."

"No, it's a very good disguise. Think of it like that. A disguise." She adjusted the scarf. Frowned and retied it. "Better," she said, standing back again, head cocked. "Hmm."

"What?"

Mouse gestured to her chest. "We've hidden the man bumps, but you need some woman bumps. Got a pair of socks? You can stuff them down your under-tunic. They should stay in place."

Spider groaned and went to rummage in the knapsack by his bedroll while Mouse admired his posterior. He really did have great legs. And a nice bum, too. She wondered why he didn't look as good in his own clothes. Perhaps because they were so loose and baggy.

Spider stood and held out two socks.

"Bunch 'em up and slide 'em in," Mouse ordered. "Want me to help?"

He wadded up the socks and crammed them down his tunic front, glaring at her the whole time while he shook his hair out of his eyes.

Mouse bit down hard on her lip, enjoying the flash in his deep brown eyes.

"Well?"

"Looks good to me. Your shoulders are a little broad, but I don't think people will be looking at your shoulders."

"Stop smiling."

"I'm sorry," Mouse said, coughing to cover a snicker, and then giving up and laughing out loud. "I can't help it. It's good. Really. I don't think anyone will suspect you're a man. Come on. Let's go find Flick and tell him where we're going."

They descended the stairs in silence. At the bottom, Spider opened the door and waited for Mouse to go out.

"Don't do that," Mouse instructed. "We're both women, remember?"

Spider sighed and they exited together.

"No clomping, either."

"Clomping? I do not clomp."

"Trudge, then. You trudge."

"I do not trudge either."

"Can you walk a little more lightly at least?" she asked as they crossed the square. Mouse noticed one of the eyes on the rooftop attentively checking out Spider. She grinned at the eye when he mouthed, *Who is she?*

"I'll do my best, Mouse."

She reached the door first and opened it, making sure they stepped inside together.

"Flick?" she called. "You close by?"

"Aye," he said coming out into the hallway. "I was just going over to check on our food supplies and—Helloooo there," he said when he noticed Spider. "Who have we here? Pretty lady, I'm Flick. Where have you been all my life?"

"I know who you are, Flick, and I'm not interested," Spider said.

"I-uh-S-spider? Wha—?" Flick looked at Wren and back at Spider and back at Wren, who was now completely doubled over, hugging herself while her laughter echoed down the hall.

Flick scowled at her, as did Spider, which sent her off into a fit of giggles and snorts.

"See?" she said when she caught her breath. "I told you it was a good disguise. I'm taking Spider with me to hunt for Max," she explained to Flick.

"Isn't that risky?"

"As risky as anything else we do. It has to be done, Flick. I've hit a dead end. Spider's the only one who knows the UpperUpper."

"If it has to be done, then be careful…and have fun, you two—and whatever you do," he turned to Spider, "don't talk. It's a definite giveaway."

"He won't," Mouse said. "Or if he needs to, he can whisper. C'mon, Spider. Let's go."

Spider followed her out.

"Nice legs!" Flick called after them.

"Asshole," Spider replied. He made a rude gesture as the door was closing, shutting off Flick's answering guffaw.

"I think whispering would be the way to go," Spider said after a while.

"Best let me do the talking."

"Sure, but I know the speak, you know? If I ask the questions they'll see an equal. Less attention drawn."

Mouse flashed him one of her rare smiles. "Good point, Spider. And thanks."

"For what?"

"It's been a long time since I've laughed that hard. Haven't felt much like laughing, you know?"

He glanced at her in sympathy. "Yeah, I know."

"So whisper for me. Let's see how it sounds."

By the time they had arrived at the City, Mouse was satisfied. "Okay, this is as far as I've ever gone. Wren used to be all over the UpperUpper, but me? No. I hope you know where you're going, because I'm already lost."

"I know exactly where I am," Spider whispered.

He sounded hoarse and husky and female.

"Just a warning now," Mouse said. "With that voice and those legs, be prepared for some serious flirting. You're going to have to pretend you like it. Flip your hair and bat your eyelashes and stuff. I'll do my best to run interference."

He nodded thoughtfully. "Okay, then. Let's go."

The two strolled into the busy foot traffic of a bustling metropolis. Mouse quickly learned it was a great deal easier getting around in the UpperUpper with an UpperUpper by her side. She was grateful for it. The beauty of the smooth, columned buildings with their store displays of products she couldn't believe anybody could afford intimidated her. And the way they spoke! How could Wren ever think they would all learn to speak like that? It would take her the rest of her life to get rid of her low-birth dialect. Without realizing it, she had snaked her fingers into Spider's hand.

He looked down at their entwined hands and then at her face. "What's this about?" He asked. She was looking a little wide-eyed and unsure. "Everything okay, Mouse?"

She shrugged. "It's different here."

"You're right," he said, giving her fingers a slight squeeze. "Good thing girls hold hands all the time, eh? We can support each other." He drew her to a shop display and stopped. "They do this, too. Stop to look at the merchandise. We can stand here for as long as you'd like."

Mouse nodded up at him, her eyes huge. This was a different Mouse, he mused. The Mouse he was used to was all lethal self-control. This Mouse looked small and frightened, just like her namesake. He squeezed her hand again. "We're doing well, Mouse. Nobody's paying attention, and we've almost reached our first stop."

She took a deep breath. "You're right," she said with one emphatic nod. "Let's get on with it. I'm being daft."

Without replying, he led her to a grimy-looking side street.

Grimy only by UpperUpper standards.

He paused in front of a small shop with blacked-out windows. With a nod to Mouse, Spider led the way up the two steps to the door and pushed it open. Inside, they found themselves in a small waiting area with dingy, frayed furniture placed carefully around an equally dingy, frayed rug.

"May I help you ladies?" a slight man asked. He smiled and nodded when the two turned around.

Spider cleared his throat. "We were told this was a good place to discreetly procure certain documents," he whispered huskily.

"We do have our limitations, but I'd say we could provide nearly anything you two ladies could have in mind." The man answered with an appreciative smile. "For the right price," he added.

"What price for new identifications, a whole set of documents?" Spider asked.

"Oh, nothing illegal, I'm afraid," the man replied. "I want no trouble."

"What about a change in birth year?" Mouse asked, lowering her eyes. "We lied about our age—"

"At our local drinking establishment," Spider finished.

"Ah, that I can do," the man said with a wink.

Spider smiled and shook his hair out of his eye.

The man cleared his throat and blushed.

"What about new identifications? We have another friend we wanted to bring to the pub with us," Spider explained. "You know what it's like. Some places wouldn't accept her if—" he paused. "Well, I don't want to say anything further, since you indicated you didn't wish to risk attracting trouble. Could you recommend someone? I've heard that Max is very good."

The man stilled. "Max? Max's retired."

Spider looked crestfallen. "Oh dear. Oh dear. Retired, you say? We went by there first, of course, but I thought he had merely relocated as he does so frequently." Spider winked. "He owes me a little favor, you see."

"And I had something for him," Mouse added. "A gratitude gift." She made her eyes large and sad, and looked at Spider, who patted her hand and nodded.

Silence filled the dingy little shop.

The man cleared his throat. "I might know where Max is," he offered.

Mouse looked up and smiled her dazzling smile.

The man blinked and looked dazed for a moment. "Do you know the UpperUpper?" he asked, naming a street.

"I know exactly where that is," Spider told the man with a smile of his own. He flipped his hair again and was delighted to see the man blush once more.

"The house number is 235. A lovely building," the man added wistfully.

"Thank you, so, so much," Mouse said and glanced down at her arm, hiding the fact she wore no timekeeper. "Goodness! Francine, look at the time. Mother will be distressed." She smiled at the man. "Thank you very much. I shall now be able to deliver my gratitude gift. It's a lovely gratitude gift. I know Max will be so happy."

She nearly pushed Spider out the door in her haste to leave.

When they reached the main street, Mouse began to retrace their steps.

"Wait, the street is the other way," Spider told her.

"We'll go in a couple of days. Or, you'll draw me a map and I'll go alone, I haven't decided."

"But didn't you want to find Max?"

Mouse shushed him by putting a finger to his lips.

They quickened their pace but not enough to draw attention.

"Can you take us down a couple of side streets?" She asked Spider. "We're being followed. No, don't turn around," she ordered. "They're far enough back that if we turn off the main street and run, we'll be fine."

146

"Come," Spider said. He grabbed her hand and pulled her down the next side street and broke into a run.

The rest of UpperUpper passed Mouse in a blur as Spider threaded them through the streets. He finally tugged her into a doorway in a quiet street. "We can go down this street and end back at the street where we entered UpperUpper, or we can go up. You mentioned you liked up."

"Always, if there's a choice." Mouse gazed upward, looking for the easiest way to access the rooftops. "Here," she said, leading him over to a fire escape. "Our rooftop highway awaits."

She swung up and then reached down to assist Spider, who scrambled up beside her, nearly unseating her from her perch.

"Sorry, I'm not the most coordinated."

"Not to worry. You've got other strengths. Let's go. Follow exactly where I put my feet, or as near as you can, to avoid any loose tiles. We'll go slow."

They moved down the row of roofs in silence. When they came to a cross street, she showed him how to swing himself over. He balked at first, but she kept encouraging him. "Just don't look down. It's easy if you don't look down."

To Spider's surprise, it was.

He landed with a little laugh and Mouse clapped him on the back. "Well done, there." She looked around behind them. "I think we've come far enough, if you want to take off some of your disguise. She produced a cloth sack from her tunic's pocket.

The first thing Spider did was yank the wadded socks out of his under-tunic and finger comb his hair so it lost its part.

With a grin, Mouse took the socks from him and placed them neatly in the bag. "It really was a fine disguise," she said as she watched him take off his skirt and neck scarf. She accepted them, then pulled the bag closed. "Now you're back to your spoiled UpperUpper self," she declared. "Although I've never known you to ever wear such…bold…colors."

"I'll return the leggings and tunic later, if you don't mind," he answered dryly. "May I borrow your cape to hide the pink?"

"Are you sure?" Mouse asked as she unfastened her cape and handed it to him. "Pink looks rather nice on you. Brings out your rosy cheeks."

Spider snorted. "Oh, I'm sure."

"Admit it, it was fun wearing a disguise."

He nodded reluctantly, then felt a slow grin spread across his face. "I made him blush. Twice."

Mouse laughed.

Someone called out softly and he shot an anxious look at Mouse.

"S'okay. It's just Wings, one of my eyes. He's called Wings 'cuz it looks like he can fly over these rooftops. I've never seen anyone so fast. Even beats me."

Mouse waved at someone pressed against a chimney. Spider could barely make out the slight figure in the shadows. Wings would have been invisible had he not known where to look.

"We're nearly home," Mouse said after a little while.

"Could have fooled me. It all looks the same from up here."

"You start to pick out landmarks after a while. See that broken window? That's one of my landmarks. You did well today, Spider. We make a good team."

Spider smiled. "A good team, huh? Wish I had a different disguise."

"Two women are less threatening, I'd hate to give that up, but for your sake, I bet we can think of another disguise."

"Just wish we could have gotten to Max."

"It's okay. I'll wager Max already knows we were asking about him."

"The people following us?"

Mouse nodded. "If it was me, I'd have people posted at all active forgers' places of business. That's why we didn't go to Max right away. I didn't want to go as a prisoner. No, when they question the nice, blushing man, he'll pass along the code word and Max will be expecting Wren."

"Code word?"

"Gratitude gift. That's Wren's code when she wants to see Max. We'll be expected, and we'll be welcomed."

"You're so clever, Mouse. You've thought of everything."

She laughed. "Not me. Wren. Wren thinks of everything." She stopped suddenly. "By the Gods, I miss that woman. I feel so lost without her. I just hope I don't screw it up."

Spider put an arm around her and patted her shoulder. "You've got Flick, Mouse. And me. Perhaps the three of us together can equal one of her."

Mouse leaned into him, surprising them both. "Perhaps so."

Chapter 10: Max

Max frowned, his grizzled white brows nearly meeting at the middle. *So the clever girl finally found me.* He had a soft spot for Wren. Unfortunately, he owed her a lot of favors he'd rather not pay back. "When was this?"

"Yesterday," the small, nondescript man answered.

All Max's people were nondescript.

"And you lost them?"

The nondescript fellow nodded. "They were good. Knew the streets up here as well as me. Perhaps better."

"Interesting," Max sat back and steepled his fingers, his elbows resting on the arms of the large wing-backed chair he used almost like a throne. "Well, she'll give me a couple of days to settle down and then we'll have a visit from her. What else do you have for me?" *For a retired man, I still seem to have a lot to manage.*

It suddenly occurred to Max that he had become a KinLord of sorts for all the riffraff who managed to escape the bowels of SubCity. He'd never been down there, and he thanked all he held sacred that he had not. What he heard was enough to convince him to remain right where he was, Above and on the fringes of the UpperUpper. Although with this last move, he mused, he'd finally crossed the line into a more resplendent atmosphere, where he was determined to remain.

"Sir?"

Max blinked. "Sorry, you were saying?"

"I was telling you about Wooster. He was arrested and wants you to help him."

"Again? What for this time?"

"Embezzlement."

Max tsked and shook his head sadly. "That I cannot do. Not unless I wish to fall with him. Tell him I will do what I can to lighten his sentence, and I will ensure his family is cared for. It's all I can do. Wooster can't expect me to clean up after him every time he gets into trouble."

The nondescript man, Ingot by name, nodded and referred to the list in his hand. "I believe that's it for today."

"Good. Maybe I'll have some peace and quiet. Why don't you make yourself scarce, Ingot? There's a good lad."

Not waiting for a response, Max got out of his chair and strode over to the window. He stretched his back to get the kinks out while he looked across the Above.

In the distance the government buildings' spires gleamed like sharp needles in the light. If he craned his neck he could see the spaceport, where shuttles circled like birds waiting to land. If he ever decided to move again, which was more than likely, he wanted a full view of the spaceport. He enjoyed watching the little bursts of light when the shuttles exited the atmosphere. One day, he again promised himself, he would visit some of the other Ring planets.

"One day," he said aloud and turned from the window. "But not today," he muttered while returning to his desk to read the mail.

He'd tried to retire. He really had. But he had been too bored. He liked being in the center of things. He liked knowing what was going on. In fact, truth be told, he was looking forward to Wren's visit. He'd heard rumors of a huge Kin war in SubCity a few weeks back. The Martials had been called in to intervene, so his sources had said. Wren was a KinLord. She'd fill him in, he thought with satisfaction.

Putting Wren out of his mind, Max refocused on his correspondence. He wanted to be finished before lunch.

~~~

"Show her in," Max said, linking his hands. He had decided to treat Wren as a special guest. The teacakes were already artfully arrayed on a gilded platter centered on his living room coffee table. The tea would be provided when his guest arrived. Which was now.

"Bring the tea," Max said as he strode over to the wide entrance to his room.

She was dressed in her assassin's greys with the hood up so her face was in shadows. How like Wren to make a dramatic entrance and remind others of her deadlier qualities, qualities Max had often made use of.

"Wren, my dear!" he exclaimed, holding out his hands. "How good it is to see you."

She stepped into the room and pushed back the hood.

He gasped as the hood settled about her shoulders.

The woman was the same height and build. Similar coloring as well, but where Wren's dark auburn hair grew in thick, coiled mats which fell to the middle of her back with a friendly bounce, this woman's hair was sleek and dark and tied back in a braided tail. Her dark eyes gazed at Max soberly.

"You're not Wren."

The woman shook her head and gave him a sad smile. "No. I am Mouse, Wren's eyes. "

"I've heard of you, Mouse."

His voice had chilled perceptibly. Someone not as skilled as Mouse would not have noticed. She was suddenly very glad she had brought extra knives and had left Spider at home. Despite his amiable appearance, this man was as dangerous as an unchained sniffer.

"I've heard of you as well, Max."

'Then it is time we met and got to know each other. Please, sit."

In silence, they sat and faced each other, two professionals sizing up a possible opponent.

Sitting in her greys, Mouse felt like a pile of soot while she gazed at Max's multi-colored brocade smoking jacket tied loosely about his softening middle. He was an older man, medium height. A shock of white hair topped his affable features. Below bushy white brows, the deep brown eyes studying her were keenly aware, reminding her of Wren. Her spirits plummeted.

"Perhaps you would like a teacake while you tell me why Wren has dishonored me by sending you in her stead," Max said gesturing to the pretty plate.

"No, thank you," Mouse said. "I assure you, if she could, Wren would be here in my stead. When last I saw her, she told me to come to you for help. She also told me not to trust you. I wonder, Max, how do you ask for help yet not trust the help you might receive?"

Max's laugh was big and booming. "I like you, Mouse. I do. But then, Wren always knew how to pick her friends. How is our Wren?"

"Dead. At least we think so. It's been more than two months."

The man sagged and his eyes lost some of their predatory gleam.

"How can Wren be dead? It's just not possible."

154

Mouse looked at her hands. "It's been more than two months since we saw her," she repeated. "We would have heard something by now."

"What happened?"

"There was to be a Culling."

"Yes, I heard about that, but then a KinLord war broke out and the Martials were sent in to keep the peace."

"That is not exactly what happened."

"Please, tell me what really happened. I prefer to know the truth of all things." He grinned, the cunning light suddenly back in his eyes. "I prefer to be the one doing the deceiving."

"We all would prefer that," Mouse agreed. "The thing is, Wren was betrayed."

"Impossible."

"Possible. She has a weakness. Her compassion, as you probably know."

Max grunted.

"No one was turned away from her KinLands, and she was a just Lord. Word spread. The number of Kin increased. Soon we were the largest KinFolk tribe. And Wren knew how to govern. We had a good system. We were thriving," she paused. "At least as well as one *can* thrive in SubCity. Anyway, Wren's power appears to have worried the two lords who bordered her KinDom. As a result, Fergus and MacMichaels banded together with the Martials."

"Wait. You said with the Martials? The Above knew what was going on down in SubCity?"

"I believe they organized it," Mouse said. "Fergus and MacMichaels are both too greedy and dumb to plan anything like what happened. On my solos, I saw a lot of Martial traffic back and forth. There was to be a Cull. Wren knew. She says she has no knacks, but she knew there would be a Cull before we heard a word about it. I just had to verify it, and I did. Flick and I. Flick's Wren's Second," Mouse explained.

She worried she'd said too much, but Max had this way about him. It made it easy to say more than you should. A knack? She wasn't sure. What she was sure of was if he was going to help, he needed to know all of it. So she continued.

"The thing Flick and I found out was, yes, there would be a Cull, but they'd only be Culling Wren's Kin. And we prepared for that. We were all set for a long hide. We pre-Culled, so we could give the Martials something to take back with them, the Kin with the knacks the Martials look for. That way they'd leave the old, young'uns and injured alone, you see. Wren's that smart." Mouse stopped.

"What went wrong?" Max asked softly.

Mouse sat back and looked up at the ceiling. It was painted, full of fat cherubs and clouds. "Turns out one of our runners, a young kid, got caught," she said to the cherubs. "Turns out the kid was our Grainer's boy. Turns out they threatened our Grainer, and he ratted us out. They massacred us," she told the cherubs and hoped the tears would stay inside her head if she kept looking up.

She swallowed to help them stay hidden. "All those old folks, young kids, all settled down for a nice, cozy hide. The Martials came in, went directly to Tunnel Two like they'd known all along—and they had— burned the ropes we had trussed up to keep everyone from the damp. Trapped the Kin and burned them too. Then they came for the rest of us. House to house." Suddenly she didn't care if the tears fell or not. Losing Kin was a crying matter. She tore her eyes from the ceiling and looked at Max again.

"What happened to the Grainer?"

"Skip? Oh, Wren, she was so angry—but not at what he'd done. She understood the why of it. No, she was angry because he didn't come to her, didn't trust her enough to know she'd make things right or die trying. She stood there shouting at him and at the same time making up a plan for how she could have bent the bad to our advantage." Mouse looked at Max again, her eyes hard as onyx. "She should have killed him then and there."

"She didn't?" Max asked, surprised.

"Course not. This is Wren we're talking about. She cut out his tongue and let him live." Mouse snorted. "Thing is, he's now so loyal, he'd die for our Kin, even me, and he knows how I feel about what he did."

"And after that?"

"That's when the other two KinLords got involved. They started recruiting. I don't blame those who went. It was a fearful night." She grew silent.

Max watched a tear track a path down Mouse's cheek. "And Wren?" he prompted softly.

"Wren told us to get out. She'd planned for that, too. A few days before, she brought Flick and me through the tunnels to the Above. A safe place. When we saw what was happening, Wren made us get out. Had Flick blow the tunnels when we heard the sniffers."

"Sniffers?"

"Yeah. Never heard of sniffers being let loose in SubCity before. Wren drew them away so we could escape. She's deadly, but against a pack of sniffers?" Mouse shook her head. "We still have hope, Flick and I, but that's only because we're fools. A fool's hope."

"And how do you want me to help?" Max asked. "Surely Wren has a plan."

Mouse smiled for the first time, delighting Max with her sudden beauty. "Of course Wren has a plan. Turns out it was her plan all along. The Cull just hurried things along. Do you know there are parts of the City that still haven't become Rubble? A kind of in between?"

"I have heard tell of such places, yes. They're abandoned because the City has moved on."

"But since the Ring," Mouse said, "the City really hasn't moved on very often. Instead of moving on, it's moved off. That's a quote from Wren. Anyway, she found a place—a square of buildings around a fountain where water still flows. It's far enough away that no one would notice us. Yet it's close enough for us to go about our business. We mean to stay there. Never go back to SubCity. It was Wren's wish."

"And you all need new identification," Max guessed. "How many are we talking about?"

"Forty-five Kin and me and Flick."

"That's a lot of idents."

Mouse thought of nearly the five hundred Kin who'd died or were now a part of other KinDoms. "Not so many, really," she answered.

Max leaned over, snatched a teacake, and took a bite. He chewed on it thoughtfully. "I couldn't do it all at once. Forty-five new idents, even for me, would draw too much attention. That's the equivalent of a small army brought from a Ring planet to do some mischief, according to the authorities. It's how they think." He took another bite. "These are delicious," he said still chewing. "You must take one."

"No thank you. I'm not very hungry."

"Tea, then. I insist."

A teacart had been rolled in by one of Max's nondescript attendants while Mouse had been telling her story.

"Tea?" Mouse twisted around and spied the cart. "Please," she said and silently berated herself for letting her guard down.

Max got up to pour them both a cup. "Cream? Sugar?"

"Neither, thank you."

Max reached over the back of the couch and handed Mouse a cup.

"Ah," he grunted as he reseated himself. He took a sip. "Nothing like a nice cup of tea. This one is from Galanta. I imported it myself. Been expanding my businesses. Which reminds me, we are conducting negotiations, are we not?"

Mouse relaxed into the cushions with her cup. "So you'll help us? I'm calling in Wren's favors."

"Enjoy your tea. We're still in negotiation."

He watched Mouse take a sip before he joined her. "It's nice, isn't it?"

She smiled again. The sun on a cloudy day.

"Wren warned me you would negotiate. She told me to tell you I know all about the ivory."

"She would have to tell you about that messy debacle, wouldn't she?"

Mouse nodded. "Of course. She saved your life that time."

"Yes, she did." He placed his cup on the table. "I loved Wren like a daughter, Mouse. When I first met her she was a helpless kitten, weak, frail, and all claws. I watched her grow into the woman you and I know to be a remarkable person. And I marveled. I truly marveled. And this is her last request of me, to help what's left of her Kin. Of course I will help."

He watched the tension seep from Mouse's shoulders. "However, you will then be in my debt, and I will expect to use your services, Mouse, whenever I have the need."

They studied each other warily.

"I can't promise that," she began. "The Kin must come first. But after that, I'm yours."

"Deal." He spat on his hand and held it out to her.

Mouse spat on hers and clasped his hand.

"Good, that's settled," Max said and handed her a napkin. He took one for himself and wiped his hand before helping himself to another teacake.

"I will need a month to organize. Are you sure you don't want a teacake? These really are exceptional."

"I'm sure they are, but no, thank you."

"Then you must take some with you when you leave." He popped the last bit of cake into his mouth. "As I was saying, I will need a month. Come back in a month, and we can make further plans. I will need images of all your Kin. Not all at once. A few at a time. I'm warning you again, this will take time. It's safest to draw it out over a year at the very least. We'll see how it goes."

"A year?"

"I'm afraid so. A few here, a few there. I have other clients. Paying clients."

"I see."

He laughed as he got to his feet. "For someone who is retired, I am a very busy man. I'll see you out."

He led her down to the kitchens, stood with her while forty-seven tea cakes were placed in a box and tied with string, and watched her smile again before she left his home through the service entrance.

The crowd swallowed her up in seconds.

Even though she carried a large white and red box, he was pleased to note he could not spot her.

Like Wren.

Max nosed around the kitchen a bit, teased a couple of scullery maids and made his way back upstairs, very pleased with the results of his negotiation.

Chapter 11: Stardust

"It's not getting any better," Wren stated through clenched teeth while she eased carefully down onto one of the two benches that now graced the entrance to the encampment. "It just won't take any more of my weight." She threw up her hands and growled her frustration. "And it still looks like a Sausage. I thought it'd stop looking like that by now."

Eloch stopped his hammering and sat beside her. He stretched out his long legs and tapped Wren's healthy leg with his own. "You were badly damaged."

"I know that. Don't you think I know that? But it should be getting better now. It's been four months. It just stopped getting better." She pondered the Sausage. "I'm afraid to take it out of its casing. I'm afraid it will just fall apart."

"A lot of healing has to be done. Veins and nerves. Muscle."

"Yeah. I'm just bored, is all. I'm not used to being idle." She nudged him. "And everything you're doing isn't helping. Look at the place. It's got benches and beds and counters. It's turning into a home. What are you working on now?"

"A table."

"But we've got a table."

"A better one."

She nodded. "You're bored, too."

Eloch shrugged. "There are still things holding my interest." He flashed her a smile and delighted in her blush. "I've learned a great deal from you about how this planet functions." His smile dimmed. "But nothing about Spur, other than She is feeding us while She feeds Little Sister."

"How so?"

"The prey Little Sister brings to us. I have an idea," he stood abruptly.

Wren watched him go inside and rummage through one of the packs he'd found. She was always amazed at what he brought back from his forays into Rubble. As soon as she was better able to fend for herself, Eloch had left for a few hours at a time, searching for items that could make their lives easier. She glanced down at her crutch. That had been a find. A crutch! Of all the things to find in Rubble.

"Here," Eloch said. "Why don't you go practice?"

She looked at what he held out to her. "My last two throwing knives!"

"I thought it safe to return them to you, now I know you won't kill me or Little Sister."

Wren bit back her retort when she realized he was teasing her. "Thank you. And I can get exercise as well when I have to retrieve them," she sassed.

"It will make you more accurate," he told her. "You'll be more careful not to throw wild."

She cocked her head at him. "Excellent point. Thanks! I'll just rest awhile and then try my hand."

"Would you like a target?"

She lifted an eyebrow. "You volunteering?"

She couldn't stop herself from laughing when he did. Eloch's laugh was contagious. Deep and rolling.

"I thought I'd put a post up for you to practice on."

"No need, but thanks. There are plenty of things to aim for." She glanced around and threw. It landed with a solid *thunk* in the center of the table Eloch was working on. "Oops. I'd better get that." She giggled and stood, using the crutch to steady herself before she hobbled over and pulled the knife out. When she turned to face Eloch again, the knife had disappeared into one of her tunic pockets, along with the other one.

Wren resettled herself beside him on the bench.

"What food do you miss most of all?" Eloch asked out of the blue.

"Gods, anything that doesn't come from a wrapper or has to be butchered."

He smirked.

"Bread. I would love to sink my teeth into a warm loaf of bread."

"Bread. That's good. I would like some bread as well."

"My mouth is watering just thinking about it." She sighed. "Back in SubCity, we'd be so happy when one of the runners snatched a bread cart filled with rolls, all crispy on the outside and soft inside. Didn't happen often. I'd gather the Kin and we'd dole them out and have a celebration right then and there. Nothing better than fresh bread," she said dreamily.

Eloch grinned. "You look like Little Sister when she's getting her ears rubbed."

Wren laughed. "Well, I kind of feel like Little Sister. We were talking about bread, after all."

Eloch stood and ruffled her hair. "I want to finish the table before it gets dark. Have you noticed the days are shorter now? Getting even colder, too." He strode away, not waiting for her answer, and resumed his hammering.

She hadn't noticed. Why had she never paid attention to the seasons? There had been no need down in SubCity. But what about the years she lived Above? She honestly hadn't noticed much difference from day to day. She shook her head and looked at the broken buildings and streets of Rubble. So much sameness. She shivered slightly and rubbed her arms. It had been getting colder.

The hum of a shuttle brought her back from her reverie. "Uh, Eloch? We've got company. If it's Martials, I'd rather they didn't know I'm here." She grabbed her crutch, scrambled up, and hobbled into the shadows of the encampment just as the shuttle circled to make its descent.

"It's okay," Eloch called over the noise. "It's Aiko." He raised his arm in greeting.

"Caution first," Wren shouted back and remained where she was.

She watched the shuttle land a short distance from the encampment, kicking up a whirlwind of dust. Eloch made his way over after the whine of the engines slowed and stopped. A few moments later the hatch opened and two people emerged, one a small, slender woman who reminded Wren of Mouse, and a tall, well-built man, though she noted he was not as tall or as well-built as Eloch. The man gripped a reading device loosely in one hand as he peered about curiously. They were both wearing dark green uniforms with orange detailing. Wren let out her breath. Not Martials, then. Something better. Ring Colonizers.

"I leave you alone for a few months and you make yourself a castle," the woman said to Eloch with a smile. "Thought you were heading south."

Eloch smiled at the woman and nodded to the man. "I was, but something came up." He glanced back at Wren.

She tried to nudge herself deeper into the shadows near the bed, but it was too late. Both the woman and the man had seen her. "May as well go on out then," Wren grumbled. She hobbled out into the evening light. "Hi," she said lamely.

"This is Wren," Eloch said. "I've been helping her heal."

Wren shot Eloch a look of gratitude. She didn't want too much said about her until she had formed her own opinions about these people.

"And these are Aiko and Genji, the people I've told you about," Eloch said, continuing with the introductions.

Wren nodded.

"Wren," Aiko said. "You've the look of SubCity."

Wren nodded. "You too. Eloch said you're a pilot. Culled?"

Aiko snorted. "I didn't wait for a Culling. I volunteered when a recruitment team came through."

"Really? Takes guts to volunteer. If they don't like what they see, it's all over." Wren smiled. "I've got to say I'm impressed, and it takes a lot to impress me."

Aiko smiled in return. "It wasn't guts, I assure you. If I hadn't made it, I might well be dead by now. I wouldn't have lasted much longer in Sub. Speaking of which, I heard there was some trouble down there a few months back."

"There's always trouble down there." She recognized fishing when she heard it.

"Your leg," Genji said, his reader in his hand. "May I take a look at it?"

Wren shot a glance at Eloch.

"You can trust them, Wren," he told her. "Genji brought me out of hibernation. He knows what he's doing."

She squinted at him. "You a Med?"

He shook his head. "Not a trained one, but I've got a knack."

"We don't need a Med when we've got Genji. Saves me from feeding one more person," Aiko said.

"May I take a look at your leg?" Genji asked again.

Wren shrugged. "I don't suppose it'll hurt." She hobbled over to the bench and lowered herself gingerly, keeping the crutch close by.

Genji began scanning her calf.

"You had enough food, I take it?" Aiko asked Eloch. "We brought some more supplies for you."

Eloch nodded. "Wren had some meal bars with her. We made do, but we'd appreciate the food."

Aiko glanced at Wren, who was deep in conversation with Genji. "Looks like she could use a set of clothes. That tunic she's got on comes down to her knees."

Eloch chuckled. "She's a little thing. I cut the leggings to fit her height, but that's my only spare tunic, so she rolls up the sleeves."

"Where'd you find her?" Aiko said.

Eloch hesitated. "I think she should tell you her story if she wishes."

Aiko smiled. "A little protective of our new friend, are we?"

"She's a private person," Eloch replied. "How was your trip?"

168

Aiko smiled to herself. She thought it rather endearing to see Eloch blush. "It was good. The Colonizers liked my efficiency, and I think they'll be using me more often. With my small crew, I'm cheaper to utilize. And I'm ready to do some shorter trips. They don't pay as much as an intergalactic one, but they're not as exhausting, either."

"What of Entean?"

"Still next in line for colonization. There's an election coming up, so the Board of Colonizing is more focused on getting reelected at the moment. Which is a good thing. No second scout ship scheduled. You've got more time to act, if that's what you're planning."

"My plan is to go south when Wren is better," Eloch said.

Aiko was about to ask if Wren would accompany him when Genji called them over, his expression serious. Wren's eyes were wide, her face pale.

"I was just explaining to Wren, here, that her leg needs surgical attention if she wants to keep it. Sooner the better."

"I didn't think it was infected." Eloch said looking over at Wren.

"It's not. It requires grafting and laser surgery. It can't heal on its own."

"But she's using it."

"Her grit and determination are using it. If it weren't in the healing casing, it would be impossible."

"We can drop her off to a MedLab on our way home," Aiko offered.

"No!" Wren exclaimed.

Aiko looked at her, one eyebrow raised. "It's your leg."

Wren glanced at Eloch.

"You can trust her, Wren," Eloch said, reading her expression. "I do."

"Okay, then." Wren looked up at Aiko, her face a mask. "I can't go to a MedLab because I don't want the Martials to know I'm still alive. Not until I get back to my Kin and see how they are."

"Wait, you're *that* Wren? The KinLord?"

"I am *that* Wren, yes.

"You did a great deal of good down in SubCity."

"I did what I could while I could," Wren replied.

"You took my people in when nobody else would," Aiko said.

"Who are your people, Aiko?"

"Gem and Echo, my little brother and sister. Orphaned after I'd already gotten out of Sub."

Wren smiled. "They're good kids," she said softly. "Gem looks like you."

"I'm grateful you took them in."

"Don't be too grateful. I have no idea if they're still alive. You probably know more than I do about what happened, and Eloch tells me you've been off planet."

"Don't know much. The spin will never be the truth. I do know Gem and Echo are with the MacMichaels Kin now. They're not allowed to say more than that they are there and they're okay."

"They're alive," Wren said with a gusty sigh. "That's good news."

"It's hard. The not knowing." Aiko said.

"Very hard."

"Ma'am? The leg? Sooner the better." Genji said.

"Right. Genji, you think you could manage it back on board *Stardust*?

Genji glanced at Wren. "She'd do better at a MedLab."

"Not a choice I've got," Wren said.

"True," Aiko said. "The Martials are saying you're dead and they're very happy about it. They haven't painted a very pretty picture of you."

"Didn't think they would."

"Genj?" Aiko said. "You up for it?"

He nodded. "I'll do my best," he told Wren. "I'd have to see it out of the casing before I know for sure."

"What's the worst that can happen?" Wren asked.

"You could lose your leg, but that's not really so bad when you think of what they've done with the animateds."

Wren snorted. "Not only not in my budget, but I like my own leg and want to keep it."

Eloch put a hand on Wren's shoulder. "It will be fine, Wren."

She glanced up at him with a small smile. "Come with me?"

"Of course."

Aiko clapped her hands together. "That's settled then. We'd better move. It's getting dark. Anything either of you need before we go?"

Eloch shook his head and looked at Wren. "You?"

"Not really. I doubt we'll be gone for long. Got my crutch, so I'm good to go."

"Let me bank the fire, then," Eloch said to Aiko. "I'll be right there."

He watched them help Wren to the shuttle and then focused his attention on Little Sister, explaining what was happening. He felt her pleasure at the prospect of being able to stay and hunt longer. If he concentrated, he could feel her lying on cool grass. His stomach fluttered. *Must go south to see for myself.*

Eloch hurried to catch up with the others and climbed into the craft. As it banked, he looked south. As far as he could see, it was all Rubble. How far had Little Sister traveled?

~ ~ ~

The Stardust was small, but to Wren it was a palace. "This is the most beautiful piece of equipment I've ever seen!" she exclaimed as *The Stardust's* hatch closed, swallowing the shuttle.

Aiko huffed as she berthed and shut it down. "Then you've never been on a ship before."

"Well, no, I haven't. I've never even been off-planet before. But my words stand."

Eloch glanced at her and smiled. When she learned Aiko's ship was docked off-planet in an orbiting space station, Wren had been like a child, barely able to contain herself.

"I'm pretty pleased with her," Aiko said. "I own her outright."

"But you're part of the Ring Colonizers, right? I didn't think anyone owned anything."

"Pilots are special. We put in a certain amount of time and, if we're still up to piloting, we can buy our own ship and work on consignment. It's cheaper for the Colonizers that way. Once we own a ship, it's up to us to maintain it to code and pay the crew, even though they still assign them to us. We don't get to choose our crew."

172

"Doesn't sound like such a good deal to me," Wren said.

"It is. I've got my own bird to fly. I know her inside and out, all her sounds, quirks, what she can do, what she can handle. Makes it much easier when I take her through the wormhole jumps."

"I've always wondered what it would be like to fly through one of those things."

"It's like nothing else. Genji, do you need any prep time?"

"An hour at most."

"Then why don't I find you some clothes that fit, Wren, and you can freshen up? I'm sure a hot meal would be welcome as well."

"Not until she's out of surgery," Genji said. "I need her to have a fairly empty stomach."

"Fine. Eloch, you still attached to those skins you wear, or would you like to see if I can find something for you, too? I'm warning you, the pants may be short."

"I prefer my own clothes."

"Well at least let me get them cleaned for you. Follow me, you two. Genji can button up the shuttle." Aiko glance at him, her eyebrows raised. "Have time?"

"Sure I do. I'll see you in an hour, then," Genji said to Wren.

She swallowed and nodded.

Wren hobbled to catch up with Aiko as she led them through the shuttle bay doors and to the elevator. "Sick Bay is two floors up, and there's a room on the same floor you can use," she told Wren.

"I'd like a room as well, if I could?" Eloch asked.

"Of course. Sorry, I assumed…"

"He found me, that's all." Wren said.

Aiko glanced between the two of them. "If you say so." She hid her grin.

Silence filled the elevator after the doors hissed shut.

"Why are you being so nice to me?" Wren asked suddenly.

Aiko glanced at her. "You took care of my people. They were actually happy. That's saying a lot for someone living in SubCity. I'd heard you'd gotten out and then went back. Became a KinLord."

"You heard right."

"Why'd you do it? Go back down there I mean?"

Wren shrugged and leaned heavily on her crutch as the elevator bobbed to a stop. "Ouch," she said.

"Sorry. One of the ship's quirks I was telling you about. This way."

They exited, Aiko leading the way.

"There's Sick Bay," she said, pointing at a double door they passed by. "Two doors down is for you, Eloch, and here," she said when she halted in front of another paneled door next to the Sick Bay, "is yours, Wren."

The door slid open to reveal a standard recovery room.

"Behind that curtain is a shower. Need any help?" she added as Wren hobbled into the room, making a beeline for the shower.

"Nope, I'm good, thanks."

"Sure about that?"

Wren laughed. "Tell her, Eloch."

"She has learned to manage my bath and shower creation, and this will be much easier. Her only complaint was she couldn't take one more than once a week. It's been taking the water longer to heat. I offered to heat water for her over the fire and carry it to her while she bathed, but she said she'd wait."

"Modest, are we?" Aiko asked.

"Modest we are." Wren answered. She didn't like people to see what her parents had done to her.

"Well, I'm very impressed that you managed to bathe at all."

"Don't be," Wren replied. "I'll do anything to be clean."

"Then I won't try to stop you. I'll be back in twenty with some new clothes. Enjoy that shower." Wren was already getting ready when the door slid shut.

"This way," Aiko told Eloch and started down the corridor. "She doesn't like to talk about herself, does she?"

"She's wary," Eloch said, thinking again how much Wren reminded him of Little Sister.

"I wouldn't expect less of a KinLord."

"What is this KinLord? She hasn't mentioned it. She talks about her Kin. She grieves for them and worries, although she doesn't know I know. She doesn't talk much about what she did in SubCity."

"From what my brother and sister described when I managed to see them, Wren is not the typical KinLord. KinLords are usually monsters, evil and greedy. SubCity is divided into at least twenty KinLands, each ruled by a KinLord. There are lesser Lords as well. Quite a hierarchy down there. To become a KinLord, you would have to challenge and destroy the current KinLord. Which is what Wren did. Then she

175

started making changes. Had Kin meetings. Let people say what was on their minds. Was known to be tough but fair. And never turned anyone away."

"Wren has killed? She doesn't have the look of a killer." But he thought again of Little Sister.

"She's killed. Many people. She has a reputation to go with those skills. Before she went back to SubCity, she made her living as an assassin. She made a very good living at it as well. Dangerous woman. Even I've heard of her, and I never ran in those circles. I hung out strictly with the Ring Colonizers." She glanced at him. "This bothers you?"

"How can I say what is right or wrong? I am not Spur's Champion. Back home I have killed. Never a human, but I have taken life, and to me, that is the same."

They reached the room and paused as the door slid open.

"Look familiar?" Aiko asked.

"My same room." Eloch said with a nod.

"I never bothered to return the clothes I lent you and you never wore. So wear them now, and we'll get your leathers off to sanitation. Leave them on the bunk, and I'll have one of my crew collect them while you're with Wren and Genji."

Eloch nodded. "My thanks."

Aiko studied him. "You look good, Eloch," she decided. "More settled, I guess I'd say. Welcome aboard." She smiled. "And now I've got to go. A ship doesn't run by itself. Most everyone's on shore leave, but *Stardust* is due for her overhaul, and nobody touches my bird unless I'm right there with them. I'll stop by later to see how well Genji did with your Wren's leg."

~~~

"Oh, the Gods," Genji exclaimed, trying to keep down the bile when he finished removing the medical casing from Wren's lower left leg. "I don't see how she survived this."

Eloch hissed and swallowed hard. "Why isn't it healed?"

"A wound like this needs to be changed quite frequently. Has the casing ever been changed?" Genji asked as he gingerly sprayed the area with a sanitation ointment. "This has got to be excruciatingly painful." He glanced over at Wren's unconscious face. She had put up a fight before she allowed him to put her under. It wasn't until Eloch promised he wouldn't let them take her leg that she complied. "I sure hope you won't have to break your promise," he said looking up at Eloch. "You okay? Want to sit down?"

"I'll be okay in a minute," Eloch said and took a steadying breath. "What promise?"

"That her leg would still be here when she wakes up."

"You can't fix it?"

Genji sighed and shrugged. "It's oozing, but it's not bleeding. That's a good sign. But if I move it in the slightest, I'm afraid it might just fall apart. It should have been changed and aired out on a daily basis, cauterized, grafted, lasered, or removed. This poor limb. How she must have suffered."

Eloch flinched. "Can you laser it closed now?"

"Let me think about this for a little while," Genji told him. He draped sterile gauze over the wound. "In the meantime, we can let it air and not have to look at it."

Eloch looked at the white gauze already showing signs of pinkish orange. "Won't the wound stick to that?"

"More than likely if we leave it on too long," Genji checked Wren's vitals. "She seems to be doing fine. Would you tell me how she got this and what you did to dress it?"

Eloch nodded and stroked Wren's hair. "A sniffer caught her by the leg and tried to drag her back into a tunnel."

"There must be more to that story. I've never heard of anyone surviving a sniffer attack. They're vicious and hungry. Trained to kill."

"Wren survived," Eloch said simply. "I only had the medical kit you left with me. Used a whole can of the sanitation ointment and then a whole can of the liquid bandage. For the fever, I gave her all the antibiotics I had."

Genji nodded. While Eloch spoke, he applied a surgical mask and lifted the gauze to study the wound again. "You did what you could, and the fact that she's alive tells me you did exactly the right things. Too bad you didn't cauterize the wound." He fell silent and bent closer to Wren's leg. "If I laser it closed, it still might not heal. Not if her wounded cells aren't getting enough oxygen to them. If I remove it and she gets an Animate for the lower leg, she'd almost be as good as new. That's the route I would take."

"But you're not Wren."

They both stared at the leg for a few moments. It oozed sluggishly.

"Can you laser it closed and then let Wren decide what she wants?"

Genji scanned his patient again. "Could do. I suppose it could be removed later. I'm going to try to mend any involved arteries as we go. Other than the lack of blood to the cells, the biggest concern is to get her wounds closed so they can heal without infection. She's been lucky. Very lucky under the circumstances."

He reached for the laser pen, then set it down on his table of tools. "She's too pale. I'm going to give her a blood transfusion. And while I'm doing that, you put a mask on and then go sterilize your hands and glove them as you saw me do. I'm going to need you to help me keep it blotted so I can see what I'm doing. This is going to take some time. Need to go slow."

It took four hours. But when Genji finally parked the laser and re-bandaged the wound, all the ribbons and tears had been closed and the leg looked more like a leg. "The scar tissue will have to be massaged so the muscles and bones don't stick to the skin," Genji muttered. "Think you're up for that?"

"She can't do it for herself? She hates being touched."

"Unfortunately not. If she wants to keep the leg, it's going to be a painful process. But," he said as he took off his mask and stripped off his surgical gloves, "at least it won't get infected. And it was in better shape than I thought. Many veins were severed, but not major ones. The calf is still attached to the bone. Time will tell if she's getting enough blood to the cells. And if she's not, then the limb will have to go."

He checked Wren's readouts. "She should be waking up soon. You staying here? I want to go wash up at my cabin. Here, I'll take that." Genji reached out for the mask and gloves Eloch had taken off.

"Thank you. Yes, I'll be here when she awakes."

"Have some water handy. She'll be thirsty. I'll be back a little later."

Eloch watched Genji sweep through the surgery doors. Then he drew up a chair to begin his vigil.

She looked pale. The dark circles under her eyes stood out, and he wondered if she had felt anything during the procedure. The leg must have been painful, not just the procedure, but to have been using it continuously. All this time. All that pain. She hid it well. He had blocked their empathic connection so he could be strong for her. But now he understood how it must have been. Such stoic determination. He reached out and pushed her curls off her forehead.

Such a little thing, fierce and proud. He thought about what Aiko had told him about being a KinLord. Fierce, proud, intelligent, fair. He'd had to change her clothes when she was fevered. He'd seen the scars. He added survivor to his list. He thought of their conversations and added curious and open-minded. And funny. She made him laugh. He liked her. He liked her very much. Maybe even too much. Three friends, now, on Spur. Aiko, Genji and Wren. And he should add Little Sister. Four friends.

Eloch went to the sink he'd used to wash and sterilize his hands. He filled one of the cups in a container over the sink with water and by the time he had returned to his chair, he noticed her eyelids were fluttering. "Wren?" he whispered.

"Eloch," she mumbled, still with her eyes closed. "I'm afraid to look."

"Your Sausage is still there. How are you feeling?"

She opened her eyes and immediately closed them, her hand coming up to her head. "Bright." She opened her eyes again and squinted up at Eloch, her hand shielding her eyes. "So he didn't cut it off. I'm glad. Oh," she groaned. "I hurt all over."

Eloch held out the cup. "Water?"

She reached for it and Eloch helped her sit up. She leaned into his strength and sipped the cool liquid, feeling it glide down her throat. "Mmm. Good. Thanks."

"More?"

"No, I'm good."

Eloch helped her settle down again and tossed the cup into a waste receptacle.

"How do you feel now?"

"I've felt better and I've felt worse, but I'm feeling more awake. So the Sausage is still with me. What did he do?"

"He lasered it closed. He said it was a miracle it hadn't become infected."

"I'm glad it's over. I'm glad it's all closed up. Hurts like a sonofabitch. More than before."

The sick bay's doors swooshed open as Genji and Aiko entered the room.

"She awake?" Genji asked as he came around the curtain to where Wren lay.

"She is," Wren answered for herself. "Thanks for leaving my leg."

Genji shrugged. "I wanted to take it. You would heal much better with an Animated attached.

"I prefer my own parts."

"There's still a chance you'll lose the leg."

"But there's a chance I'll keep it, too."

"Either way, it's going to take a lot of rehab."

"How long?"

"A couple of months if you work it every day. I can affix a permanent brace, which should help speed your recovery. It will require another surgery."

"When?"

"In about a month."

Wren looked at Eloch. "I'd be keeping you from your purpose."

Eloch opened his mouth to answer, but Aiko interrupted. "You can stay with us, Wren. We've got equipment to help you regain your strength. We've got the medical if you need it."

"But wouldn't I be in the way?"

"Not at all. We're docked here for the next couple of months while *Stardust* gets her overhaul. Got a skeleton crew on board. You couldn't have picked a better time."

Wren looked at Eloch, eyebrows raised.

"It is your choice, Wren."

She nodded. "Can I sleep on it?" she asked Aiko. She had already decided it was best for everyone if she stayed, but she needed to settle into the idea.

"Sure. Why don't you rest now, Wren? Eloch, you know where the galley is. I'll meet you there."

"I'm going to give you something to help you sleep," Genji told Wren. "It's a painkiller as well."

Wren nodded. "That would be nice. To not feel any pain for a while."

With a nod Genji went to get the injections.

"What do you think?" Wren asked Eloch. "About me staying here for a couple of months?"

"You will get the care you need," he said slowly.

She wrinkled her brow. "I don't know these people. Don't know if I can trust them."

"I trust them," Eloch said. "They could have abandoned me after the Board of Colonizers got through with me. Instead, they took me where I wanted to be and bring me supplies regularly."

Wren nodded. "True." She reached for Eloch's hand. "I feel wounded and vulnerable, and I'd rather be holed up somewhere nobody can find me until I'm better."

He squeezed her hand. "I think you will be safe here, Wren. I do."

"And nobody from below can find you in a ship docked off planet," added Genji, returning with a prepared injection. "For now, sleep." He shot the drugs into her vein.

Wren sighed as she felt them taking affect, pulling her under. Her hand would have slid out of Eloch's had he not continued to hold it.

"Now she is unconscious again, we should move her to her cabin, where she'll be more comfortable." Genji said.

Eloch nodded and gathered her into his arms, carried her next door and gently laid her in her berth. As he covered her sleeping form, he noticed how bony her legs had become, how prominent her ribs. "She should stay here and heal," he told Genji, who had followed him in. "Rubble is no place for the injured."

"I agree with you. Aiko is waiting in the galley for you. I'll come too."

"How long will she be asleep?"

"As long as she needs. I gave her a mild sleep aid. If she weren't so exhausted, it would have taken her longer to fall asleep."

~ ~ ~

Wren had been dreaming of bread when she slowly came awake. She still smelled it as she lingered between sleeping and awaking. Then she opened her eyes.

It took her a while to realize where she was. On a ship docked at a space station orbiting Spur. Imagine that. Her, a SubCity dweller, orbiting Spur in a ship. And the room wasn't half bad. It was small but had a bed which felt like heaven compared to what she'd been sleeping on for the past four months, a shower and head only a few steps away, a small desk (was that actually an info console on the desk?), a couch where Eloch sat watching her, and a coffee table.

She focused on the coffee table. Was that—? "Bread!" she exclaimed happily. "I was dreaming of bread, and there it is!"

Eloch chuckled deep and low. It felt like a ripple over her skin. "You have been sleeping for nearly twenty-four hours. I thought you might be hungry by now."

Her stomach growled and she grinned. "There's your answer." She scooted up to a sitting position, and tugged her blanket up to cover her front. Securing it under her armpits, she held out her hands, ignoring the familiar pain that radiated up her leg. "Gimme."

Eloch handed her a slice slathered with nut butter.

"It's still warm! Oh, and it smells so good." She took a bite and purred her pleasure.

Eloch watched her with a grin. He'd never seen anyone take such pleasure in the smallest things the way Wren did. "Feeling better?"

She nodded, took another bite, and kept chewing as she answered. "The sleep felt good."

"How's The Sausage?"

"Hurts. But it seems to only hurt when I move. That's new. Until now, The Sausage has been a constant complainer."

"When you finish, we'll have Genji come and take a look at it. Tea?"

At her nod he poured her a cup and handed it to her. She held up a finger, popped the last bit of bread in her mouth, and accepted the cup.

"More bread?"

"Please. How do they get fresh bread and nut butter way up here?"

"The bread's cooked here, and I don't know where the nut butter comes from," he said and held out another slice. "If you stay, you will enjoy the food. Aiko told me she only lets the cook take a leave when she herself takes leave."

"Don't blame her." Wren took the second piece of bread and tucked into it.

"So what have you been doing while I've been sleeping?"

"Making plans. Gathering supplies."

"To go south?"

Eloch nodded.

Suddenly the bread lost its appeal. Wren set it down on the table beside the bed and licked her fingers.

"Wish I could tag along."

"Don't you think it would be wiser to stay here and heal?"

"Yes, of course I do. And I need to get back to my Kin as well. But still…" she sighed. "It would have been quite an adventure."

"And one I need to make alone."

"And I've delayed you, I know. When do you leave?"

"Soon." He stood, towering over her. "I'll let Genji know you're awake so he can look at your leg."

Wren watched him stride away. He paused at the door and smiled. "I'm happy to see you awake and refreshed."

She returned his smile, pretending she felt like it.

~~~

"Where's Eloch?" Wren asked when Genji came in and approached her bedside. He carried his reading device along with casing, sterilizer canisters, and a medical kit.

"With Aiko in the stores room. She's outfitting him for his journey."

Wren nodded and lifted her blanket off The Sausage. "I haven't looked at it yet," she commented.

Genji glanced at her and down at her leg while he pulled up a chair. He spread his supplies on the bed alongside her leg. "Well, we can look at it together." Taking up his scissors, he began to gently snip off the casing.

Wren flinched and willed herself to hold her leg still.

Silently they both watched while the leg was exposed. Ragged scars ran the whole circumference of her calf, but there was no more seepage.

"Wow. It looks so much better than it feels."

"Hurts, does it?"

"Like the sniffer's still attached to it."

Genji glanced at her and grinned. "It's because the muscles are busy attaching to your skin at all these laser sites. I will need to begin massaging the skin loose in a day or two. Then the muscles will recreate their membranes. In the meantime, we will keep your leg elevated for a couple of days."

Wren sighed. "That means bed rest, doesn't it?"

Genji did not answer as he scanned her leg with the reading device. Wren glanced at him when he made a sound deep in his throat.

"That sounded an awful lot like a groan. What's up?"

186

"The readouts say you're not getting enough blood flow to carry oxygen to your cells. The small arteries are too damaged. Without the oxygen, there's no way you will heal internally. The leg's got to go."

Genji watched silently as the color drained from her face. "I'm sorry," he told her and meant it.

"Why can't you heal the arteries?"

He shook his head. "I tried. And I doubt anybody could have done better at a Med Lab."

Wren, her mouth covered with her hand, looked at the ceiling and willed the tears to stay where they were. "So that's it, then. No other option."

"Death is the other option. This leg will eventually kill you, Wren. I'm sorry," he said again.

"Well," she said and let her hand fall. "If you put it that way. Do it as soon as you can. Poor Sausage never stood a chance."

~~~

Two weeks later, Wren gazed down at her Animate leg, shiny black from the thigh down. She looked up at Genji and Aiko. "So this thing never comes off?"

Genji shook his head. "Never. It's a part of you, all your nerve endings attach to it. It will work just like your old leg did. Better, in fact. It will never tire. Never age."

Wren tapped it. It sounded hard and hollow, although it wasn't. It was filled with machinery. An artificial Animate. Nothing human about it. "This must have cost your whole commission for a year. I owe you, Aiko. Both of you. I'm in your debt, and I pay my debts."

"It wasn't as expensive as you think," Aiko said. "It came from a Pawner. He'd gotten it free from an UpperUpper who bought it for his daughter. The girl never had the opportunity to use it. The grieving father wanted it out of his sight."

Wren shook her head and stroked the leg's slick surface, studied its contours. A cold, smooth replica of a human leg. Top of the line. "Poor girl. Sad story."

"Yeah, but it worked in your favor," Genji said. "And now you get to try it out. Want to stand up? I'm going to warn you, it will hurt until your body adapts."

Aiko laughed and shook her head. "The ever-practical Genji, who wants to see how this new toy of yours functions, Wren. Are you ready?"

"After, what, more than four months now? I've been either hopping, shuffling with a crutch, or lying around in agony. You think I'm ready to stand crutchless? You bet I am. And don't worry, Genji. Pain and I are old friends. Lets me know I'm still alive."

She reached for his offered hand and hauled herself up. There was a wave of vertigo, but she took a deep breath, waited it out then dropped Genji's hand. "Wow," she said. "Look at me. I'm actually standing on my own!"

"Does it hurt?" Aiko wanted to know.

"Not bad. Not bad at all." She took a step, teetered a bit and flung out her arms before she took another step. Then another. And another.

"This is amazing!" she said as she haltingly turned around to face the two. "I think I can get the hang of this pretty quick."

Genji beamed and Aiko applauded. "Now we just have to get you fattened up and healthy, and you'll be as good as new."

Getting fattened up and healthy meant days of exercise while being scanned with reading devices, followed by endless plates of food, followed by sleepless nights of pain.

But the pain wasn't the throbbing, wounded kind. This pain was the result of strenuous exercise. And she should be sleeping, but she missed her leg. The Sausage was gone. Lopped off and destroyed…and she missed it. Granted, the animated leg was far superior, and she was beginning to trust its abilities, but it wasn't and never would be a part of her body. And what was it with the sudden itching that she couldn't scratch and something Genji kept muttering about a *ghost limb*? Was she going to be forever haunted by The Sausage now?

With a growl, Wren threw the blanket back and got out of bed to begin pacing. Back and forth she strode, fueled by her anger and frustration, determined to once and for all get over her self-pity.

It was time, she decided, to stop feeling sorry for herself and her plight. Start being grateful. She was pretty lucky to be here where she was. First Eloch saved her life, then Genji had saved her life, and Aiko gave her shelter and the perfect hiding place to recover. It was time, she decided, to start paying back those who were being so kind to her, beginning with the man who saved her life. After Eloch accomplished whatever he wanted to accomplish on Spur, he was going to want to go home.

Wren was going to help him do that.

Next, it was time to rise from the dead and check out the state of her Kin.

Chapter 12: South

He missed her. It wasn't just one thing about her that he missed. It was the whole her.

The whole package.

At first he thought he missed the company. When Aiko dropped him off at the encampment, it had been stone silent. He thought when Little Sister made her appearance, when she joyfully slammed him to the ground by way of a greeting, the need for companionship would dissolve. But it hadn't. And worse, Little Sister missed her as well. There was a huge emptiness where Wren should have been.

It left him baffled. She wasn't even of Entean. She was an alien who belonged to Spur. Nothing to do with him. Yet it didn't seem to matter to his heart.

It didn't matter to his heart.

Eloch groaned aloud.

When had that happened?

Eloch sat up in his bed—her bed, for her scent still lingered—and slid from beneath the bedroll. Naked, he walked toward the entrance, careful not to disturb Little Sister where she lay at the opening. He shivered in the chill night and paused to throw a blanket over his shoulders before walking out into the black. When his eyes adjusted, he looked up and north.

Up and north was where she was.

Just after reentry, Aiko had informed him Wren had decided to have her leg amputated.

"Why didn't she tell me?" he had asked while the news squeezed his heart.

"She knew you'd stay, and she felt she'd kept you from your mission long enough. She made us promise not to tell you. Had she not, I surely would have, Eloch. Whether she realizes it or not, she needs you."

It was then when he began to realize he needed her as well. He might even have even blurted it out to Aiko if she hadn't changed the subject.

The night was clear and cold. After studying the sky carefully, he thought he could just make out the space station as it orbited above the City, despite the glow of lights.

He wondered how Wren was adjusting to her new artificial limb. He knew what giving up The Sausage had cost her. He had felt her fear, her need to keep everything together. She must have lost a great deal over her short life. A life filled with violence. He ached for her loss. If only they had been on Entean! With Entean's help, he could have healed her. Painlessly.

Silently, Little Sister slipped her muzzle into his hand. He looked down and smiled. She whined and he squatted down to give her a one-armed hug, hiking up his blanket. She leaned into him, licked his face. They stayed that way for several moments. It was a comfort.

"We should sleep, my friend," Eloch finally said, his voice rough to his ears. "Tomorrow we go south."

Her excitement was palpable and that helped him smile.

Everything was packed. Aiko had given him the same instructions she'd given him nearly five months earlier—she would occasionally fly by to see if he was back, and if he ran low on supplies he should go to the City and look for Manabu...and did he still have the plastic card to give the Martial at the gate?

He had. It was stored safely in the pack.

Aiko promised she would look after Wren and return her to her Kin. But when he had gone to say good-bye to her, Wren had other plans. She told him she'd see him when he got back from the south. He had smiled then, and he caught himself smiling now.

He would see Wren again.

With that thought, Eloch folded himself back into the Wren-scented bedroll and drifted to sleep.

The early morning hours brought the first frost the pale sun refused to warm away. The gravel under Eloch's boots crunched and crackled as he made his way south through abandoned streets and buildings, which sparkled under their frost blanket. Little Sister darted back and forth across his path, chasing various scents, her breath puffing little clouds, and he frequently got glimpses of green and free-flowing water from the sniffer's mental projections. How in all this rubble had she found green grass and flowing water?

At midday he stopped, took off his pack, and stretched to ease the kinks out of his back. He leaned his pack and staff against a wall and slouched against it. Little Sister came back to lean against him while they shared a meal bar. It felt warmer to Eloch, but the sun still shone pale against a pale sky. This far from the City, the rubble was more broken down, less easy to recognize, the buildings more fragmented, and none of them had a roof. After he ate, he used his staff to look under stones and chunks of concrete as he sought for any sign of life. Little Sister whined, eager to be on her way.

By the third day, Eloch was beginning to lose hope he would ever find anything other than abandoned and collapsed buildings. He paused on a small rise to see into the distance. All he saw were piles of stone, concrete, and rebar exposed like ribs. There was no wind. Just the same pale sky. It smelled of dust and age. Cold and empty.

By day four, Little Sister was scampering loops around him like a puppy. She kept urging him on, first racing away and then coming back to nip at his heels. Eloch laughed. "So I am your flock now?" he asked the excited beast.

She looked at him and *woofed,* then dashed off till she was no more than a faint dot on the horizon. Eloch watched her disappear into the shadow of a high-rise building that looked as if it would topple any moment, its broken glass like mirrored teeth reflecting back the pale sun. When she didn't reappear, he stepped off the road to follow, rounding into the shadow where he had last seen her.

Eloch stopped in his tracks, astounded. Here was a place as beautiful as Entean. Here was the green and the flowing water he'd glimpsed in Little Sister's mind! Trees, flowers, a perfumed breeze and…was that birdsong?

A fast glimpse of this paradise was all Eloch was allowed before Little Sister attacked, catapulting herself onto his back and threw him to the ground, her teeth straining for the neck kill while she clawed at the backpack which kept her from reaching it.

Foreigner! Not of me! Not of me! Foreigner! Not of me!

The words rang in his ears, repeating over and over.

"No!" Eloch shouted.

Using all his great strength, he flipped himself over, pinning Little Sister and knocking the wind out of her. Without hesitation, he twisted so he could kneel over the sniffer. With his staff on her neck, he kept her from his throat, although her claws, no longer blunt from when he'd clipped them, were doing their best to break through the leather of his tunic and reach his flesh.

194

She was so much more powerful than when they'd last fought. It wouldn't be long before Little Sister succeeded in ripping him to shreds.

"Stop! Lady Spur!" Eloch shouted. "You must let me speak with you. I am the Champion of Entean. She sends Her greetings to Her Sister! Please! I have nothing but peaceful intentions."

Was Little Sister hesitating?

Hope flared.

"Oh, lovely Lady," Eloch continued, using the courtly manners Entean had instilled in him. She called it the Language of Planets. "Your sister sends Her salutations. I am to present them to You. Please allow this!"

Little Sister stopped her struggles but remained coiled and ready.

Eloch remained just as ready and waited.

Entean? A voice spoke in his head. *It has been millennia since any of My sisters has sent salutations. And from One so far.* "I apologize." The gentle, melodious voice said, no longer in his head. "You may rise and deliver Entean's salutations. Your creature will not try to harm you."

Eloch slowly released Little Sister and used his staff to help himself up. Little Sister whined and got to her feet as well, then licked the blood from his hand, blood from her bite. He glanced down and smiled at her, hoping she knew he understood the attack was beyond her control. Then he looked up and his smile faded.

Before him stood a Woman, ethereal in Her beauty, who shimmered within a gossamer gown.

Eloch went down on one knee, bowing low. "My Lady, you have awakened. I am most glad."

"So it was you," she said. "You who have been calling me. You who sent the hungry beast for me to nurture."

195

Was she angry? Were those accusations? He could not say.

"It was," Eloch said. "For I cannot return until I ask Entean's question of You and receive Your answer."

"Then rise, Champion, and ask."

Eloch rose but still kept his head lowered.

"You hesitate. Are you afraid?"

"I am, Lady, yes. I do not think You wanted to be awakened, nor do I think You will like the question. I must lay emphasis on the fact Entean has been concerned about You. And I, as her Champion, feel no judgment toward You. You may search my soul if You choose."

The lightest touch on his shoulder filled him with blistering fire. He bit his lip to keep from crying out. It was never clearer to him than in that instant; he did not belong to Spur.

"Your heart is pure, Champion. Entean has chosen well. Please do not fear Me," she soothed. "Perhaps at first I did resent your interference, but I was glad to feel the joy I rediscovered in caring for this beast. I created all sorts of creatures for her to feed upon. And then I created even more creatures, just for the pleasure. What does my Sister wish to know?"

Eloch took a deep breath and gathered his thoughts, grateful for the vine which flourished inside him and held him. Claimed him. Reminded him he was not alone. "I am here for two reasons. The first is to ask the people of Spur to cease their plans to colonize Entean." He hesitated and groped for the proper wording. "The second and more important reason is to learn why, my Lady Spur, You would allow any of Your creatures to leave You."

As the silence grew, so did his fear.

When he finally lifted his head to face his fate, what he saw filled him with so much sadness he ignored the burning pain as it seared through him when he gathered the weeping Being to him.

A part of his mind witnessed in disbelief. How could this powerful Being be so filled with despair as to accept comfort from someone who did not belong to Her? Yet, here he was, stroking Her back, and here She was, weeping in his arms.

Little Sister threw back her head and howled her grief. From the cracks and crevices and out of the shadows of the little oasis came all species of creatures. They created a circle around the pair, predator and prey alike.

"Where is your Champion, my Lady?" Eloch asked softly. "Your Champion should be administering to You, not I."

"I have none," Spur sobbed. "I am forgotten. Only here, in this tiny part of Myself, am I known. All others turned their backs on Me. They abandoned Me."

Like a summer storm that came and went in an instant, Spur ceased Her grieving. When She looked up at him and smiled, no evidence remained of Her tears.

"Thank you, Champion, I am much better now." She stepped back, gently releasing Herself from his care. "I have caused you pain!" She exclaimed when She saw him flinch.

"I believe it is because I am not of You, my Lady."

"I can adjust Myself. I am sorry." She reached out and touched him again. This time, it soothed, and they both smiled as Little Sister's bite marks disappeared from his hand. "It seems I have forgotten so much. I truly have been asleep." She turned and shooed the creatures back to where they belonged. "Come, Champion, bring your beast friend and rest beside the waters with Me."

Eloch fetched his staff and followed Spur, Little Sister trotting ahead of them both. They stopped at a sandy beach. With a sigh, Eloch slid the pack from his back and leaned it against a tree in the full leaf of summer, his staff beside it.

Spur had settled Herself on the sand. She glanced at Eloch and patted the sand beside Her. "Sit, Champion, please." She smiled.

He sat, leaned back on his elbows, and stretched out his legs, enjoying the warmth of the sun, a vibrant sun, on his face. "This is a beautiful creation, Lady," he told her.

She smiled and leaned back on Her elbows, emulating him.

"Tell me," She said after a time. "Will you return to Entean now you have your answer?"

Eloch hesitated. "If You will, my Lady, I desire to stay a little longer, serve as Your Champion, and help You find a Champion born of Spur whom I can train."

Her face shone. "You are so very kind. Entean has chosen well." She repeated with a sly smile. "And I feel She guessed you might wish to do this. The plant I sensed growing within you makes a perfect conduit between us."

She sat up straight again. Eloch followed suit. "I told you it has been millennia since I last had contact with any of my Sisters. It has nearly been as long since I had a Champion."

He masked his shock. "What happened?"

She shook her head. "I do not know. Or, if I did, I have forgotten, as I have forgotten so many things. What is your name?"

"I am called Eloch."

"Eloch, Champion of Entean, will you serve as My temporary Champion?"

"My Lady Spur, I will."

Suddenly Spur was standing, looking down on him, Her hand outstretched.

"Then rise, Champion of Spur, borrowed from and to be returned to Entean."

He grasped her hand and stood. Spur's power filled him as he rose to his feet.

Once again the power of a planet surged within his being, filling him, knowing him, consuming him. As the power seeped into each cell, he exalted.

I am born for this!

This is why I breathe! This is why my heart beats! This is why I live and I move and I speak!

This!

Eloch raised his arms, threw back his head and cried out his pledge, cementing the bond.

"I am Eloch, Champion of Spur and Champion of Entean. Spur, I carry Your sweet power. Spur, I am Your will. Together, we serve and nurture. Together, we guide and teach. Together, we return the balance. This I do pledge."

Eloch opened his eyes. Spur was no longer before him. She was within him, as Entean had been before their connection was severed. He felt Spur as he had felt his Entean.

As Eloch rejoiced, so did Spur. She giddily explored each thought, each memory, each action and word within his mind. *I have yearned for this, Champion. I had forgotten how much I have yearned! In this small amount of time, you have become quite precious to me, my Champion. I shall take good care of you until you are returned. From your memories with Entean, I now know how.*

Eloch felt her sifting through those memories. *Champion! You love!* The delight She took in Her discovery shimmered through his body. *And she is one of My own!*

Eloch laughed out loud, her joy contagious. "I do love. And I don't know what to do about it."

You love, Champion. You love. That is all.

"It is that simple, isn't it?" Eloch laughed again. He promised himself when he saw Wren again, he would do exactly that. Love her. She would know how he felt.

Now rest, My Champion, and let Me feed you. We have much work to do, much planning. I want My people back. I must reclaim them. Some will need punishment. Some will need care. All of them will know Me.

~ ~ ~

The days flew into weeks while Eloch shared with Spur what he had learned of Her surface. He quickly realized the difference between Entean and Spur. While Entean spoke with him in all different ways, using all six of his senses to get Her point across, Spur was direct and very verbal.

An argumentative, impatient, and quick-to-anger Being who questioned almost every suggestion. Yet She listened to reason and was quick to forgive.

I wish to walk among them, My creatures who have forgotten me.

"And You should, My Lady. They need to remember You, feel gratitude for Your presence. Taste Your power."

Perhaps destroy and begin again.

"I serve You, My Lady," Eloch replied. "But I do believe there are many who deserve to keep their lives."

The one You love?

Eloch smiled. "And others. Many good people. And, perhaps many driven to do bad things out of desperation and ignorance. They need to love You, respect You, but not fear You." As he was speaking, Little Sister had wedged her muzzle into the palm of his hand. "Little Sister loves and respects. Otherwise, she would be very dangerous."

I must tame these creatures, then.

"I think it would be a good way to begin. I have an idea."

What is your idea, Champion? She could have searched his mind for the answer but had discovered Eloch preferred to keep his thoughts private until he was ready to present them to Her.

"We prepare a new habitat for a group of these people, the ones yearning to escape from their unbearable lives. Because they have forgotten, they do not realize they can remain here on your surface and be fulfilled."

A habitat such as what I've created for My new creatures? She searched his mind for the images he projected for her. *Ah, I see. This exact place.*

"Yes, Lady, and perhaps a barrier so only those You choose will be able to come here.

And the others? I will destroy them.

"But perhaps they can learn?"

He opened his mind and felt Her searching his memories and learning how Entean brought situations into balance.

My people are not as settled as Your people, Champion. I believe some will be destroyed. And some will be able to learn.

"I agree with You. We may have to cause fear until the respect is achieved. We will have to make a point in order for You to regain control, I believe."

Let us return, Champion. Have you rested sufficiently?

"I have."

Let us begin.

Chapter 13: Returning

"I need a break," Wren gasped.

"Wouldn't mind one myself," Aiko puffed.

Wren sat heavily on the bench and sighed as she took off her sparring gloves and wiped her face with the towel she'd draped around her neck. After little to no exercise for months, not only was she teaching her new leg how to respond to the signals from her brain, she was slowly getting back into shape. Slowly being the crucial word.

Aiko handed her a glass of water before joining her on the bench.

Wren nodded her thanks, tilted back her head, and drank deeply.

"That's good. Wow, I am still out of shape."

Aiko raised an eyebrow at her. "I'm rather glad you are. Otherwise, this wouldn't be a fair fight at all." She rolled the water glass along her brow.

Wren snorted. "Oh you'd do just fine. You've still got those SubCity street moves."

"The only good thing that comes from that place."

Wren nodded. "Unfortunately."

The two sat in silence while they regained their breath and rehydrated.

"May I ask you a question about Eloch?" Wren said.

"Of course. Not that I know very much about the man. You're the one who's been with him the most."

"What do you mean? Doesn't it take a year to travel from there to here?"

"It does, but most of that time he was in a coma."

"He called it hibernation. But I know him as Eloch-on-Spur. You saw him on Entean. What was that like?"

"Frightening. He still frightens me. That man is chock-full of knack, the likes of which I have never seen before. There we were, the three of us—Genji, Etsuo…who is still on leave with the rest of the crew or you'd know who I was talking about…and me. We'd just touched down and were only yards from the shuttle when this giant man comes out of the woods carrying that staff of his, the plants and trees shifting out of his way. And then strange, unexplainable things happened."

"What kinds of things?"

"Things like our firearms turned into piles of dust, took 'em right down to their individual elements, he did. And in just moments our shuttle was covered with vines. And I gave him a translator which he gave right back to me. And then suddenly he had his own. Frightening. Then he tells us we can't leave. And that he will be back and we should eat. He turns and walks away as trees erupted from the ground and surrounded us, a living cage. I'll never forget it. And the food he tells us to eat? It's right there with us in the cage, hot and steaming and delicious."

Wren was silent for several moments.

"So, it's all true, then," Wren finally said. "What he's been telling me. It's all true." She laughed suddenly. "I thought he was a crazy man with a knack for animals. Harmlessly sweet and crazy. I just humored him, went along with it. After all, he took me in, patched me up, and helped me. But he's everything he says he is! Gods, I feel so stupid."

204

"How could you not think he was crazy? If I hadn't seen it with my own eyes, I would have thought him as nuts as some drugged-out person in Sub. Of course you thought he was mad. Any sane person would have."

"Thanks," Wren said. "I was a little frightened at first. He's big and I was helpless. But he was so patient and kind to me that I relaxed. During the trip back here, he said he ate a seed that contained all the knowledge Entean had gathered from your shuttle." Wren decided to leave the matter of waking Spur for another conversation. Even better, let Eloch tell it if he wanted to.

"Is that what happened? One of my crew took him to the shuttle, where he had some sort of choking fit. She gave him water and then then left him at a table in the ship's galley. We found him there, lying on the floor. Thought he was dead. Decided his species couldn't survive being separated from the home planet." Aiko huffed. "Turns out he was in a coma. Genji pulled him out of it. And when he came out, he could talk to us. In our own language. And he knew things like he'd lived on Spur all his life, yet it seemed all jumbled in his head. I had Genji work with him to sort it out."

"Genji. He's an interesting character."

Aiko laughed. "I think most who sign up for interstellar exploration are interesting characters. I think Genji walks around with a head filled with one giant question mark that he lives to satisfy. A valuable asset."

Wren frowned thoughtfully at her. "I think we're more alike than I first realized. Not because we've survived SubCity, but rather because of what SubCity made us become."

"You mean cautiously nice?"

Wren laughed. "That's a good way of putting it. And appreciating the worth of worthy people. I miss mine."

"Your worthy people?"

"My Kin, yeah. I think I'm nearly ready to come back to life." She hesitated. "There's one more favor I need to ask."

"And that would be?"

"Can you help me get Eloch back to Entean?"

"Already working on it, although why you'd want him to leave is beyond me. It's obvious he's become one of your worthy people, the worthiest of them all, is my take."

Wren went still.

Aiko watched the telltale flush rise from her neck up to her cheeks as Wren's expression changed into one filled with wonder. Aiko sat back with a grin. "I knew it!" she exclaimed. "I could see it."

"You knew? I didn't realize just how...um... worthy until right this very moment."

Aiko reached out and touched her hand. "Well, as I said, I don't know Eloch well, but I do know there's something very special about him. And frightening. So much knack stuffed inside that handsome exterior. But good. His knack isn't the kind that hurts people."

"So you'll help me get him home? We can combine our resources?"

"You still want to send him back?"

"I don't want to, but it's where he belongs, like I belong back with my Kin."

"I suppose it is, Wren, but for your sake? I sure I wish it weren't."

Wren looked at her and shrugged. She set down her glass and reached for her gloves. "I suppose we should get back at it," she said and tugged on a glove. "Oh, and the matter of Eloch's worthiness to me? Can that be our secret?" she asked as she tugged on the other.

"Of course."

~~~

Over dinner, Aiko resumed their conversation. "You say you're going to return to your Kin. Do you have a plan?"

Wren reached for a slice of bread and buttered it slowly. "I first need a new ident," she mused. "Although I haven't figured out who to ask. There's someone I *can* ask, but I'd rather not have to. He'll want a favor in return."

Genji looked up from his meal. "What if we provide her with ident?" he suggested.

Wren looked at him and then at Akio, who nodded.

"You could be a new crew member we picked up on Talamh."

"That'd work," Genji mused. "You've got the look. You could have been born and raised there," he eyed the bone on his plate and picked it up. "Gonna need a new name."

Two sets of eyes turned toward Wren. She tried not to squirm.

"Let's make her blond and call her Chirp," Aiko suggested.

Genji shook his head. "Chirp's too SubCity. Making her blonde's a good idea."

Wren rolled her eyes. "How about jet black? Matches my new leg."

"Your eyes would pop bright blue," Aiko said.

"You'd look dangerous." Genji said.

"Dangerous is good," Wren said.

"Name?" Aiko asked Genji. "Make it a good one." She winked at Wren.

"Nakami," he said and gnawed at the bone.

Aiko raised her eyebrows at Wren. "Nakami with jet black hair. What do you think?"

Wren grinned. "It's a far cry from Wren, that's for sure. Yeah, I like it."

"Only thing, we're going to have to take a short trip to Talamh and get your background data. I happen to have an old SubCity friend living there who can help us out. She runs a brothel."

Wren barked out a laugh. "Of course she does."

~~~

Wren walked through the City like she had the right. She found it the best way to go unnoticed. But it was strange to feel so jumpy on her home turf. She felt like an outsider, and it wasn't because she had a new identity. No, it was more because over the past nine months since she had walked this stretch of street, she'd been near death, met an alien, been on a ship, and even been to a different planet. She just didn't feel like Wren, KinLord, anymore. The Universe was so much bigger than that. She thought *she* might want bigger.

Before Aiko dropped her off at the City's spaceport, she'd taken Wren on a flyby of Rubble to see if there was any sign of Eloch. To Wren's disappointment, they found none. The encampment he'd shared with her was undisturbed, neatly cleaned and stored, awaiting Eloch's return. Wren was grateful to Aiko for giving her time to wander through and reminisce. Before she left, she wrote him a message to tell him where she was and placed it on the table, anchored by a heavy piece of rubble. If she was lucky, he'd find her. Otherwise, it was time for her to dive back into her life as KinLord.

If it was even possible anymore.

She felt ready to find out.

Two of Mouse's eyes had been shadowing her for some time, skirting the rooftops, one on either side of the road she'd chosen for her approach. She heard their whistles high above her, mimicking the birds that nested in the eaves and doorways of abandoned areas. They were talking to each other and calling ahead, alerting her Kin, alerting Mouse, by what the whistles were telling her, of an approaching stranger, a stranger who walked with purpose. A stranger who walked like she knew where she was going.

She'd spent five days nosing around the spaceport and around the UpperUpper. She might no longer be wearing her assassin's greys, but she knew how to disappear. Her uniform, now currently hidden by her cloak, was a good disguise. No one really wanted to mess with Ring Colonizers, even if their rank was low. Wren had learned that Colonizers were, in a way, considered nearly as important as the UpperUppers, because they could get people off Spur. Funny thing, though, the lower ranks of Colonizers didn't even realize how important they were. Took someone like her to notice.

She'd been tempted to go to Max, but chose not to. There was some somebody or somebodies who wanted to wipe her and her Kin off the face of the planet. She decided it was more prudent for them to believe they'd succeeded.

If she was wise, she'd just disappear and truly become a part of Aiko's crew. Travel, learn. Perhaps relocate on Talamh or one of the other colonies. There was lots of space on Talamh, she mused, and she'd fit right in with that rough and ready crowd. But she hadn't stayed.

She missed her Kin too much.

The closer she got to the square with the fountain, the more eyes were following her. They were circling around her like a pack of sniffers. Hopefully they were just as lethal. She wanted them to survive.

A small woman dressed in assassin's greys slipped from the shadows and blocked her way. Wren saw the glint of a throwing knife where she'd palmed it.

"Halt!" the woman commanded. "What business have you here?"

Wren found it impossible not to smile. Slowly, as to not startle anyone, she lifted her hood off and revealed her face.

"Hello, Mouse," she said, and felt a laugh bubbling up. "Long time no see."

Mouse went white and Wren laughed again, so happy to see her friend and supporter again.

~ ~ ~

Mouse had been trailing the stranger ever since she was alerted to a trespasser at the border of the territory they'd mapped out for themselves. It had unnerved her to watch the stranger walk directly to their new KinSpace, as if the trespasser knew where they were.

It also unnerved her that the woman seemed vaguely familiar. Was it someone in Max's employ, a messenger of sorts? But they had been so careful. How could Max even know where their new KinLands were? If he did, it was one other hold he had over her, over them. His silence would need to be bought. Her knife and what she did with it the payment.

Mouse whistled a command to Wings, her best eyes, to see if the stranger was as alone as she appeared to be.

Wings nodded and dropped out of sight.

The stranger kept coming with quick, sure strides. A green uniform peeked out from under the cape with each step. Not a Martial's uniform, then.

A Colonizer.

Why?

Again, Mouse thought of Max. He knew lots of people. Perhaps it was someone who could help with the idents.

Whatever the purpose of this mysterious trespasser, she was getting too close. It was time to make introductions.

Mouse whistled to Feather, her next-to-best eye, and commanded her to alert Flick and Spider. She wouldn't put it past the Martials to send this stranger as a decoy while they flanked the KinSpace and attacked. After what had happened in SubCity, Mouse, Flick, and Spider were doing their best to prepare for anything, to think like Wren. *Caution First.*

Wings whistled a message. The stranger was traveling alone. Mouse sent him back to his watch. She would handle things now.

With barely a wasted movement, she dropped off the roof and into the path of the trespasser.

"Halt!" she commanded. "What business have you here?" She readied her throwing knife.

The trespasser stopped and very slowly lifted her hood from her face, letting it drop back onto her shoulders. She laughed and shook her thick, ink-black hair. "Hello, Mouse," she said. "Long time no see."

Mouse nearly dropped her blade as her field of vision narrowed to a pinpoint and her ears rang. She tried to speak, but could only gasp while the woman stood, hands on her hips, and laughed. *It couldn't be, could it?*

"Wren?" she squeaked. "Wren, is that you?"

"In the flesh." Wren held out her left leg and thumped it. "Well, nearly all of me. You thought I sucked at math before. Now I'm *really* going to suck. I'm down five digits, only fifteen left to count with."

Mouse shook her head. She couldn't quite make the ringing go away. "But you're dead."

Wren laughed again and stepped closer to her friend. "Hardly, though I was close to it for a time." She reached out, her brow furrowed. "You don't look so good, Mouse. Why don't we go over to that building there, and you can lean against the wall." She started to put her arm around her friend.

A voice rang out. "Hold! Don't touch her! Step away!"

Wren froze and cocked an eyebrow at Mouse.

"I-I'm okay," Mouse called and tried to keep the quiver out her voice. "Stand down. I-I'm okay." Her voice sounded so thick. "Go, bring Flick." She commanded. She watched her eyes scurry to do her bidding. When the two were alone, Mouse collapsed into Wren's arms. "Gods, Wren!" she sobbed. "I know you don't like to be touched, but I have to. I have to touch you to be sure you're real."

Wren smoothed Mouse's hair and held onto her. "It's good to see you too, Mouse. I came back as fast as I could. I'm sorry it took so long."

Mouse straightened and stepped back so she could see Wren's face. "You lost a leg."

"I lost a leg. Got all chewed up by a sniffer."

"Oh, Wren," Mouse rubbed at her eyes. "I'm sorry."

"Better than being dead, but I'm not going to lie. It's been rough. I've a story or two to tell."

Mouse's smile was watery. "No doubt." She reached out and ran her hand down Wren's hair. "Your hair, it's so—"

"Black? Straight? I know. It's my disguise. I'm Nakami, born and raised on Talamh. I'm a new crew member of *The Stardust*."

"Nice to meet you, Nakami of Talamh. I was going to say your hair is smooth. Must have hurt getting all those coil mats out."

"Hurt like a bitch, let me tell you. I almost cut them all off. It would have been easier, but," she shrugged. "With the leg gone, I wasn't going to lose any more body bits, even though hair grows back." She had to blink. *Why can't these damn tears stay where they belong?*

Silently Mouse reached out and hugged her friend again. Hard.

"Don't," Wren muttered and tried to push Mouse away.

Mouse clung harder.

Finally surrendering, Wren wrapped her arms around Mouse in return.

That's how Flick found them.

He couldn't tell if they were laughing or crying, or maybe a little of both. He folded his arms to wait. Feeling a presence draw near, he glanced over and saw Spider.

"What's going on?"

"Not sure," Flick answered. "But from the way they're carrying on, I think that black-haired woman in the colonizer uni is Wren."

Spider's mouth gaped open, and he looked from Mouse and Wren, to Flick and back again. "And you're just standing there?"

Flick shrugged and grinned. "If I went over there, I'd become a blubbering fool. It's more manly to wait, get a grip on my feelings and all."

Spider swallowed and cleared his throat. "Yeah, I get what you mean." He looked up at the grey sky. "Think it will get colder tonight? More fluffy rain?"

Flick looked up as well. "Fluffy rain? That's what it's called?"

"Dunno. It's what I call it. Can't really call it ice rain, though it is frozen. I've never heard of it before," He scoffed. "I bet it's got all the UpperUpper's university professors in an uproar."

Flick nodded and rubbed his chin. "I expect they would be puzzled."

"Flummoxed."

"Yeah, that too. Ready to join the group? I think I'm in control now."

"Let's do it, then."

The two crossed over to the women. Flick tapped Wren on the shoulder and she glanced up at him, beaming. "'Bout time you got back here, Wren. Some holiday that must have been."

Wren flung herself into his embrace. "I had a couple of hiccups, but I'm here now. Needed to make sure you know what you're doing."

Spider wrapped an arm around Mouse, who leaned against him. "Good to see you survived, Wren," he said.

Wren extricated herself from Flick and looked over at Spider. "Good to have survived." She arched an eyebrow. "And what's this I see? Mouse, you going after schoolboys now?"

Mouse reddened and Spider grinned as he tucked Mouse more securely to his side.

Wren winked at Spider and then glanced at Flick. "Any other couplings I should know about?"

Flick shook his head slowly and grinned. "Not when they'd have to compete with you."

Wren lowered her eyes. "Oh, Flick." She couldn't bear to see the light in his eyes, not when she knew it would never come to anything. "Shall we go someplace? Fill each other in? I'm not ready to make myself known to the Kin."

She flipped up her hood and tucked in her hair.

"Allow me to escort you to the Narrows," Flick said with a courtly little bow.

~~~

"How are you managing?" Wren asked, scanning the square as they headed toward a more private area. "In all this cold?"

Flick looked over at her again, his eyes bright. "Blankets and wood until Mr. Wizard over here got the heaters going. Now we're all fairly snug."

"That would be me," Spider said. "I'm the wizard. But I didn't do it on my own. Flick gave me considerable input."

Flick shrugged. "Living in SubCity all my life where everything breaks makes one creative."

"What about the energy drain? Won't that draw the attention of the Martials?"

"Max helped," Mouse said.

They paused at the door of one of the buildings facing the square. Flick opened it, allowing the others to go ahead of him. Mouse took the lead up the stairs to Flick's office space.

The room was filled with a trio of battered desks. Two of the desks were fairly neat. The third had papers strewn all over its surface, a pencil parked haphazardly in the center.

Wren nodded at the third desk. "Looks like my resurrection is keeping you from your work."

Flick rolled his eyes. "Scheduling the watch can wait. It can wait forever, as far as I'm concerned. Pull up a desk and have a seat."

Wren took off her cape and blew on her hands before she sat at one of the neat desks. "It's warmer in here, but not by much."

"The heat comes on later in the day," Spider explained. He drew up a chair and sat near Mouse, who had taken the other tidy desk.

Flick sat at his desk and idly picked up the pencil, twirling it between his thumb and forefinger.

"Tea?" Mouse asked. She went into an adjoining room. "It helps keep us warm," she called over her shoulder.

"You found Max?" Wren asked while they waited for their tea.

Spider nodded. "Only Mouse has met with him, although I went with her the first time to the UpperUpper."

"Tell her about your disguise." Mouse called from the other room.

Spider went red and groaned as Flick laughed.

Wren looked at the two and crossed her arms, stretching out her good leg. "I think I need to hear about this disguise."

"He made a most fetching girl," Mouse called over the sound of a whistling teapot.

Wren chuckled. "Did I hear that right?" she asked Spider.

Spider groaned again and rubbed his face. "I think I'd better tell you. The others are bound to either play around with or ignore the facts." As they waited for Mouse to return with steaming mugs of tea laced with sweeteners and hot powdered milk, Spider told of his experience as Mouse's guide into the UpperUpper.

"Flick actually made a pass at you? That I would have liked to see," Wren said when Spider finished.

"It wasn't exactly a pass. I was just being friendly," Flick explained.

Entering the room, Mouse shook her head at him. "His definition of friendly is a lot friendlier than mine." She handed Wren a mug of tea and another to Spider. "Careful. It's hot. Be right back."

Wren nodded and held the mug to warm her hands while she waited for it to cool. "I like what I see here," she said after Mouse brought two more mugs from the adjacent room and handed one to Flick before she took her seat by Spider. "You three have become quite the team. And you seem to have settled well into governing the Kin."

Flick glanced at her and blew on his mug. "We followed your lead."

"Yeah," Mouse agreed. "You told us what to do, and we did it."

"But I'm sure you ran into things I hadn't thought about."

"Not really," Flick laughed suddenly. "You told us to talk to Spider, here, and we did!"

"Are you flirting with me again, Flick?"

He barked out a laugh.

"The Kin? How are they?" Wren asked when the laughter died down.

"Surviving. Not thriving yet. We're all still pretty jumpy. Afraid we'll be discovered and tossed back into Sub at best. At worst?"

They all knew what at worst meant.

Wren nodded. "And Max? Is he helping with the idents?"

"For a price," Mouse said and held Wren's gaze.

"I'm sorry, Mouse. I know you want to get out of that line of work."

Mouse shrugged. "We do what we need to do. The idents are taking a long time. Max is being cautious."

"Good. Good," Wren said thoughtfully.

"He was really shocked when I told him you'd died. It sincerely shook him up. I know he'll be very happy to hear you didn't."

"I think," Wren said slowly, "we should let me be dead for a while longer. Until I can figure out what really happened."

"We know what happened," Flick said. "We got ambushed and massacred."

Wren shuddered. "But who instigated it? Fergus and MacMichaels are too stupid to pull off something like that. Someone didn't like what I was doing down there in Sub, and I want to find out who and why."

"The why would be you were wrecking the status quo, Wren," Spider said. "It's pretty obvious the community you were building down there was giving people hope. It's harder to control a tribe filled with hope."

"So the somebody would be the Board of Culls?"

"It's where I'd start looking."

"Hmm. I wonder how I can use my new ident to get into that group? I wonder what my excuse should be?"

"I think you need to go to Max, Wren," Mouse said.

"Maybe. But not as Wren. Maybe as Nakami." She shot a glance at Spider. "How much power do the Martials really have?"

"Not as much as you think. They're not a governing branch. They receive orders."

"So someone ordered the Martials to work with the other KinLords to destroy my Kin? And because I was the KinLord, I had to go as well." She shook her head. "And now it's going to just get worse down there."

"Already has," Mouse said softly. "No matter what happens, I'll never go back there. I'd rather die."

"I think that's the feeling of all the Kin right there," Flick said. "So," he continued after a while, "if you're not going to show yourself, who's going to be KinLord?"

Wren glanced over at him and smiled. "I think you have been doing a great job, don't you?"

"It's not the same, though. They need you, Wren. What you give them, they need."

Wren looked at the mug in her hands. "But the thing is, I'm not sure I've got what they need anymore."

Mouse reached across her desk and covered Wren's hands with her own. "Want to tell us what happened? How'd you survive the sniffers?"

Over Wren's bent head, Mouse looked at Flick with raised brows. She had never seen Wren like this before.

Flick had. *Give her time*, he mouthed.

Mouse nodded, unconvinced that time was what Wren needed.

Wren looked up. "I nearly didn't survive the sniffers," she said. "Eloch saved me."

"Eloch?" Flick said. "Who's Eloch?" His scowl deepened when Wren's mouth curved up.

"Eloch is the Champion of Entean, and I guess I need to begin with when I saw you all last."

Apparently the story couldn't be told without interruptions, but after several answered questions, mugs of tea, and bathroom breaks, Wren finally brought her friends up to date.

"I can't believe you've been off planet," Spider said.

Wren nodded. "I can't believe it myself… first on a Space Station, then on Talamh. I actually got out of the ship and walked around on Talamh."

Spider hiked his elbows on the table and leaned toward Wren. "What was it like? Talamh?"

"The gravity was lighter. People were more nimble, but on the small side. I'd swear they all had SubCity blood and not UpperUpper. I'm actually a little taller than some, if you can imagine that. Do you know the history of that first colonization? Were they Subs? An experiment maybe? Subs are always the ones considered expendable. They act like Subs to my mind."

"Not sure. I'll find out if you like. May take some digging, it being some thousand years ago. I always wanted to go off-planet and explore," Spider added.

"It's always been my plan," Wren said. "To get the Kin to one of the other planets."

Flick's head shot up. "Since when?"

"Since always."

"How come you didn't tell me?"

Wren sighed. "Because, Flick, I wasn't sure it could work. But now? Now I've got some contacts. Now, it's possible."

"With Max's help, it might work," Mouse said.

Wren gestured at her uniform. "Not just with Max's help. I've got a couple of new friends."

"What if the Kin don't want to go?" Flick asked. "*I don't want to go*. I have no desire to go anywhere except away from Sub. Why can't we move the Kin to Rubble? You and this Eloch person did just fine in Rubble."

"But we were dependent upon Aiko's supplies and what Little Sister brought us," Wren countered.

"We could make it work," Flick said.

"Fine, Flick. Come up with a plan, and we'll see if it can work."

Mouse's head whipped around at Wren's tone. "If you don't want to be KinLord, Wren, then don't jump down Flick's throat. It would be easier to live in Rubble than to try to blend with the UpperUppers and eventually become colonized."

Wren sighed. "I'm sorry. I'm tired."

"Then rest," Flick said. "Mouse can lend you her room since she's not there that much."

"Sure. Come with me, Wren."

Mouse all but dragged her from the room.

"Why'd you jump all over Flick like that?" she hissed as soon as they were out of hearing distance. "He's under a lot of pressure, here, trying to fill your boots. You cast a long shadow, Wren. We hear it all the time. If the Kin don't like something it's all 'But Wren this and but Wren that.' Got annoying a few months ago."

They stopped in front of a door at the end of the hall. "Here's my room, make yourself at home. I finally got a bed a week ago."

Wren shot her a look but said nothing. "Thanks," Wren said as they crossed the threshold. "I'll just nap and then I'll leave when it gets dark." She sat on Mouse's bed and pulled off her boot.

"You're not leaving yet," Mouse said and drew up a chair. "You can't just come back and go away in the same day. What's happened to you? We need to finish up that conversation at least."

Wren squinted at her and shook her head. "Wow, not quite the homecoming I was expecting."

Mouse softened. "Look, we've all been through a lot in a very short time. You should hear the three of us squabble, and Cricket gets in on the act, too. It's just that Flick…" She paused. "Well Flick has feelings for you, Wren. You shouldn't be so hard on him."

"I shouldn't be, I know. But when I look at him and he looks at me that way, I just feel guilt. A tremendous amount of guilt to add to all the other guilt I'm carrying around. I feel like I used him, all those nights he used to cuddle with me so I could sleep. He's one of my best friends, and I've treated him horribly. And now—" Wren broke off.

"And now?" Mouse prompted.

Wren shook her head, her mouth a tight line.

"It's this Eloch person, isn't it? This alien?"

"I've got to help him get home. I owe him my life, Mouse, don't you see?"

Mouse studied her friend. "Oh, I see. I see plenty. And," she rose and rested her hand briefly on Wren's shoulder, "it's really none of my business, is it? Rest well, and we'll talk more over a meal." She turned to leave.

"Speaking of none of my business," Wren called after her. "What's going on with you and Spider? I've never seen you this way."

Mouse laughed weakly. "Neither have I, and I'm not sure what's going on with us. It started out as a challenge for me to even like him. I only made the effort because you told us to trust him. I wanted to know who I was trusting, and…well, I guess I like what I found out."

222

"I guess so," Wren said. She absently scratched her thigh where it was connected to the animated.

"Hurt?" Mouse asked and gestured to Wren's leg where she was scratching.

Wren shook her head. "No. Itches. I don't understand the technology, but where it interfaces with my flesh, it itches. Used to itch worse. I thought my leg had come back to haunt me."

Wren pulled up the leg of the uniform and exposed the animated. The two looked at it silently for a few moments.

"It works just as well as a real leg. Better, actually. I can never damage it. But I miss my flesh. I tried so hard to keep it, Mouse." She shook her head and added, with a smirk. "I suffered a lot of pain and agony for nothing." She waved a hand. "I'll try to rest now, Mouse. Perhaps you'll show me around when I wake up?" Wren hiked herself onto the bed and pulled up the throw before settling into a comfortable position, facing away from Mouse.

"Of course," Mouse said. "I won't be far. And Wren, don't be too hasty about leaving here. We're happy you're back. You can't know how happy."

"I've missed you all, too. I've worried over you all. Wake me in an hour if I don't wake myself."

"Rest well," Mouse told her and closed the door behind her softly.

"Well?" Flick said when Mouse reentered the room and took a seat beside Spider.

"Well what, Flick?"

"Well, what do you think? How's Wren?"

"Resting. When she gets up, I think I'll show her what we've accomplished."

Flick shook his head. "It's not what I meant and you know it," he said darkly.

"Wren's been through a lot, Flick. We all have."

"She's in love with him, this Eloch bloke," he said bitterly as he twisted the same pencil between his fingers.

"Flick, he saved her life. I'm sure she's got some feelings of gratitude for him. And she told me she owes him. Wants to help him get back home. But love? Wren doesn't let people get close to her, you know that. Besides, she's here with us. She's not with him." But she did wonder if Wren had fallen for the alien. It sure seemed like it to her.

Flick harrumphed and focused on his pencil-twisting.

Mouse sighed. "Don't you have a meeting with Skip? We're going to need to get more wood or coal or something. Blankets?"

"I don't think Wren's staying, Mouse. Going to go off with this Eloch. Mark my words."

Mouse frowned. "And what of it? We've been doing fine here without her. Maybe it's for the best."

"I'm barely doing fine without her, Mouse. I'm barely doing anything. And now she's back, and then she'll go. Maybe it would have been better if she let us think she was dead. Maybe it would be better if she actually was dead. We could mourn her, pick up the pieces, and move on."

"I've thought that myself," Wren said, leaning against the doorframe.

The pencil flew from Flick's fingers and landed on the floor, forgotten.

Wren glanced at Mouse and shrugged. "Couldn't sleep. You were right about some things." She crossed the floor to Flick, pulled up a chair, and sat, straddling it, her face so close to Flick's that all he could see were her eyes. Her familiar, alive eyes.

"Thought about just leaving you all, letting you think I was dead. Nearly did. But you see, I couldn't. I'm a selfish bitch, Flick. I knew I wasn't dead, and I needed you, all of you, to be okay. I needed to see with my own eyes that you were all okay."

She reached out and tugged his forehead to hers. "I'm sorry, Flick, that things can't be the way you want them to be between us. They never could be. But that doesn't mean I love you less, need you less." She drew back so she could see his whole face. "And it does my heart proud knowing the Kin are in your capable hands, Flick. They're yours. You're their KinLord now. If you say they go to live in Rubble, then that's where they'll go."

"Wren, you can't mean—"

"No, Flick, they're yours, and I do mean it. And since we're talking truth, I don't know how I feel about Eloch. Maybe I do love him. Scares the crap out of me if I do. Probably won't do anything about it, either. But I owe the man my life. The Board of Colonizers threw him away. He deserves to get home. It's the least I can do to help him. And if that hurts you, then I'm sorry, but I can't make myself be what you want me to be anyway. I've been through too much, now, and it's changed me."

Flick drew her back to him and kissed her forehead as Wren threw her arms around his neck.

"I'm sorry," he said.

"I'm sorry, too."

"What now?" Mouse asked after a while. She reached into her pocket, retrieved a handkerchief, and tossed it. "Here, catch. Clean yourselves up."

Wren caught the handkerchief, careful to use only half when she wiped her eyes and blew her nose. "What now?" she asked Flick after he used the other half.

225

"Now I figure out how to survive in Rubble," he announced, shoving the handkerchief in his pocket. "Didn't think you'd want it back, Mouse."

"Not now. When it's cleaned."

Wren smirked, her heart suddenly lighter. "Since I've lived in Rubble, perhaps I can help."

"I'm counting on it."

CHAPTER 14: REUNION

Wren threw a snowball and watched it explode when it smacked against the wall across the street from Eloch's encampment. Rubble was blanketed with snow, a first in her lifetime. Maybe even a first in several lifetimes. She'd never known rain could turn into anything other than rain. The only place not covered with several inches of the white stuff was the circle of melted snow rapidly icing over where Aiko's shuttle had touched down.

She puffed out a breath and retreated to the warmth of the encampment, grateful for the solar heater and extra blankets Aiko had left with her. She dug out the paper-thin solar blanket and busied herself attaching it to the doorway. She didn't like not being able to see anyone approach, but the warmth it provided was well worth it. Already she felt her muscles relax, and she could no longer see her breath. She decided to make a cup of tea before she went back out into the cold to create some sort of warning system, not that she expected any unwanted visitors.

Still. Caution First meant survival.

She hooked up the portable kitchen, another gift from Aiko, turned on a burner under the teapot, and waited. She caught herself grinning as she thought back to the rustic encampment Eloch had devised. Hadn't he known about all the equipment Aiko kept in *The Stardust's* storage?

She looked around and felt a little pang as its emptiness sank in. A thin layer of dust lay on the table, chairs and counter spaces. As if on cue, she sneezed and decided she'd clean after she had her tea.

"Why wait?" she asked herself and picked up a cloth, moistened it with the tea water warming in the kettle, and wiped down the table and chairs.

The pot whistled. The rest of the cleaning would wait.

As she sipped her tea, Wren's thoughts drifted back over the past three weeks. She was grateful she had released her Kin to Flick. All agreed it would be better to keep it secret that she was still alive. For the moment. So Wren had only stayed a few more days, to help Flick fine-tune his leadership skills and devise a migration plan for the Kin. As long as it was cold and the Kin were healthy and safe, they would remain where they were. When the weather changed, they would begin their move.

Wren had returned from the visit to Aiko's ship with a list of even more requests, and the catalog of debts she'd racked up made her extremely uncomfortable. She didn't like owing anyone anything, even though Aiko assured her repeatedly that she owed nothing. "I guess we keep different books," Wren had replied. Somehow she'd pay the woman back.

"So now that's settled, what do you need?" Aiko had asked.

And Wren told her.

Before they moved, she wanted to make sure the Kin had a secure and inconspicuous supply line. Wren volunteered to explore the tunnels not destroyed by their escape from SubCity. But the Martials would be aware of those tunnels, and she wasn't sure what she'd find. A shuttle would be better. A shuttle with a cloaking device, even better. A shuttle with a cloaking device and a pilot would be perfect. Aiko had a pilot in mind.

It was a start.

Wren took a sip of tea and played with different scenarios in her mind until she caught herself drifting toward other issues she had put off, namely Eloch and what to do with her life now she was no longer a KinLord and assassin-for-hire.

She set her cup down and began to pace. Whenever she thought of the man, she got so twisted up inside. It wasn't fair. What can one do when a force the likes of a hurricane blows into your life? She kicked at the earthen floor with her Animated, the constant reminder of what she'd gone through with Eloch's help.

Another person she owed.

She'd discussed how to help Eloch with Aiko as well. But, as Aiko pointed out, there was no way to plan Eloch's return to Entean until Eloch reappeared from the south.

Which was why Wren was back at the old encampment.

Not only did it offer her the solitude she craved when she had decisions to make and events to plan, but Wren would be the first to know when Eloch returned.

And until he returned, Wren could spend the time plotting the next steps in her life. Did she want to find out who had massacred her Kin, or did she want something else for herself? Or did she even need to choose?

~ ~ ~

She happened to be out gathering wood when, out of the corner of her eye, she saw a dark blur coming straight at her. Dropping the wood, she reached for a knife and turned just in time to be hit by the full force of Little Sister's enthusiastic greeting. With a half laugh, half cry she found herself flat on her back, wood scattering in all directions, and her face being washed to the chorus of yips and joyful rumbles.

"I've missed you, too. Let me up, Beastie." she laughed and pushed the sniffer off.

She stood and brushed the snow off her leggings while Little Sister burst into a series of circles and figure eights around her, kicking up plumes of snow.

It made her laugh. "You've got some new moves there, looks like," she told the delighted creature.

And then she felt him, turned toward him as inevitably as a full Animated responded to a nerve signal, and locked with his magnetic gaze.

Somewhere in the back of her mind Wren recognized the difference in him. It would have frightened her, but his intensity first overwhelmed and then consumed her. Eloch strode up to her, his cape swirling behind, and dropped his staff to sweep her up in his arms.

He gave her no chance to think, just started planting kisses, beginning at her forehead, then her eyes, her cheeks, lips, neck, and back to her lips. They began as gentle, butterfly kisses, but gradually deepened. Some were short, some he lingered over. All pushed her into a fire, a heat she'd never felt before.

No longer able to think through the firestorm of passion, she gasped his name in surrender and burrowed her face into his neck, inhaling his scent as he carried her into the warmth of the encampment.

Did the doorway's curtain part for them? Surely not.

He set her down, smoothed her hair and said not a word.

He didn't need to.

His bold eyes, burning deep and green, told her enough.

With gentle yet insistent hands, he helped her undress. The clothes seemed to melt away, with the occasional *clink* from one of her knives. If she had been able to think, she would have been amazed at how they disappeared like magic.

But she was too focused on touching and touching, *finally* touching that broad chest and those strong shoulders. All that beautiful golden skin that had tantalized her for so long was now offered to her to explore. In the candlelight his skin was even more golden. And he smelled so good, so wonderful, like a deep forest, or what she imagined a deep forest would smell like, all clean and damp and musky warmth.

And when had he lit candles that made the most amazing little patterns on his belly, that line of hair that drew her eyes downward? But no matter, his hands, his beautiful, strong hands were so warm and doing amazing things to her insides as they circled and stoked the small of her back and at the same time holding her so close.

He laid her down upon the sleeping cot. And what was he doing with his lips? Oh, the Gods! His warm, nibbling lips were finding all her most sensitive places. And what were those clever hands doing now? Touching, caressing. She could smell her passion. She could feel her moistness.

She moaned. She was being filled. Had she been empty? Filled with what? The warmth was seeping into her through his touch. Power was filling her, that's what it was. And passion, too. Oh yes, the fire was way out of control now. No going back. His power filled her. His passion filled her. Power and warmth and, and, oh it was so much, and there was more flooding into her, and she wanted to give back to him. Fill him with her warmth in return—

"Beloved," he whispered. "My beautiful beloved." His velvet voice sent tendrils of need to her core. There, it kindled.

Enflamed.

Ignited.

This is important. Somehow I know this is important, and I'll never be the same. But it didn't matter. Within the safety of his strength, feeling his hands and his lips and *her* lips and *her* hands. Lips, hands, breathing and being breathed, in that moment, it just didn't matter.

And it just all felt so good, to be consumed like this. So right, and so very perfect. It felt holy, even. Sacred.

With a laugh, she realized it wasn't that she didn't like being touched, it was she didn't want to be touched by anyone but him. Ever again. Only him.

All this time she had been waiting for this, for him.

"Please," she breathed. She parted her thighs even further, arched her back even higher and guided his erection toward her core. "Please."

She laughed when he entered her, and gripped him with all her might, enveloping him with her being, giving as much as she received.

~~~

"In the south, did you find what you were looking for?" Wren asked, and smiled when Little Sister nuzzled her hand, demanding to be petted.

Eloch's eyes took on the intensity she had noticed before. It made her feel uncertain. Cautious.

"That and more," Eloch answered, and he told her how Spur had used Little Sister to attack him, his conversation with Spur, and the result of that conversation. "I spent the rest of my time solidifying my bond with Her," his look softened, "and then I felt you return here and came as fast as I could."

She melted into his gaze, had to shake herself to refocus. "So you are now the Champion of Spur? Is that what I feel from you? That intensity?"

He nodded. "The power of your planet fills me. I am Her vessel until I find Her true Champion."

"And you can do those things here that you said you could do on Entean?"

232

Eloch laughed. "Of course I can. It is part of being a Champion." He reached out, tugged her closer, and gave her a great, smacking kiss on the mouth. "I know you don't believe me, but you will."

"But I do. After I had that little talk with Aiko you so wanted me to have. I really like her, by the way."

"Then I will show you just to show you." Eloch reached his hand out and the staff he'd dropped outside materialized in his hand.

Wren gaped.

He flicked his wrist and the table held two bowls of stew, crusty bread, and two flagons of beer. The quality of the food was such as she had only seen on *The Stardust* or at a banquet in the UpperUpper.

She leaned over to sniff it and closed her eyes at the succulent aromas, finding herself suddenly ravenous. "Handy trick, that."

"Not a trick, Wren, a gift. A very handy gift. Come, sit with me and dine while you tell me of your adventures since we parted."

She sat beside him, watched while he made a candle materialize, already lit. His eyes were shadowed when she looked at him. "I'm feeling so many different emotions right now, Eloch."

He took her hand and gently rubbed his thumb over the back. "I imagine you are. Tell me, love." His voice was soothing.

She shook her head and felt the soft fuzz of a coil mat brush her ear. "Oh?" She reached up with her hand and fingered the soft coil matted style she usually wore. "My hair is back to normal."

"They suit you better than the straight black."

"True, but the straight black was part of my disguise. Not sure how safe I'd be if it the Martials knew I'm still alive."

"By my side, you are safe. Very safe. Safe enough to be yourself. Eat, love. We need the nourishment."

She hesitantly spooned up a mouthful of stew and followed it with another. It steadied her, the ordinary task of eating. She accepted the bread Eloch offered, took a bite, and enjoyed the crunch of the crust and soft, yeasty flavor. She smiled at him and nodded.

Eloch toasted her with the beer.

"Thank Spur for me. This is better than anything I've ever tasted."

"Your delight and appreciation are all She needs. All She has ever needed. That's what happened. The people forgot Spur is the source of everything on Spur. It grieved Her more than She could bear, so She disappeared. But now? Now things will be different. The people of Spur are in for a rude awakening, Wren. As Her Champion, I have been empowered to punish those who refuse to respect their living planet." He took a long draught from his flagon.

"When you say things like that, I'm afraid, Eloch."

"Don't be. It has nothing to do with you. But there are some who should fear. And fear my successor as well. Tell me of your adventures."

She looked down at her animated. "Obviously, I lost The Sausage."

"I would have been there if you had told me." He gripped her hand, hard.

"I know. But I'd kept you from the south long enough. I made Aiko promise to say nothing until you were back."

"She kept her word."

She grinned. "Figured she had, since you weren't there."

"And without The Sausage? Are you in less pain?"

"Much less, although it took me a while to adjust. I got to go to Talamh." Her eyes sparkled. "Through an actual wormhole! Aiko allowed me up on the bridge when she used her knack to set the coordinates. No offense to Spur, but I loved it, seeing how people live on a different planet."

"Spur wants to know if you sensed the spirit of Talamh."

Wren chewed her lip and looked off in the distance for a moment. "I don't know. I don't know how to sense something like that."

"Spur told me to teach you so you will know." Wren wondered what that meant, but before she could ask, Eloch continued. "And your Kin? Have you seen your Kin?"

Wren felt her lips curve with her answer. "I did, and they are doing very well, although only Flick, Mouse and Spider know I survived." She paused. "I turned the leadership over to Flick. We thought it best if I didn't distract the Kin from accepting him."

"You are no longer a KinLord?"

"Nope. And it feels like the right thing to do. I want different things than they do. I didn't realize it until I really listened to what Flick was saying." She paused and gathered her thoughts. "They never wanted to leave Spur. That was me, because of my past. But for the Kin? They only ever wanted to escape from SubCity, and the Culls, and the horrific life, all of it."

She paused again, her face alight. "Eloch, they want to live in Rubble. When I left, we started making plans for how to do it. I'm going to help them. Of course, they'll need to know by then that I'm alive, but enough time would have passed for them to feel secure with Flick."

"And then? After you help them relocate?"

"And then? I haven't a clue. I've been thinking about it since I've been here. I'm hoping I'll know when the time comes."

"I'm sure you will, Wren."

She smiled. "I'm glad one of us has faith in me." She wondered if returning with him to Entean would be an option, if he asked. Knowing the heat of love still flowed in her veins, she'd never make a decision until time had passed and the newness had settled into something that either worked or didn't.

"Flick. Tell me more of your friend, Flick."

"He's the best friend a person could wish for. He's like a brother, a loyal, patient, kind brother. Peaceful by nature, but a good fighter if he needs to be. Being a leader is difficult for him. He never wanted to be KinLord. But he's doing fine. He will make a very good KinLord."

"And perhaps more. I would like to meet this Flick."

"You're thinking he'd make a good Champion, aren't you?"

"Not I. Rather, Spur. She senses something about him. She appreciates his desire to remain on Her surface."

Wren frowned.

"What is it?"

"I was wondering if Spur is offended because I'm trying to leave Her."

"She calls you a Daughter of Spur, so I don't believe She is offended. Besides," he said intently, "you were born to be with me."

Wren laughed. "How can you say that? You and I were light years apart. You had no idea I existed or even if there were other planets with life."

Eloch joined in her laugher. "Isn't the universe a miraculous place?"

He swept his hand across the table and the remains of their supper disappeared.

Wren's eyes widened. "I'm seeing this, yet it's still unbelievable."

"Then I'll keep at it until you do believe. Come." He reached out his hand to her, helped her rise to her feet. "To bed."

She stared as their small cot as it transformed into a large bed covered with soft down bedding. "A very lovely gift. Thank Spur for me."

"Thank Her yourself, with your heart. She doesn't need me to mediate between Her and one of Her own."

He scooped Wren up again carried her to their bed. "I know you can walk, but I love holding you."

She leaned into him. "And I love being held by you. Eloch?"

"Hmm?"

"This…thing…between us. It's important, isn't it?"

"Very."

She nodded and remained silent as he lay her down and crawled in beside her, then covered them both with a silky down comforter. Snuggled in the warm bed with Eloch on one side and Little Sister curled beside the bed on the other, Wren fell into a dreamless, peaceful sleep.

In the morning she woke to soft kisses trailing down and across her back. Slow, deliberate kisses. It took her a few moments to realize the path of the kisses. The sensation demanded she pay attention to it and not the pathway the pleasure took. But when he reached her buttocks and the crisscross of scars there, she finally recognized the trail his lips followed.

Pleasure was swallowed by shame.

In the bright morning light there was no darkness in which to hide her ugliness. The puckered scars running the full length of her back, the black shiny leg so unlike skin.

He must have sensed she was awake and lifted his eyes to meet hers, the smile fading when he saw her face. "Wren."

She rolled over and reached for the bedclothes, yanked them up to her chin.

Eloch pulled her into his arms, threw his leg over her torso, his body held tightly against hers.

His tawny, perfect body.

"Wren, what troubles you?"

She nestled into his shoulder, breathing in his scent. "I never wanted you to see the ugliness."

"Ugliness? I saw no ugliness. I saw the body of my beloved. Her beautiful body that has suffered much but survived because of the spirit it houses. Look at me, Wren." She burrowed further. "Love, look at me," he said more gently.

After a moment, she slowly lifted her face to him.

He used his thumb to wipe the tears as he spoke. "I love this body, Wren. It is glorious and strong and so tiny and graceful and it pleasures me beyond anything I have ever felt."

She smiled at that. "I am rather good in the sex department, aren't I?"

"So good that I will never let anyone else experience a single moment of the pleasures you gave so freely to me. I am keeping you all for myself."

"And I have no say in it?"

He kissed her, thoroughly. "Do you wish to have a say?" he asked several moments later, his green eyes dark.

She grinned. "Not really." Her mouth found his and she hugged him close, allowing him to slowly remove the bedding in order to lie skin to skin again. She sighed into his mouth, enjoying the soft prickles of his chest hair on her breasts.

"I can erase them if you wish. The scars." He said, relishing the feel of her in his arms.

She drew back to see his face. "And my leg? Can you give that back to me as well?"

"Unfortunately, no. But I can make it so it no longer causes discomfort."

"That I would appreciate, but I will keep my scars to remind me where I started and what has made me strong," she said, nestling the covers over them again.

"I'm glad. And I say again, I love you the way you are." He put a hand over her clenched fist. "There is no need for shame, Wren. Please, let me love you the way I wish. In the daylight, neither of us hiding from the other."

She sighed and stroked his face. "I can try, but not today. I'm not ready yet."

He grinned. "I could make you ready," he said wickedly.

She laughed. "I'm sure you could, but for now, just hold me."

He did, and she drifted back into sleep.

"I can radio Aiko to come get us when we're ready," she told him over breakfast, a rather late breakfast. More like lunch.

239

He nodded. "I love you, Wren. With all that I am, I love you."

Wren felt heat creeping up into her face and she felt shy suddenly. "Where did that come from?"

Eloch laughed. "From me. I want you to hear my feelings when we aren't busy with lovemaking. I want you to know and believe I want you to be by my side for the rest of our lives, and I want you to know it is my choice. You, too, have a choice to make. I am patient and can wait for your answer, but before I take action, I want you to know my intent and my feelings. Whatever happens, whatever you decide to do, I will always love you, Wren."

She opened her mouth to speak, but the words couldn't pass through the thickness in her throat. She put her hands to her chest, felt the fullness there, closed her eyes, and tried again. "Whatever happens, whatever I decide to do, I will always love you, too, Eloch," she laughed as the truth made her free. "I do believe you are the Champion of my heart."

He sat back and grinned. "Now that we have disclosed our hearts, Spur wishes to meet Flick. Our priorities may be different, but as Her Champion, I do Her will."

"Will Spur help the Kin relocate?"

"Of course She will."

"And keep them safe?"

"Just wait until you see what She's got planned."

~~~

Mouse happened to be looking south and saw their approach. Wren still wore the green uniform of the Colonizers beneath her fluttering cape, but her hair was back to its customary coilmats and color. She wondered at that briefly, until Eloch lifted his head and gazed intently at her. *How could he know he was being observed? And at such a distance?* She

240

watched as he leaned over to speak with Wren, who looked up and waved at her. A sniffer darted from around a corner to trot between the couple. *Stranger and stranger,* Mouse thought, assuming the sniffer must be the Little Sister who had nearly killed Wren.

Mouse didn't raise an alarm, even though the pair made no pretense of stealth. Instead, she slipped from her post and went to fetch Flick, who was meeting with Skip.

"We've got guests," she whispered to him but didn't wait for him to follow.

"Guests?" he asked when he caught up with her.

"Wren and what I suspect is the Champion of Entean."

Flick grunted.

"They're coming from the south. Just walking along, visible to anyone who chooses to look."

Flick grunted again.

"Thought we'd go out an' meet them. See what's up."

"Think it's a good idea, Mouse. Lead on."

"You're going to be okay with this Eloch fellow being here?"

He shrugged. "I'm going to have to be, aren't I? I want Wren happy. If he makes her happy, then I'll be fine. If he doesn't, well, he'll have to answer to me."

Mouse glanced up at him. "Then I'd better warn you, he's pretty large."

She led Flick through a maze of unfamiliar streets until they rounded a corner and he saw them. "Holy stercus, Mouse, the man is colossal! Look at how tiny Wren looks," Flick squinted. "Her hair—"

"Apparently our Wren feels safe enough to go undisguised."

"I wonder what changed her mind."

"Walking next to the biggest man who's ever existed *and* a tamed sniffer probably would help with the mind change."

Flick stilled. "Hadn't noticed the sniffer."

"They're a rather impressive trio, aren't they? And it's time to put on our welcome smiles."

It wasn't hard. Flick grinned. "Miss us that much, Wren?" he called when they were within range.

"You know it!" she called back. "Thought I'd check in with my KinLord replacement."

They met in the center of the street, where Wren happily skipped into Flick's and Mouse's combined embrace.

Flick looked up to find Eloch watching him, his expression a mask. A wave of energy passed over him, like a breeze. It left behind gooseflesh. The hairs at the back of his neck raised.

That man had some major knack.

"And you must be Eloch of Entean." Flick said cautiously, as he studied the alien. "Wren told us you saved her life. Thank you."

Eloch watched Wren cross back to his side, his expression softening. "Her life is precious," he said, drawing her to him.

Mouse raised an eyebrow and grinned at Wren's blush. "Interesting," she said. "I'm looking forward to some girl talk with you, sister." She burst out laughing when Wren actually giggled.

Flick swallowed his jealousy and instead concentrated on the happiness he saw on Wren's face. "Did you just giggle? When did you ever giggle, Wren?"

She giggled again and clamped her hands over her mouth. "Not another word about giggling. Don't forget, I've got a sniffer on my side."

Mouse took a step back when Little Sister stepped forward, her head cocked, ears pricked.

Wren looked up at Eloch. "Should we introduce Little Sister to a couple of new pack members?"

Eloch smiled. "Don't be afraid," he told the two and sent a mental signal to Little Sister to greet the new pack members.

Moments later, both Mouse and Flick were stroking soft, black fur and listening for the very first time to a sniffer's rumbles of pleasure.

"I wonder if all sniffers are like this, deep down," mused Flick.

"Under the right care, of course they are," Eloch replied.

Little Sister rolled over on her back for a belly rub.

"She's so trusting," Mouse said, her voice filled with amazement. "I just never imagined."

"How could you?" Wren said angrily. "The poor things never knew another way to be," her voice softened, "until Eloch."

"And now Spur has reawakened, there will be more changes," Eloch said.

Flick looked up. "Spur reawakened? What do you mean? How can a planet be awake?"

Eloch grinned at him. "Prepare yourself, Flick, for Spur has chosen you to be Her Champion."

Flick gaped at Eloch. "I-I don't understand," he stammered as he jumped to his feet and backed up a step.

Wren touched Eloch's arm. "Maybe this is too abrupt. Maybe we could backtrack a little."

Eloch glanced at Wren. "What do you suggest?"

"Let's duck into one of these buildings, where it's private, and you can show them exactly what it means to be a Champion of a planet. Maybe even begin by telling your story."

Eloch studied Flick and Mouse, who had also risen to their feet. Both looked a little dazed. "I see I've assumed too much. You're right."

"Spider should be here," Mouse said.

"Then go get him," Wren told her. She pointed to a relatively safe-looking building. "We'll be in there, first floor."

Mouse took off at a run while the other three entered the building and crossed into a dusty, vandalized living room. With a sweep of Eloch's staff, the room was sparkling clean. Candles from bronzed wall sconces cast a warm glow. A fire crackled merrily in the fireplace. In front of the fireplace were five comfortable-looking chairs arranged in a half circle.

"Let's sit and get warm," Wren said.

Gently, she helped Flick out of his cloak and guided him to a chair, draping his cloak on the chair behind him as he sat. She laughed quietly as she watched him run his thick fingers through his shock of hair. "I know exactly how you're feeling," she told him. She took off her cloak and flung it over the chair next to Flick, then sat. "It seems like magic, but Eloch assures me it's not."

244

Eloch leaned his staff against the wall and sat in the chair next to Flick. "First you need to understand Spur," he said. "And then you need to understand the relationship between the spirit of a planet and Her Champion. I know you feel like I am pressuring you, but it's because Spur is pressuring me. She thought it would take months, maybe years to find Her Champion, but the moment She saw you, She decided Her search had ended."

Flick looked up. "The breeze I felt."

"Was Spur scanning you."

"And she has picked me to be Her Champion?"

Eloch nodded.

"So what are you? Aren't you Her Champion?"

"For only a little while longer. I am Entean's Champion."

"The planet he's from. It's light-years away," Wren interjected. "He has to get back there and be Entean's Champion."

"Right," Flick said. "Wren told us you came because your planet wanted you to represent Her." He grinned suddenly. "She said she wasn't sure if she believed you, but then the pilot," he shot a glance at Wren. "Aiko, right?" At Wren's nod, he continued with a grin. "Yeah, Wren called you crazy until Aiko confirmed you weren't."

Eloch chuckled. "You saw what I did with this room. How can you explain it and not believe?"

"True," said Flick.

"A planet's reason for being," Eloch continued, "is to care and provide for its creatures and maintain a balance. It is what She does. And all She needs in exchange is gratitude and acknowledgement. For some reason the people of Spur forgot Spur was their provider. They no longer believed in Her. She lost Her Champions and the planet fell into…"

He paused. "It fell into rubble, and Spur's creatures were suddenly filled with malice and barely surviving. It pained Her so much She turned Her back on Her people and hibernated. While I've been here, and seeking Her since I arrived, She gradually became aware that someone knew of Her, someone was hunting for Her, wishing to see Her.

"Unfortunately, the someone was not even one of Hers. At our first meeting, She tried to have me killed, Her disappointment was so great. But then She realized She had need of me. In truth, we needed each other, because I cannot be who I am born to be without the spirit of a planet to Champion."

"And what does a Champion do, exactly?" asked Flick. He leaned forward.

"A Champion helps the planet maintain the balance among all things. And since Spur has chosen you, I should warn you, this planet is extremely imbalanced, and dramatic measures will have to be taken to restore Her balance. The first will be to teach Spur's people to respect Her and Her power. I have an idea how to begin, but then I will step aside and it will be up to you to continue."

"But I don't know what to do. I'm not ready."

Eloch laughed. "It's almost exactly what I said when Thaif, the Champion before me, told me Entean had decided I was ready, and I will tell you what he told me. He said it wasn't up to us to determine our readiness. It's up to Her, and She says it's now. Spur will have me do this one thing, begin the process to rebalance, and then it will be your time."

"But why me?"

Eloch briefly closed his eyes and then smiled. "It appears Spur wishes to answer you Herself."

"How?"

Eloch held up a finger. "Watch." He leaned back in his chair and closed his eyes again.

Both Flick and Wren gasped when a fine gold mist began to rise from Eloch, like an overlay separating from its base. When fully separated, the mist rose above Flick and then hovered a few feet away from him as it began to take form. When the beautiful woman was nearly solid, She lightly touched down to stand before Flick. Both Flick and Wren fell to their knees, not daring to look directly at Her.

"Please, my Champion" Spur said in Her melodious voice. "Do rise and look upon Me. I wish to see your sturdy face. You as well, Daughter of Spur and Lover of Entean," she said to Wren.

In unison, the two friends did as their planet requested.

Spur stood quietly before them, Her hands folded neatly in front of Her. They could actually feel Her power. They felt Her scan them, like gentle fingers flickering in and about their bodies.

"Blessings to you, My son and daughter," Spur breathed. "At last. At last."

Wren glanced at the sloppy grin on Flick's face and wondered if hers looked as silly. To have a planet acknowledge her! Gooseflesh rippled over her skin. *Acknowledged by my planet. No wonder Eloch feels so much more complete as a Champion. The feelings go so deep, words can't even find them.* She touched her face, finding it wet with tears.

"I am not worthy to be your Champion," Flick was saying. "I'm nothing. I'm nobody. Born from scum and raised in dirt. I can't even talk right. I can't ever be like him," he said pointing at Eloch.

247

"I don't want you to be like Entean's Champion. I want you to be like Mine. And to Me, you are beautiful. To Me you are perfect. To Me you are worthy. The work ahead of us will take years of steady building and repair. I have abandoned My people for too long. But I will make it right and I need you, Flick. I need your humility. I need who you are. The people of this planet are too used to abusing the little power they wield. I know you will not abuse what we will become together." She reached out and touched her new Champion. "Within the next few days, Entean's Champion and I will begin great works. Watch him. Learn from him."

To Wren's surprise, Spur addressed her, alone. "Daughter, there is something I would have you do. Now is not the time to discuss it, other than to say I am well pleased with the choices you are making, and I bless your union with Entean's Champion. When the time comes for me to speak of it, I shall give you a gift to celebrate these choices."

Wren felt her mouth tremble. She searched for words but couldn't think of anything to say. Impulsively, she knelt in front of Spur and took Her hand and kissed it. With that kiss, she felt a surge of energy run through her before Spur gently withdrew Her hand.

"I am returning now," Spur said.

She dissolved into the golden mist and Eloch breathed her in. He stood and stretched. "Your planet's Spirit is beautiful, is She not?" he asked.

A scuffling of footsteps announced Mouse's and Spider's arrival. "Wow, look at this room!" Mouse exclaimed. "What'd we miss?"

Wren looked at Flick. Their shared grin dissolved into laughter.

"Not much," Flick replied. "Only the Spirit of Spur, Herself."

~~~

Eloch smiled down at Wren when she unconsciously slipped her hand into his while they walked to the Kin. She was so engrossed in telling Spider and Mouse about seeing Spur, she wasn't even looking at him.

248

Which gave him the freedom to study her. She was attuned to what was going on around her, it was usually hard for him to enjoy watching her without her noticing and becoming self-conscious.

The hand he was not holding was alive with gestures. Her eyes were bright, cheeks glowing pink. Her head swiveled back and forth between Mouse and Spider, sending her coils dancing. She glanced back, caught him studying her, and winked. This time, there was no self-consciousness. She kept right on chattering. But she had noticed his scrutiny and was aware of him. He sighed. Not nearly enough time to enjoy his Wren.

They were close to the square where the Kin lived, and Wren started to take the lead. He watched her hesitate and allow Flick to move ahead. Once a leader, always a leader, Eloch supposed. He released her hand and slowed his pace so she could enter the square with her friends. At the entrance, Eloch came to a full stop and commanded Little Sister to sit beside him.

This was Wren's time to shine.

His would come soon enough.

The square looked like a small town he'd find on Entean. The lower levels of half the buildings were makeshift shops where supplies were stored according to categories. The upper levels, he assumed, were living quarters. The other side of the square looked lived in as well, although not as many of the rooms looked occupied. The side where he stood still had an air of abandonment. He sensed more than saw the people positioned on various rooftop locations. Wren had called those on lookout *eyes*. He liked that.

In the center of the square stood the fountain of a woman who poured water from a pitcher. Several women were gathered and chatting with one another as they drew water. As he watched, they quieted and turned toward their KinLeader and his entourage.

Someone cried out and pointed at Wren. From one of the shops came a heavyset man with his arms outstretched, followed by two boys. The man scooped Wren up and swung her round and round as the crowd began to gather around her. The man let her go and she was enveloped by another pair of arms, and then another and another. Her laugh rang out in the frosty air. Then they were all talking at once. Even though Wren said few had survived that hellish night in SubCity, forty-five people still could make a lot of noise.

Eloch watched Flick raise his hands and shout for order. It took a few moments, but the crowd calmed down enough for Flick to call for a KinTalk in forty. Flick saw him and gestured him over with one hand as he gave a sign to the rooftop eyes with the other.

Eloch glanced at Little Sister, whose ears were pricked with interest. "Stay close to me," he commanded and strode toward the crowd. The crowd gave him plenty of space. He suspected it was more because of Little Sister, who was behaving quite properly, than he.

"This is Eloch of Entean," Flick said, "and his sniffer, Little Sister. They are friends of the Kin. Eloch saved Wren from death. And," Flick paused, "you're not going to believe this until he proves it to you, but he is the Champion of our planet, Spur. Go get yourselves ready. We'll continue this discussion at the KinTalk. Skip," he said to the man who had swung Wren about in welcome, "open up the storehouse. We'll have a communal feast tonight, when Wren will tell you her story."

The man smiled and saluted his KinLord, then motioned to the two boys to follow him. When he smiled, Eloch suddenly realized the man had no tongue.

Mouse caught his glance. "Wren cut it out. By all rights she should have killed him."

He shot a glance at Wren, who shrugged. "KinLord's not a job for the faint-hearted, Eloch."

"Neither is Champion."

Flick gestured for Wren, Mouse, Spider, and Eloch to follow him toward the less inhabited side of the square. Eloch went last and saw Mouse send a quick signal to the eyes on the roof.

When they reached an office room with three desks, Flick grabbed a chair and sank into it. "That went well, I think."

"You did great, KinLord," Wren said.

"Thanks, but we both know they would have quieted down a lot faster if it'd been you."

Wren drew up a chair, sat beside him, and smacked his leg. "Nonsense. They'd be that way to any KinLord if one of theirs had just returned from the grave." She ran her hand over her coils and flipped them off her neck. "Whew! It was quite the reception. Here, Eloch," she reached over and pulled forward another chair for him.

Eloch rested his staff against the wall and sat as directed. Little Sister poked her head under his hand and allowed her ears to be fondled until the new smells in the room became too much and she had to nose around.

"What now?" Mouse asked as she sat beside Spider on the couch. She knocked his long legs to the side so she could have a little room.

"Now," Flick replied, "we've got less than forty minutes to decide how to introduce Eloch and Spur to the Kin." He brightened. "Do you think She'll come forth again?"

"I don't know," Eloch replied. "Spur is different from Entean. Entean never showed Herself, preferring to work through Her Champion. Perhaps it is because I'm not Spur's permanent Champion, but She does like to make an appearance. If it were up to me, I would caution Her to remain within. This meeting should be about the Champion championing Her and not about Her revelation."

Flick grimaced. "I had hoped that Mouse and Spider would be able to see Her, though." He looked at the two. "You have no idea how beautiful She is."

"If She doesn't show Herself this time, there will be other opportunities, I'm sure." Eloch said.

"Tea?" Mouse asked and moved to rise.

"Can't we have something else for a change?" Wren asked and looked pointedly at Eloch. "I had the most wonderful ale the other day."

Eloch glanced at her sideways and tried not to smile. With an exaggerated sigh he gestured to the table placed before the couch.

"Oh—" said Mouse, and sat back.

"—my," finished Spider while reaching for two of the tankards. He handed one to Mouse, who looked at it suspiciously.

Eloch reached over and handed a tankard to Wren, another to Flick, and picked up the final one for himself. "To your health, and thanks be to Spur," he said and drank deeply.

~~~

Flick deliberately waited for all the Kin to be assembled before he stepped up onto the raised platform and waited for the noise to die down.

"I learned today," he began, "that our planet, Spur, is alive." He looked at the raised eyebrows and scowls of disbelief on his Kin's faces and laughed. "Your faces! I musta looked the same when I first heard it. And, no, I am not a crazy KinLord."

He paused again. "Spur's spirit and power dwell in this man," he motioned for Eloch to join him. "Before there was the City, before there was SubCity and Rubble, the people of Spur lived differently. They lived as one giant Kin, and Spur's Champion was their KinLord. I don't know what happened, what went wrong, but Spur was forgotten. And She, in turn, left us. But now," he paused and stepped aside, "I think I will let Spur's Champion speak on Spur's behalf."

Eloch nodded to Flick before turning his intense gaze upon the Kin. For a brief moment he stood, staff in hand, and allowed the people to feel the power that filled and emanated from him. Its impact was so powerful that Flick felt compelled to walk off the stage and stand with Wren and the others. So powerful that the Kin in the first row stepped back as well.

Eloch already knew his great size made him seem formidable, and now he put his full power—his knack, as Aiko called it—on display, so these people would always remember this moment, the moment they learned the truth of Spur.

"I am Eloch of the planet Entean and Champion of Spur," he said in his deep, quiet voice. "I came as Entean's Champion to stop your people from colonizing Entean. Entean also instructed me to ask Her sister planet, Spur, a question, and in order to ask, I reawakened the living Presence of your planet Spur.

"No planet should be without Her Champion, abandoned and ignored. No people should be without the wisdom of their planet. And now Spur has awakened, things are about to change, beginning with you, Flick's Kin.

"In the south, in Rubble, Spur has created a new place for you to live. Flick informed me you Kin are already prepared to move into Rubble. In Rubble you will find the safe place Spur has created where the Kin will thrive. Spur will teach you how.

"I also must warn you that in the next few days tremendous shifts will occur in the City. It will be dangerous for a span. Listen to your leaders. Prepare now to leave for your new home."

When he finished speaking he scanned every face in the crowd, all of them still gaping at him in disbelief.

"Who are you, an alien, to tell us these things? Where's our proof?" a woman demanded. Her voice trembled as she tightened her grip on the child huddled in front of her.

"How can we trust something we can't see?" another of the Kin piped up.

"How far south? We need to stay close to the City for food and clothing." An old man with white hair exclaimed. "We'll starve and freeze."

"You will do neither," Eloch told him and waved his staff at the man, who looked down to discover he was now wearing a thick, woven cloak. In his hands, he clasped two loaves of bread.

The Kin gasped. Eloch again waved his staff and every one of the Kin found themselves wearing woven cloaks of different patterns and colors. Eloch joined in their delight when he saw the cloaks Spur had created for them.

From within his memories, Spur must have located the weavers' clan patterns of Entean.

Flick rejoined Eloch and addressed the crowd. "As you can see, Spur is very present. It is time we all acknowledged and welcomed Her back into our thoughts, our hearts, and our lives. But tonight, we feast. And tomorrow we get ready to move."

"I thought you'd do more," Wren told Eloch when he rejoined her.

"The Kin needed to know they would be cared for. That's what I demonstrated for them. If I had done more, it would have instilled fear, and Spur wants love."

Wren nodded thoughtfully. "As Flick said, Spur's Champion is a KinLord, a very powerful KinLord."

"Exactly. He put it well."

"And will this very powerful KinLord be providing all the Kin with some of that lovely ale at tonight's feast?"

"I think he might do even better," Eloch mused.

Chapter 15: The Reckoning

Eloch had walked this corridor before, gone through the glass doors that hissed so softly when they closed behind him. He had faced the same bored faces before, faces marred by greed and malice. Imbalanced faces. Last time he was thrown out. This time there would be a more satisfying conclusion.

This time he was not as alone.

Not only was Aiko standing beside him on the right, his Wren and Flick were on the left, Genji and Etsuo behind him, and behind them, Spider and Mouse.

And within simmered Spur.

The Chairman scowled at Aiko. "Who are all these people?" he grumbled as he scanned the group. He caught sight of Eloch. "Oh, it's you again, the Entean fellow," the Chairman drawled. He leaned his elbows on the table, as if to keep himself awake. "What did you call yourself? Champion, I believe?"

The woman sitting next to the Chairman snickered.

The Chairman scowled. "Aiko, why have you brought him back? We have finished with this…what did I call him? Bone puppet?" He chuckled. "Bone puppet, that was it! We're finished with you, Bone Puppet."

"But I have not finished with you," Eloch said. "You did not listen before. You will hear me now." He paused and scanned the six board members' faces. "I am Eloch, Champion of Entean," he said again.

The woman tittered.

Eloch ignored her. "But I come to you today as the Champion of Spur."

"Enough!" The Chairman shouted. "I will hear no more of this madness. This man is seriously delusional and needs help. You have wasted enough of my time." He adjusted his glasses and glanced at the agenda at his place. "Who's next?" he asked his neighbor.

"For too long Spur has been ignored. Mistreated. You have spurned Her and decimated Her, and it ends today," Eloch continued. He pointed his staff at the agenda. It turned to dust.

The woman gasped.

As did Mouse.

Wren glanced back at her friend and winked.

The Chairman's face reddened, and he jumped to his feet. "Cheap parlor tricks! I don't have time for this. Take him away." He flapped his hand at the two Martials guarding the doors. He glowered at Aiko. "And you," he jabbed a finger at her, "no more of this, or I will ground you. Confiscate your ship."

Aiko gulped.

Satisfied, he'd made his point, the Chairman sat.

"I have not finished," Eloch said calmly. He pointed his staff at the guards aiming their weapons at him.

The weapons dissolved in their hands, returning to their basic elements. Their faces froze. They cried out when the metal flooring snaked up and trapped their legs.

Etsuo nudged Genji. "This is what I've been waiting for," he whispered. His eyes glimmered while he grinned hugely.

Mouse's hand crept into Spider's.

Eloch swept his staff across the four other guards who had only now realized their companions were being attacked. Their weapons dissolved. Metal snaked up their legs and trapped them. He aimed his staff at the intercom the Chairman had slapped into life. The man's eyes widened when it dissolved. He went white when the arms of his chair wrapped around him, forcing him back into his seat.

Cries of alarm went through the boardroom as the rest of the Board members were gripped by their own chairs. The snickering woman's scream was high and thin while her chair captured and held her securely, despite her struggles.

"You have imbalanced your planet. You have imbalanced yourselves," Eloch said, his voice filled with power. "Look south," he commanded, gesturing with his staff.

All eyes gazed out the huge window that commanded a view of the City's skyline.

A rumble began in a range too low for their ears to pick up, but they felt it in their chests. It built to a crescendo until the very ground swayed and bucked beneath them.

Wren gasped, trying to keep her balance, and she reached for Flick, whose eyes were alight with excitement. Genji stumbled to one knee while Etsuo leaned heavily on Genji's back for support. Spider and Mouse clung to each other and grinned. Aiko grabbed whatever was closest to steady herself. It happened to be one of the imprisoned Martials.

"*That's* what I'm talking about!" Etsuo hooted.

Outside, toward the south, a mountain range formed, huge, jagged peaks like teeth surging out of the ground. It pierced through Rubble and formed a barrier, ringing the City.

"Here is where you will stay," Eloch said, "behind that wall, until you have learned to honor your planet and her Champion. Those who already understand this will be allowed passage through the mountains. Spur will know who they are. Spur will provide for them." Eloch pointed his staff at the spaceport. They watched as the light from the conning tower flickered and went out. "As of today, colonization is no longer an option. Trade between planets is allowed, but colonization is abolished, and self-government is now the order of the day." He looked at the Chairman. "This Board is dismissed. Permanently." He glanced at Flick and nodded. "When the time comes, I will return to Entean. But know this. When I leave, it will be because Spur's new Champion will be ready, and that Champion will also, as I am doing now, wield the power of this planet."

A movement caught Wren's eye. "Eloch!" she said urgently.

He ducked, preventing his death, but the knife sank deep into his back. He groaned. The staff clattered to the ground.

Flick and Wren caught Eloch as he slumped and eased him to the floor.

The Chairman barked out a laugh as the chair arms relaxed enough for him to free himself. "Get more Martials," he shouted to the one who had thrown the knife.

The Martials had already kicked free of the loosening metal and rushed to the doors.

"And sniffers!" The Chairman called after him.

"I can't get out!" the Martial said while he hammered on the door panel.

A worried Martial peered in and began to pry the door open from the outside. It didn't budge and he ran off to get help.

Eloch's unconscious form stirred.

Wren glanced at Flick and back at Eloch. She watched, fascinated, as a shimmering, golden mist lifted away from his body, and knew Who was about to appear. The fog solidified into a woman.

A very beautiful Spur.

A very angry Spur.

"How *dare* you!" Spur snarled, her power crackling around her. Her usually melodious voice rumbled like the earthquake had moments earlier.

The room dimmed and transformed into an impenetrable vault.

She pointed a finger at the Martial who had thrown the dagger. "How dare you attack my Champion! You do not deserve to live."

In an instant, a pile of carbon lay in a puddle of brackish water where the Martial had been standing seconds earlier.

She pointed a vengeful finger at the Chairman, who held his hands up in surrender, his mouth a dark hole in his ashen face.

"And you! No respect. If you value your life, you will learn respect. I *will* see balance restored to Me. I *will* have harmony again. I *will* be loved once more." She crossed over to Eloch and gracefully knelt beside him. "This beautiful and brave soul has reawakened Me."

Spur reached out a hand and lovingly caressed Eloch's pale face. She smiled when it began to regain color.

Eloch opened his eyes. "My Lady."

"Are you healed, Champion?"

"I am."

"Then rise. We still have much work to do." She smiled up at Flick and allowed him to assist Her to Her feet.

With Aiko and Wren's support, Eloch got to his feet and stood between them. Catching sight of Wren's expression when she handed him his staff, he put an arm around her waist and pulled her close. "I am well," he whispered.

She leaned against him and tucked her head against his chest.

Spur turned and looked at the Board members. "Your ignorance is not entirely your fault. I accept some of the responsibility. However," she gestured to the newly formed mountain range, "I believe it will be many years before I see any of you on the other side." She touched Eloch's shoulder. "This Champion," She touched Flick's shoulder, "and My future Champion, are under my care. I will allow no harm to come to them. You will do as My Champion bids, because he speaks for Me."

With that, She shimmered and dissolved, again merging with Eloch.

Eloch sighed and briefly closed his eyes. When he opened them, he looked directly at the Chairman.

"What do you want?" The Chairman asked, his face still ashen.

"A ship with a shuttle," he nodded at Aiko. "This pilot and one other. Freedom to take supplies across the mountains to those living beyond until they have learned to work harmoniously with Spur and prosper on their own." Eloch became aware of growling and scratching coming from beyond the vault Spur had created. "Freedom for all sniffers." He paused. "In order to restore balance, I will be in command. And when the time is right, Flick will be in command."

Flick straightened, locked his gaze with the Chairman's, but said nothing.

The Chairman nodded at Flick before returning his attention to Eloch.

"And when balance is restored?"

"You will be free to self-govern as before, with one exception—from this moment and through eternity, you will do everything you can to maintain balance on this planet."

Eloch directed his staff at the walls, which became as before. He pointed to the doors and they opened.

Hackles raised, the pack of six sniffers walked stiff-legged and growling toward Eloch's group.

"Stop!" he commanded.

They stopped.

"Sit," he told them.

They sat.

Not one of them growled when he approached them. Eloch smelled like Spur. And a bit like Little Sister. The pack's leader caught the scent, cocked his head, and let out a happy *woof*, his tail curved elegantly around his haunches.

With his mind, Eloch directed the sniffers to go to the newly formed mountains and hunt.

In unison, they leapt upon him, slathered him with grateful licks before they darted out through the doors and scrambled down the building's halls toward freedom.

Genji grinned and nudged Aiko when he saw the sniffers' dark shapes wend their way through the City, racing toward the southern peaks.

Eloch motioned his companions to follow him as he strode toward the exit.

"Where are you going?" the Chairman called after him.

"To SubCity," he answered. "There are souls who need rescuing."

"What do you want us to do now?"

"Dissolve this Board of Colonizers. And the Board of Culls. We will put someone else in charge of your government."

~~~

Wren hurried to keep up with Eloch. Although she had promised herself she would never step foot in SubCity again, this was one promise Wren was happy to break.

He glanced at her, gave her a quick smile. "Who controls SubCity?"

"The KinLords. You know that. Slow down a little, Long Legs," she puffed. "You're losing your posse."

Eloch slowed to the pace she wanted. "But who controls the KinLords?"

"That's what I've been trying to find out. I suspect it's got something to do with the Board of Culls, but this is all new to me. Obviously, since my Kin were massacred, I was out of the loop. Why? What are you thinking?"

Eloch stopped to allow the others to catch up. "I'm considering how to resolve this situation. Sometimes it's best to find the key players and neutralize them. Sometimes, it's best to neutralize their minions." He gazed at the crowds around the entrance to SubCity, and at the teams of Martials stationed at various checkpoints. "Are there normally so many Martials?"

"Not until Wren was ousted." It was Mouse who answered, having arrived in time to overhear Eloch's question.

"And is it normally this crowded?"

"Not at this time of day," Flick said as he joined the group.

"I suspect the new view has got something to do with the frenzy," Wren commented dryly as she tilted her head in the direction of the towering, jagged peaks now separating the City from Rubble.

Eloch grunted.

"Looks like there are more people trying to get back into SubCity than ones wanting to get out," Spider said uneasily. "I'm wondering if it was a good idea for me to come here." He tightened his cloak's hood closer around his face.

Mouse looked up at him and looped her arm through his, giving it a little squeeze. "I know you're without a disguise, but I doubt very much people are looking for you, considering the circumstances. Looks more like they're concerned for their families."

"I'm going in," Eloch decided. "I think SubCity could use some modifications." He glanced at Aiko, Genji and Etsuo. "Perhaps you three should return to *The Stardust*.

Aiko shook her head. "The ship is fine. I radioed. The port is nearly vacant. Everyone's heading to the City's center to see what's going on. I'm staying with you. My brother and sister are down there."

"If there are injuries, I can help," Genji said. "I'm coming, too."

"And I have *got* to watch the show," Etsuo grinned.

Eloch nodded. "Then follow me." He aimed his intent focus on SubCity. They could feel his power beginning to build.

"Wait," Wren said and waited for Eloch to refocus on her. "What is your plan?"

"I am going to open SubCity to the sky."

"But—"

"No one will be injured, Wren," Eloch said gently.

Eloch swept his staff in front of him and strode forward, the others hurrying in his wake. The crowd parted for them just as readily as the trees and shrubs back on Entean. He loved the feeling of Spur's power rushing through him. But Spur wasn't Entean. Where Entean was patient and nurturing, Spur was dramatic and impatient, nurturing in a less subtle and more up-front manner. He understood, then, that her people would be much the same, like Wren. Or Flick, who had been so good at providing Wren the balance she needed. Flick was the perfect choice for Spur's Champion. Eloch could imagine the kinds of conversations he and his planet would have. It made him smile.

His mind felt full of clamor. His thoughts were being shoved around, yanked apart, and reorganized by Spur, who wanted her own Champion, and She wanted him NOW. Eloch understood her impatience, and her need to move forward after so many centuries of disappointment. She was like a person dying of thirst, but—"Now is not the time for this, My Lady," he muttered. "Let me finish what we have planned."

Wren's hand stole into his and he gave it a squeeze. He glanced back and smiled at her before he released her hand. "I'm fine, my love," he told her. "It's just Spur and I have different timetables."

Spur had heard him and understood. He felt Her pressure lessen, and it allowed him to collect himself for the next confrontation with the imbalanced peoples who governed her planet.

They had reached the gates.

"Halt!" a Martial commanded. "Get into line with the others." He punctuated each word by poking his weapon at them.

"I think not," Eloch replied mildly.

The weapon disintegrated into dust.

Before anyone could react, the Martials or the crowd, Eloch again swept his staff. "Sleep!" he commanded.

The people of the City crumpled where they stood.

Eloch strode forward toward SubCity and the first set of stairways.

"But aren't they going to get cold?" Wren asked, picking her way through tangled limbs.

"They are Spur's. She will care for them," Eloch replied as he crossed through the checkpoint and pressed on into the SubCity's shadows. "Some she may wish to keep asleep."

"You mean She will kill them?"

"That is between Spur and each individual, Wren. Remember how Flick described it? Think of Spur as a KinLord, if that helps, a KinLord such as yourself." He glanced at her. "You are like Spur in many ways."

"Oh, God!" shrieked Etsuo. "I think I just stepped on someone's hand."

Genji groaned while Aiko hissed. "Watch where you're going, Etsuo. They're people, not carpets."

The light dimmed and the smells of SubCity began to make themselves known, Wren unconsciously reached for Flick's hand.

Flick glanced at her and gave her hand a squeeze. "Never thought we'd be down here again, eh?"

"Wish to the stars we weren't," she replied. "I keep wondering if I'll ever be done with this gutter."

"Yeah, I'm ready to take the Kin to Rubble. No matter how it turns out, we'll be living above ground."

"That's a positive step right there."

267

They'd reached the bottom, crossed through the last checkpoint, and stood at the all-too-familiar hub of SubCity. Wren glanced at Mouse and Spider, who were gazing off to their right, toward the old KinLands.

Mouse caught Wren's eye. "Don't bother going there, Wren. I did, and I'll always regret it."

From her expression, Wren could imagine what Mouse had discovered. She shook her head. "Don't worry. I want to get in, get out, and get on with my life. Eloch?"

He was gazing at the ceiling, oblivious to the sleeping bodies lying haphazardly about.

Genji shivered. "It's like a cold, dark tomb in here."

Aiko glanced over at him. "Welcome to SubCity." She rubbed her arms, wrapped them tight across her. "I have no idea how I'm going to find Gem and Echo."

Wren shot her a sympathetic glance but said nothing, because Eloch had begun his remodel.

He lifted his arms, directing his staff in a wide arc. The same low rumble resurged while they felt the power building. Wren felt the hairs on the back of her neck stand on end, and she clung to Flick's hand. Flick arched an eyebrow at her and she shrugged. "Waaay beyond my comfort level."

Flick gave her hand another squeeze, returned to observing Eloch, and quickly forgot everything else. The energy continued to build until the ceiling exploded outward with a deafening roar. Debris scattered across miles of rubble, and for the first time in hundreds of years, light flowed into SubCity.

Dust gently floated to the surface, covering everything and everyone in a soft film.

Eloch's audience fell into fits of coughing and sneezing.

"The people," Wren choked out. "Won't they smother?"

Eloch looked at her, his eyes still sizzling with power. "They are Spur's. She will care for them. Watch."

A gentle wind blew. Not the cold winter wind of Above, but soft and perfumed. It gently caressed those lying there. Soon they were swept clean.

"It's magic," Mouse whispered, her smile lighting her face. She held out her hand and let the breeze caress it. She glanced at Spider when he curved his arm about her waist. "Pure magic."

"It's Spur," Flick said, and he released Wren's hand so he could hold both his up to feel the gentle breeze.

"Look!" Genji said. "Some of them are waking up."

"Flick will lead those who awaken now with his Kin to the oasis in Rubble," Eloch said. He pointed his staff in the direction of the square with the fountain, where Flick's KinFolk were living. A path formed where the tunnels had once been. "I suggest you lead them there."

"But what of the others?" Flick asked.

"They will have to earn the privilege," he answered. "Go, Flick. It's time to leave." He glanced at Aiko. "How soon can you ready the shuttle for transport?"

"As soon as I get back," she answered as she frantically searched the crowds. "There!" she cried and pointed to two figures clinging to one another. "It's Gem and Echo!" She started toward them but Eloch's voice drew her to a halt.

"No time, Aiko, I'm sorry. The people need to move so I may seal the way behind them. You will greet your brother and sister back at the square."

"I'll make sure they're first in line, Aiko," Flick said gently before he walked directly toward them.

Aiko frowned, but nodded. "Genji, Etsuo, I think we should go back now." She glanced one more time at her siblings before she turned toward her ship.

"Wren and I will meet you at *The Stardust*." Eloch said.

"Isn't Wren coming with us?" Mouse asked.

"Wren and I need to find someone who can lead the City back to balance, someone who knows its ways, yet still has some scruples."

"Max," Wren said.

"Max," Eloch agreed.

"Let us go with you, then," Mouse implored. "You don't even know how to get there."

"Flick needs you both, and I will know how to get there as soon as you tell me."

Since Wren had a much better sense of the UpperUpper than Mouse, she knew exactly where Max had relocated. She thanked them and waved them off to help Flick lead his new Kin through the path Spur had created for them.

After a quick tally of the people threading their way down the main street of the KinLands, Wren estimated nearly a thousand souls. *More than I would have guessed, it being Sub and all*, she thought. While she waited for the trail of people to pick their way through SubCity and out, her eyes skimmed over the desolation. Her gut twisted. How had she managed to survive there for so many years?

She found herself gazing at the area that had once been her own KinLands. The house she, Mouse, Flick, and the others had called home was a ruin, and it was a marvel it still stood.

Bones of houses and bones of— "People!" she blurted, feeling the blood drain from her face. "Eloch," she whispered.

He glanced down at. "Wren? You're pale. What is it?" He cradled her against his side.

"My Kin who died," she said. "They never buried them, just let them decompose where they lay. Please," she whispered, "would you cover them?" she pointed to an area that still looked like a slaughterhouse.

"That was where you lived?" He couldn't keep the anguish out of his voice. "There? Oh, my love."

Keeping his arm around Wren, Eloch pointed his staff and once again the ground shook and rumbled. But this time, it seemed different. Gentler. Then the ruins and all the remains sank into the arms of Spur, leaving behind a square mile of smooth, earthen floor. From the floor, small white flowers emerged, perfuming the air that had once smelled of sewage and rot.

Across the field, at the path's edge, Wren could see Flick standing, alone. Her heart told her he, too, was grateful. She touched Eloch's sleeve and pointed at Flick. "We thank you," she told him quietly. "We thank Spur, too." She blinked so she could keep Flick in focus as he turned and followed his people.

"Let's finish this," Eloch said as he motioned for the path to close behind Flick. It was as if it had never been.

He glanced down at Wren. "You okay now?"

She smiled up at him. "I will be when we can have some time with just the two of us. I hate to say it, but I miss you when you go all Champion."

He laughed. "I'm still Eloch."

She nodded. "But a little scary. All that power sizzling around you."

He released her and reached for her hand. "All that power makes me hungry. Let's find your Max and settle who will govern the City."

"You're in luck, then. Max always served the best food," Wren told him as she clasped his hand.

Together they picked through the strewn bodies of sleeping citizens of the City and into the UpperUpper.

"Won't they be surprised when they wake up?" Wren said.

Eloch chuckled. "They will certainly have something to talk about."

"And then...what then?"

Eloch shrugged. "It's up to Spur, Her Champion, and Her people."

Wren chewed her lip. "Then you're going home?"

He sighed. "I hope so, Wren. I have been honored to serve as temporary Champion for Spur, honored to help Her remember what it is like, but Spur is not Entean. They are different."

"Different? How so?"

"Entean's people, my people, are not as technologically advanced. It seems we have focused more on perfecting our symbiotic relationship with our planet. We create art, music, we sing, dance, work with our hands. It's a simpler life. And I noticed something else."

"What's that?"

"My people are not as quick to anger as Spur's. Entean does not like conflict. Spur sees conflict as a storm that is quick to rise and leaves freshness in its wake," he glanced at her. "Unfortunately, Her people have a different interpretation."

"Interesting," Wren said thoughtfully, "that planets have personalities."

"And give rise to the personalities of their creatures."

"Am I quick to anger?" Wren asked.

"And when it passes, the air has been refreshed. It's not a good or bad trait, Wren. It's the way you are. I love the way you are." He stopped and tugged her into his arms so he could kiss her.

Wren sighed into his kiss, wrapped him in her arms, and held him tight. She allowed herself a few moments to feel the fire they built between them, a fire that made her weak in the knees and nearly helpless.

Then she leaned back an inch or two. "Let's find Max so we can continue this, uninterrupted next time." She kissed him again quickly and stepped out of his arms. "I can't believe what you do to me, Eloch. If we kept kissing, I'd just forget we were in the middle of a crowded street. I would have pulled you right down to the ground so we could use all these sleeping people as our bed."

Eloch broke into laughter. "And I would have followed you down willingly."

She led the way up the main street and glanced at the shop windows and the goods on display. "Wow," she said, coming to a halt in front of a store specializing in Ring Trade goods. "Look at all these things from the other planets in the Ring."

"How many planets does the Ring comprise?"

Wren glanced up at him, then back at the window. A glass bracelet caught her eye and she traced its outline with her finger. "I'm not sure. Many. It's been a few thousand years, after all. Aiko was telling me there are even a couple of planets where they've totally lost contact with the people."

"Hasn't anyone tried to visit them?"

"They sent out one ship to each, and when they didn't return, they decided it was a waste of money to send out more." Wren looked up at

Eloch's frown. "Hey, Spur's in control again. Maybe things will change." She gazed one more time at the iridescent glass bracelet. "We'd better go. How long are those people going to keep sleeping?"

"Until we have completed our mission. Don't worry. Spur is caring for them."

Wren nodded. "And some may not wake. I get it. The KinLord example helped."

"Max will be ready. Spur woke him. Are we nearly there?"

"A few more minutes, up this street and over two."

~~~

Max had wept when he saw she was still alive. It still surprised Wren to think of it. She'd had no idea his true feelings for her, how he thought of her as a daughter, how helpless he'd felt, never being able to keep her safe. Had she known, she probably would have used it as a negotiating tool. *Tricky old devil,* she thought, *smart to have kept it from me.* It was nice to know that, in his way, Max had always had her back.

All his helpers were still asleep, so Max led them into his kitchen to find food and drink. They talked for nearly an hour about everything that had happened since she had last seen him. It allowed them enough time to reconnect.

But of course, Max missed nothing. He had been surreptitiously studying Eloch and Wren while they ate and talked. "I heard of you, you know," he told Eloch suddenly. "Quite the laughingstock, you were."

Eloch glanced up from the sandwich he was devouring. "They are not laughing now," he said.

Max glanced over at Wren, his bushy white brows nearly touching when he frowned his perplexity. "Today is a very different day, Max. You may have noticed since you're the only one awake in your house.

274

Allow me to enlighten you." And she proceeded to relate the day's events.

"And you have come today because?"

"Because the City needs a new leader," Eloch said, licking his fingers. Wren handed him a napkin, and he grinned at her. "A leader who has a network of spies, knows the underbelly of this government, and is willing to work with the Champion of Spur. Wren recommended you.

"And the Champion? That would be you?"

Eloch shook his head. "I have been assisting Spur, but She has already selected another and is anxious to begin their relationship."

Max nodded, tapping a finger to his grizzled chin. "And I just take your word for it?"

"Just look outside, Max" Wren exclaimed.

Eloch held up a hand.

She glowered at him, but sat back with a huff, arms crossed.

Max looked at them both and grinned. "Never thought I'd see the day you meet your match, Wren."

"Don't push it, Max," she warned him.

Max winked at Eloch. "My girl's got a temper."

"Speaks her mind, she does," Eloch said and then waved his hand across the table. The food disappeared.

"Nice trick," Max said unimpressed.

Eloch waved his hand again and the table was filled with gold coins stacked neatly in rows.

"Better," Max said, and then groaned when the coins disappeared.

Eloch pointed at Max, and Wren gasped, her eyes round. "Better go look in the mirror, Max," she said with a little laugh.

Max rose from the table and paused, looking quizzically at Eloch. *Where were the aches and pains?* He bolted out of the kitchen and toward the hall mirror, Eloch and Wren close on his heels.

They watched Max pat his ruddy cheeks, now unlined, as he gazed at the thick shock of dark hair. "I must be thirty years younger," he said. "Please, don't make me old again." There was real fear in his voice.

"Never," Eloch said.

Wren tapped Max on the shoulder. "Are you convinced yet?"

Max reluctantly turned from his reflection. "I was convinced before your little miracle show, I just wanted a chance to see for myself what the Champion could do. If only I had such power," he told Eloch.

Wren looked at him sadly. "I suspect you'd probably abuse it."

Max grinned. "You're probably right. Where do you want me to start?"

"Spur and I have left you with quite a mess to clean up," said Eloch, "so I suggest you begin there. When the people awaken, they might panic. Who would you like to awaken now, so they can help you prepare?"

Chapter 16: The Champion Of Spur

Four weeks later, Flick woke abruptly from a deep, exhausted sleep and sat up, confused and annoyed. He needed his sleep.

The longer he was KinLeader, the more he admired Wren. She had made it seem so easy. The move to Spur's oasis out in Rubble with so many people to care for had been exhausting, but Wren had been there, coaching and advising every step of the way. And now, with the help of Spider and Mouse, he felt ready to lead.

Which was a good thing, because the others were beginning to arrive, those Spur felt were ready.

But that wasn't why he was awake. Something had awakened him.

Flick sat up and ran his fingers through his hair while gazing around the room. With a start he realized he wasn't alone.

"It's time," Eloch told him quietly. "I will wait outside." He turned and left.

Flick hastily dressed and joined Eloch in the hall of the new KinLord home Spur had created. The house was silent, everyone else asleep. Eloch led Flick downstairs and into the gathering room. Flick followed him to the center of the room and stopped when Eloch stopped.

Eloch turned to face Flick. "Ready, Champion?"

Flick swallowed and took a deep breath, vividly aware of the rush of prickles along his arms and back. "I suppose I am. What do I do?"

"Simply allow Spur to join with you. She will teach you everything you need to know."

Flick nodded.

"But before we begin, I have one word of advice."

"And that is?"

"Speak your mind. As Her Champion, you are Spur's equal. What you think and feel, how you view things, are very important to Her," Eloch smiled. "You'll find she is much like Wren. Treat her as you treat Wren, and you will make a superb Champion."

Flick nodded thoughtfully. "You've mentioned that before. I know how to work with Wren."

"Then you know how to work with Spur."

"And the staff? Do I get that as well?"

Eloch shook his head. "My staff came from Entean."

"Will I get my own?"

"If you want one, ask Spur. It's not necessary. Working with Spur's power is more about focusing your concentration than waving a stick about. But I have found the bigger the gesture, the more others pay attention." Eloch grinned. "And it makes a great walking stick. I suspect you will be traveling quite a bit while you help Spur restore Her balance."

"But what of my Kin?"

"What of your Kin? You have Mouse and Spider to manage things when you're gone."

"True enough."

"Anything else troubling you before we begin?"

"What will become of you?"

"I suspect I will be going home, to Entean."

He had to ask. "And Wren? Will she be going home with you?"

Eloch smile sadly. "That I do not know. We have Spur's blessing, but I'm not sure if Entean will welcome her."

Flick had thought he would be happy to hear that news. He wasn't. But all he said was, "Who wouldn't welcome Wren? I'm ready now."

Eloch nodded. "All right, then. Stand and prepare to receive Spur. Speak your promise to Spur that you will serve Her all your days, or until She chooses another to Champion her. This will be your sacred vow. Your oath. The power She gives to you should only be used to bring balance in all things. You go where Spur sends you, and together you restore balance wherever and whenever it has been lost."

Feeling Spur's impatience, Eloch knelt down, closed his eyes, and spread his arms wide, allowing all that was Spur to empty from him. He felt Her pull free, felt the power he contained diminish. Since he had never been Spur's, the separation wasn't as painful as it had been when he was suddenly cut off from Entean. Besides, as he soon realized, Spur had left him a gift that bonded with Entean's plant growing within him: some of Spur's power remained, absorbed by the plant and shared with him, its host.

Eloch opened his eyes and stood to watch as the fine golden mist enveloped Flick. Unlike Eloch's experience, there were no grand gestures or words spoken aloud. Flick simply put both his hands over his heart. Eloch saw his lips move, but whatever was said remained between Spur and Her Champion.

When Flick absorbed Spur's essence, his eyes flew open and Eloch saw the dizzying power behind them. Flick wavered, and a staff appeared in his hand, which he used to steady himself.

He glanced up then and smiled at Eloch, the knowing smile of Champion to Champion. "It does make a handy walking stick, doesn't it? I think I'll go out for a while. Take it all in." Flick laughed suddenly. "You're right She's a lot like Wren. Or, rather, Wren's got a lot of Spur in her."

Eloch nodded. "I couldn't agree more, Champion of Spur, I couldn't agree more."

~~~

"Now what happens?" Wren asked later that day. They sat on the riverbank where Eloch had first met Spur. She didn't look at Eloch. She watched Little Sister splashing around in the water with another sniffer who had shown up not too long ago. "You go back to Entean?"

Eloch hesitated. "It is where I'd like to go, but…" His voice trailed off.

"But what?" Wren prodded, hoping she was the reason for Eloch's hesitation.

"I think Spur has more work for me. When Flick comes back, I think I will know more."

"Work? I thought you were finished being Spur's Champion."

"I am, but apparently Spur and Entean have been talking."

"Talking? About what?"

"They want to know why Their other sisters have been so silent."

Wren went still. "What does that mean, exactly?"

"It means, exactly, that I have a new quest. While Spur was transferring to Flick, she gifted some of Her power and knowledge to me, and it told me I have more work to do."

He turned to her and gathered her hands within his own. "Wren, will you come with me?"

Warmth spread through her. "Me? Who's always wanted to travel to the colonies? Me, who has Spur's blessing for our relationship? Go on a quest with the love of my life? I'll have to think about this. Oomph!"

Eloch had yanked her into an embrace so tight Wren could barely breathe. "When Flick returns, we'll speak with Spur and find out what's next." His chest rumbled in her ear.

"Besides," she continued, when she could get her breath back, "I think Spur said She had plans for me, too. I wonder what She's got in mind? And a gift. She said She'd be giving me a gift when the time comes. I do so love a good gift."

THE END

The Entean Saga continues with Episode Two: Brightness Calling.

About the Author

C.B. Williams is the author of several fantasy romance books that span the subgenres of Young Adult, Space Opera, Science Fiction and Romance. While each story is a grand adventure into time and dimension, her stories are also reflections of contemporary issues such as social norms, relationships, spirituality and environmentalism. She writes with keen emotional depth, insightful observations on human nature, and a fabulously quirky sense of humor. ***www.cbwilliams.us***

Other titles by C.B. Williams

Under the name C.B. Williams:

Sky Dancers (2014)

The PeaceKeeper Corps (2014)

The Walkers Trilogy
Walkers (2012)
The Place Between Worlds (2012)
The Shield (2013)

Under the name Cynthia Campbell Williams:

This Fool's Journey, Tarot Tales for Modern Minds (2011)

Praise for The Walkers Trilogy

"*Walkers* caught my attention from the first page, and then kept getting better and better. It has just enough fantasy to stretch the reader's imagination and still make you wonder...what if it really could happen? What if other worlds are right there at the tip of our fingers? Kate and Ash are characters that jump off the page and into your heart. It's great fun to watch them interact, to question, and to begin building a relationship." ~ L. j. Charles

"While the series may be designed for the oft-overlooked young adult reader, the series is highly readable and entertaining for adults as well. Anyone who enjoys depictions of other worlds, creative creatures and well-wrought characters will have a hard time putting this down." ~ A. Adrian

"Williams obviously puts her heart and soul into her characters, and it's easy to get caught up in the action. Can we be blamed for wanting more? Let's hope we can read about these characters again in some future volume. Recommended for anyone who enjoys Celtic fantasy with brisk, lean storytelling." ~ R. Kane

Praise for This Fool's Journey, Tarot Tales for Modern Minds

"Part allegory, part fantasy, part fairy tale and very wise, it taught a tarot novice like me how to understand the tarot's archetypes through a time and space-bending journey filled with colorful characters. A delightful collection of stories!" ~ J. Caldwell

www.ingramcontent.com/pod-product-compliance
Lightning Source LLC
Chambersburg PA
CBHW061543170626
46811CB00001B/68